W9-BKJ-255

Praise for
LAWRENCE SANDERS's
"DELIGHTFUL CAD"* ARCHY McNALLY
and the bestselling series

"Archy McNally is as amusing and rich as Dorothy Sayers's great creation Lord Peter Wimsey." —*Cosmopolitan*

"As crisp as a gin and tonic." —*St. Petersburg Times*

"Insouciant . . . to be effortlessly enjoyed."
—*The Boston Globe*

"Vincent Lardo continues [the] McNally sleuth series in superb style . . . His twisted plots and humorous characters are entertaining and provide a fun, quick read."
—*The Tennessean*

"[Lardo] admirably reproduces the same frothy tone Sanders brought to Archy's misadventures . . . virtually indistinguishable from the seven Sanders churned out."
—*Fort Worth Star-Telegram*

"You're only saddened when it ends."
—**The Palm Beach Post*

"You never know what that scamp Archy will get himself into." —*San Antonio Express-News*

"McNally is a charmer." —*Orlando Sentinel*

"An enduring character." —*The Indianapolis Star*

Turn the page for more rave reviews . . .

McNALLY'S GAMBLE
Archy basks in the sun, sin, and deadly schemes of Palm Beach . . .

"Wonderfully infectious. You can't help falling for [Archy]!"
—*The Washington Times*

McNALLY'S PUZZLE
*All the pieces fit in McNally's latest case—
money, sex, and murder . . .*

"Sanders's novel is easy reading . . . amusing one-liners."
—The Associated Press

McNALLY'S TRIAL
*Archy—and his new sidekick, Binky—investigate the
deathstyles of the rich and famous . . .*

"Passion, greed, murder, and wit—they are Sanders's stock in
trade, and McNally is his most delightful character."
—*Chicago Tribune*

McNALLY'S CAPER
*Archy is lured into a Palm Beach mansion as mysterious
as the House of Usher—but twice as twisted . . .*

"Sibling rivalries and passions." —*Orlando Sentinel*

McNALLY'S RISK
*The freewheeling McNally is seduced by the very temptress
he's been hired to investigate . . .*

"Loads of fun." —*The San Diego Union-Tribune*

McNALLY'S LUCK
*McNally returns—and the case of a kidnapped cat
leads to ransom and homicide . . .*

"Entertaining . . . sophisticated wit . . . This is a fun book."
—*South Bend Tribune*

McNALLY'S SECRET
*The rollicking bestseller that introduced Lawrence Sanders's
most wickedly charming sleuth, Archy McNally . . .*

"Witty, charming . . . fine entertainment." —*Cosmopolitan*

LAWRENCE SANDERS

M^cNALLY'S BLUFF

An
Archy McNally novel
by Vincent Lardo

BERKLEY BOOKS, NEW YORK

THE BERKLEY PUBLISHING GROUP
Published by the Penguin Group
Penguin Group (USA) Inc.
375 Hudson Street, New York, New York 10014, USA
Penguin Group (Canada), 90 Eglinton Avenue East, Suite 700, Toronto, Ontario M4P 2Y3, Canada
(a division of Pearson Penguin Canada Inc.)
Penguin Books Ltd., 80 Strand, London WC2R 0RL, England
Penguin Group Ireland, 25 St. Stephen's Green, Dublin 2, Ireland (a division of Penguin Books Ltd.)
Penguin Group (Australia), 250 Camberwell Road, Camberwell, Victoria 3124, Australia
(a division of Pearson Australia Group Pty. Ltd.)
Penguin Books India Pvt. Ltd., 11 Community Centre, Panchsheel Park, New Delhi—110 017, India
Penguin Group (NZ), Cnr. Airborne and Rosedale Roads, Albany, Auckland 1310, New Zealand
(a division of Pearson New Zealand Ltd.)
Penguin Books (South Africa) (Pty.) Ltd., 24 Sturdee Avenue, Rosebank, Johannesburg 2196,
South Africa

Penguin Books Ltd., Registered Offices: 80 Strand, London WC2R 0RL, England

This is a work of fiction. Names, characters, places, and incidents either are the product of the author's imagination or are used fictitiously, and any resemblance to actual persons, living or dead, business establishments, events, or locales is entirely coincidental.

The publisher and the estate of Lawrence Sanders have chosen Vincent Lardo to create this novel based on Lawrence Sanders's beloved character Archy McNally and his fictional world.

McNALLY'S BLUFF

A Berkley Book / published by arrangement with The Lawrence A. Sanders Foundation, Inc.

PRINTING HISTORY
G. P. Putnam's Sons hardcover edition / August 2004
Berkley mass-market edition / August 2005

ISBN: 0-425-20437-5

BERKLEY®
Berkley Books are published by The Berkley Publishing Group,
a division of Penguin Group (USA) Inc.,
375 Hudson Street, New York, New York 10014.
BERKLEY is a registered trademark of Penguin Group (USA) Inc.
The "B" design is a trademark belonging to Penguin Group (USA) Inc.

PRINTED IN THE UNITED STATES OF AMERICA

10 9 8 7 6 5 4 3 2 1

McNally's Bluff

1

THE LADIES SHRIEKED IN DESPAIR; THE GENTLEMEN moaned in frustration. Couples, chosen by the luck of the draw, gasped as they turned a corner and collided with the friends they believed they had lost at the last cul-de-sac.

Wives cast furtive glances at passing twosomes to see if their husbands were hot on the trail of or suspiciously detained in a leafy nook with some mysterious young beauty. Shouts, giggles, expletives, raucous laughter and sighs were the order of the night, presided over by a crescent moon and a sky full of tropical twinklers.

A bacchanalian orgy? The Shriners' annual scavenger hunt to benefit gout-suffering millionaires? An out-of-hand church bazaar? Not at all, folks. The huffing and puffing, snorting and shouting, guffaws and wails were nothing more than the Palm Beach Smart Set traversing the Amazin' Maze of Matthew Hayes.

As a native of this island where, according to our chamber of commerce, the tropics begin, I thought I had seen it all—from Arabian princes with blond bimbos on each arm to zillionaire computer moguls who are publicly bicoastal and privately bisexual.

Now any of the above, and their ilk, who can afford the price of a luxury villa on Ocean Boulevard usually settle for the swimming pool, tennis court and nine-hole golf course that comes with the house. Be that as it may, self-proclaimed impresario Matthew Hayes chose to scuttle his backyard playground and erect a garden hedge maze which, so the Amazin' Hayes boasted, was designed by no less a person than a student of the renowned maze designer Adrian Fisher.

The scuttlebutt (created and perpetuated by Hayes's publicity factory, of which he is the sole employee) had it that the maze, one hundred and fifty feet in diameter, was fashioned after the hedge maze at Hampton Court Palace where Sir Walter Raleigh gallantly covered a muddy patch with his cloak so the first Elizabeth would not have to soil the soles of her royal boots as she and her court searched for the center of the maze—or the goal, as it is known to maze aficionados.

This doubting Thomas, otherwise known as Archy McNally, Discreet Inquirer for the family firm of McNally & Son, Attorney-at-Law, is paid, when requested, to deflect the indiscreet foibles of the Palm Beach rich before they become fodder for the tabloid press. As one whose livelihood depends on keeping a finger on the pulse of the community, I thought it prudent to delve into the life and times of Matthew Hayes. This Johnny-come-lately would not be the first upstart to descend upon our Elysian Fields preceded by his reputation and a pocket full of ready cash, hell-bent on becoming one of *us* without waiting the required half century to prove himself worthy of the honor.

Going to the delightful Lake Worth library, I perused *Labyrinth—Solving the Riddle of the Maze* by the maestro himself, Adrian Fisher. I learned that there was indeed a noted hedge maze at Hampton Court Palace; however, it was planted at the behest of William of Orange in 1690, or approximately eighty-seven years after the demise of Elizabeth Tudor. So much for the amazin' facts of Matthew Hayes.

Frankly, it's what I expected from the man who likes to bill himself on par with the brothers Ringling who, as the world knows, put Sarasota on the map; it is now home to the Ringling Museum, which pays tribute to the circus and the creators of the Greatest Show on Earth. If Hayes hoped to erect his own memorial to the less than reputable—some would say sleazy—world of traveling carnivals in Palm Beach, he has to be stopped at all costs.

I BRUSHED UP ON MATTHEW HAYES VIA OUR RESIDENT gossip columnist, Lolly Spindrift. Lolly can be coaxed into telling what he knows over an expensive dinner, provided the seeker of salacious prattle picks up the bill. Lolly tattles in direct proportion to the cost of the meal, the quality of the wine, and the popularity of the beanery.

I chose Acquario on the Esplanade, a favorite of Lolly's and, I will admit, mine. We started with the cold seafood sampler of Maine lobster, stone crab, shrimp, cured gravlax (a boned salmon marinated in dill) and smoked trout before continuing with the five-course tasting menu. As the evening was strictly business, I had no reservations about charging it to my expense account under Business

Dinners—as opposed to Miscellaneous Expenses, which accounts for an alarming ninety-nine percent of my day-to-day expenditures.

The only thing Lolly enjoys more than a posh restaurant is a love affair with one of the working class. Blue, it's been said, is the color of distance and royalty. In Lolly's case, it's the color of his latest boyfriend's collar.

"Did you get me here to pick my brain or compromise my virtue?" Lolly asked as a gorgeously garnished yellowtail snapper was placed before him.

"I thought you lost your virtue to the mixologist from Bar Anticipation in West Palm."

"He's history," Lolly informed me. "I gave the ingrate a taste of society and, tit for tat, society got a taste of him. He left me for a woman, of all things."

"You're a soft touch for a pretty face, Lol," I sympathized. "What you need is willpower."

"I had a Will Power once and would have him again if I knew where I could reach him. Are you still seeing that policeman?"

I put down my fork. Camping with Lolly Spindrift in the line of duty has its limitations. "Georgia O'Hara is a *policewoman,* how many times do I have to remind you of that fact?"

Lolly shrugged as if gender differences were too trivial to take seriously. "And where does this leave Connie Garcia, with whom you were this close to marrying not too long ago, may I ask?" "Thisclose" was about a half inch between Lolly's thumb and forefinger. With that, he spooned up a dollop of Bali risotto. It seems other people's love affairs are a tonic to the man's appetite. Lolly is a smallish fellow who can eat twice his own weight without an ounce of it turning to fat. Go figure.

"One more question and you'll pay for the dinner, Lol," I cautioned.

"As you wish, but before we leave the subject of our respective, however diverse, love lives, may I impart a word to the wise?"

"Let's have it," I answered, knowing I had no choice.

Like a cat about to lap up a dish of cream, Lolly meowed, "The widow Taylor has been seen in Miami on two occasions in the company of the hunk, Alejandro Gomez y Zapata."

It riled me that no one was able to utter Alex's name without preceding it with a descriptor—like hunk, gorgeous, dreamy or handsome. It riled me further because it was true. Last, and certainly not least, it riled me because Connie had taken up with Alex at about the time I had taken up with Georgia, thereby closing an open relationship Connie and I had more or less enjoyed for years.

By the widow Taylor, Lolly was referring to Carolyn Taylor. She is the second wife of the late Linton Taylor, a man who came into millions upon the death of his first wife, the daughter of a Texas oil baron and Chicago meatpacking heiress. Talk about being well connected.

In addition to the money, Carolyn also inherited a bungalow on the Boulevard that compares in style and scope to its neighbor, Mar-a-Lago. She is also an archenemy of Lady Cynthia Horowitz, a septuagenarian with more money than sense whose interest in young men is on par with that of Lolly Spindrift. In fact the two share during the lean summer months, when the pickins are slim. Connie toils as social secretary to Lady C, which brings us full circle to Lolly's "word to the wise." My ex's *au courant* might be getting matey with a rich, recently widowed PB socialite who is also a rival of my ex's lady boss. It had all the ingredients of a *crime passionnel,* causing Lolly to devour all five courses with unprecedented speed.

Connie is a beautiful Latina with a temper to match. Were I Alejandro Gomez y Zapata, I would safeguard my fountain of testosterone. I speak from experience.

"Your source?" I inquired.

"Sorry, my informant spoke under a guarantee of anonymity."

Lolly reports the local gossip in the manner of a Washington correspondent for *The New York Times* reporting the next Watergate. "They were seen," he hinted as he scooped up a taste of the osso buco, "at a marina in Miami."

Lolly's pal Phil Meecham operates off his yacht which is berthed here in PB, but is known to make excursions to South Beach in search of grist for his indiscriminate libido. Confiding in Lolly Spindrift is tantamount to giving a press conference. While Carolyn Taylor is a familiar personage on our tight little island, Alex is a Miami boy who has appeared in our midst only since he's taken up with the lovely Consuela Garcia. While Meecham would certainly notice Alex, it was a wonder he knew his name.

As if reading my mind, Lolly said, "Alejandro is fast becoming a political force in Miami and points north. They say he's the odds-on favorite should he choose to run for mayor."

Alex is first-generation American and has vowed, via his column in a popular Miami daily with a tremendous Cuban-American readership, to return to Cuba, rout Castro and reclaim his heritage. The Gomez family harvested sugarcane and the Zapatas exported rum. Alex isn't clear as to just how he is going to accomplish this mission, but those who hear him at political rallies (or see him bumping and grinding on the conga line) never think to ask. He is young, he is handsome, he is hope personified and that, it seems, is more than enough for his numerous followers—including Connie. Alex has mastered the art of politicking—you can fool all of the people some of the time and you run with it when that time has come.

Lolly sees all liaisons as potential love affairs so it would not occur to him to even suspect a political aspect to his informant's sighting. I refrained from voicing this interpretation for fear that Lolly would formally announce that the widow Taylor was financing an armada of luxury yachts for Alex's Cuban conquest. At this time I had no way of knowing how right I might be, nor could I predict the lethal consequences of my association with Matthew Hayes—but I get ahead of myself.

Carolyn and Alex? Curious. This very afternoon I had sat in on a meeting between her stepson, Linton Taylor, Jr., and my father. In his quest for legal counsel, Laddy, as he is known locally, told my father that Carolyn Taylor had taken up with a young man so soon after the demise of Linton, Sr., it was obvious that the affair had been going on long before old man Taylor met his maker by way of myocardial infarction. The young man, who is not Alejandro Gomez y Zapata, had moved into the Taylor abode, Flamingo Run, as the funeral cortege had filed out. This rather theatrical description of the comings and goings at Flamingo Run is taken, verbatim, from the mouth of Laddy Taylor. Client confidentiality, and the sensitive nature of this meeting, forbade me from mentioning it to my dinner companion lest he would devour the plates, glasses, table linens and silverware for dessert.

Again exhibiting his prowess in reading my mind, which was getting scary, Lolly stated, "I understand Laddy Taylor is seeking the help of McNally and Son. Do you want to confide in Lolly?"

I would rather confide in a convention of investigative reporters. So much for trying to keep a secret in Palm Beach. "Where did you hear that?" I foolishly asked.

"From Laddy Taylor, who else?" Lolly answered. "He's screaming his head off to anyone who will listen. Big Linton left it all to Carolyn, lock, stock and barrel, and Laddy Taylor is threatening to contest the will. Correct?"

An Inofficious Will, my father the lawyer had termed it. A will inconsistent with the moral duty and natural affection of the testator. You see, as the money came from Laddy's natural mother, he felt it should have been passed on to him rather than to his stepmom, Carolyn. But there were extenuating circumstances, not the least being that Laddy Taylor and his father had been estranged for years and Junior had returned to Palm Beach just in time to see Carolyn's stud enter and the cortege exit.

However, to show her heart was in the right place, Carolyn offered Laddy Taylor his late father's wardrobe, which included a dozen pairs of silk boxer shorts, all emblazoned with the image of a flamingo on the run. This did nothing so much as set the perfect stage for a crime of vengeance.

I did not want to discuss our meeting with Laddy Taylor, no matter how obliquely. Determined to get what I was paying for, I abruptly shifted gears and asked, "What do you know about Matthew Hayes, Lol?"

Lolly dropped Laddy Taylor and picked up on Matthew Hayes without missing a beat (or a bite). "Finally, the reason for your largesse," he sighed. "Did you get your invitation to the opening of the maze?"

"How did you know I was invited?"

"I worked with Hayes on the list of invitees."

Besides his gab column, Lolly does obits, weddings and

bar mitzvahs for extra cash. He is also available for "consultation" for those wishing to break into Palm Beach society, which is comprised of three strata. The old-money folks, who speak only to each other and shun trendy restaurants, dining only at their clubs, the Everglades and the Bath and Tennis. The new-money people, who will speak to anyone who is kind enough to notice them and dine out, ad nauseam, at trendy restaurants. And finally, there's the Smart Set, made up of the offspring of the former and the latter, with a soupcon of young boys and girls whose entrée is their youth and comeliness.

Don't tell father, but the McNally money is too new to be considered old, but old enough not to be labeled *nouveau*. Hence we transcend the system, which is a boon to business.

"What's the poop on Matthew Hayes, Lol?" I repeated.

"You want the official bio, or the awful truth?"

"The awfuler the better, Lol."

OVER AN OUTRAGEOUSLY EXPENSIVE BOTTLE OF BEAUjolais Nouveau (it doesn't age so well, like we humans, the younger the better), Lolly imparted what I had come to hear.

To wit: Hayes was a second-generation carny who began his professional life as a human cannonball. His stature, five-feet-four in heels as high as a man could don without arousing suspicion, made him not only suitable for the job but also had his father eyeing Manny the Midget with malevolent scorn.

Hayes was literally catapulted into the big time when the cannoneer, who was not licensed to kill, misdirected his missile, sending Hayes over the net and head first into the amazin' bosom of Marlena Marvel. To be sure, at the time of this encounter of head and heart, she was plain old Molly Malone, but unlike her namesake of song, this modern Molly did not proffer mussels and cockles, alive, alive, all. This Molly proffered alcoholic beverages in downtown Des Moines where she was affectionately known to her loyal customers as Stretch, due no doubt to the fact that she stood six-feet-two in her stocking feet. When Molly ambled about in her work shoes, towering red satin high-heeled slides, she resembled an L.A. Lakers center in drag.

Molly settled the disoriented cannonball on her lap as an enterprising photographer took a snap. When he sold it to the local press, who ran it beside a shot of the popular dummy of yore, Charlie McCarthy, seated on the lap of his creator, Edgar Bergen, a star was born.

Hayes talked Molly into joining his traveling carnival. To ensure that she didn't stray, he married her in a very public ceremony. Ever aware of photo ops, the groom climbed a ladder in order to plant a kiss on his blushing bride's cheek. The newlyweds billed themselves as the Amazin' Matthew Hayes and the Marvelous Marlena Marvel: he as the carny pitchman and she as the show's main attraction. They owned the carnival after two seasons on the road. Devoid of talent, hubby made the most of Marlena's six-two frame, flowing red mane and, naturally, the ample bosom that saved his life.

Marlena was presented as Venus de Milo before a black curtain that cleverly made her appear armless. She rode a white horse as Lady Godiva, wearing nothing more than a long red wig. She mounted a drugged tiger as Sheena Queen of the Jungle, clad in a leopard-skin sarong. As the Elephant Girl she rode—you guessed it—wrapped in the animal's ears.

Marlena Marvel was the perfect draw for the men Hayes fleeced with rigged games of chance, illegal gambling, and sex shows. A petting zoo and rides kept the wife and kids occupied while daddy lost a week's pay to Matthew Hayes's exchequer.

Now retired, rich and infamous, the couple had arrived in Palm Beach to baffle us with their hedge maze because they were unable to dazzle us with their brilliance.

"I understand," Lolly concluded, "that Amazin' was often caught in the sack with cuties he liked to pick up on the fairway while Marlena was shivering inside the elephant's ears. She threatened to sit on his lap if he didn't mend his ways."

"ONE FINAL WORD TO THE WISE," LOLLY INTONED AS I gasped at the bill just presented. "I told you the Adonis I rescued from Bar Anticipation left me for a woman."

"Yes," I said, surrendering my credit card with great reluctance.

"The woman was Carolyn Taylor."

Well! One never knows, do one?

2

LADIES AND GENTLEMEN, GOOD EVENING AND WEL-
come to Le Maze." Our host stood on a black drum
about three feet high, which I imagine was once festooned
with bunting. Matthew Hayes, dressed in a tux and sporting a red cummerbund and matching carnation, had a fine
head of gray hair and piercing blue eyes. His lean figure
could easily fit into the trousers and blazers offered in the
prep department of better men's shops. His voice, that of a
true carny hawker, belied his spritely appearance and immediately commanded the attention of the crowd of perhaps twenty couples milling about the great room of the
house just christened Le Maze.

I think the former owners of the villa on Ocean Boulevard would have been amazed to see what Amazin'
Matthew Hayes had done with it. The furniture, strictly
rental, was a potpourri of this (early hotel) and that (late
motel). The art, twelve-by-six four-color posters, depicted

scenes from Hayes's former carnival in all its gaudy splendor. A strong man, a tattooed lady named Lydia, a bearded lady, male Siamese twins joined at the hip (no doubt with Super Glue), Ferris wheels, ferocious tigers, parachute jumps, a two-headed dog, the fairway and, most conspicuous of all, Marlena Marvel in all her many guises.

There were booths offering cotton candy, candied apples on a stick, soda pop, franks, burgers, beer from a keg and a moviola advertising French films. (Really!) There was an organ grinder with a monkey, a fortune-teller (Madame LaZanga) with a deck of tarot cards, a man who guessed your age (his was a thankless job with this crowd), several pinball machines and a guy in a bowler hat and arm braces (so help me!) running a three-card monte scam across a portable bridge table. There was a knife thrower asking for volunteers (ha!), a sword swallower and a lion tamer short on lions but long on tight breeches, blond locks and whip.

There was also a platoon of boys and girls in the traditional black pants, white pleated shirts and black bow ties, passing around trays of crystal flutes (rented) filled with surprisingly good champagne.

Lolly, in his trademark white suit, painted silk tie and panama hat, breezed by munching a candied apple and whispered, "My dear, it gives new meaning to the word gauche."

"Didn't you advise him?" I whispered back.

"I suggested the guest list, not the decor. Look, there's Katie Mann with her new husband. Or is it Trish Manning's new husband Katie's got her mitts on? Oh, dear. Ta-ta, dearheart."

"Before you ta-ta, Lol, will you tell me if that's Carolyn

Taylor's beau?" I asked, discreetly nodding toward the couple in question.

The widow Taylor is a looker in her forties. She wore her auburn hair in a rather mannish cut that was surprisingly sexy on her. In a miniskirt and black satin bolero blouse knotted above her toned bare midriff, there could be no doubt as to her gender.

Her partner was at least twenty years younger and as good-looking as all the young men, usually from the Midwest, who come to our town not seeking fame (they go to N.Y. and L.A. for that) but fortune. This one came in natural blond.

"That's him," Lolly said, pouting over his loss. "Billy Gilbert. There's less to him than meets the eye, if you get my drift." With that he took off to see just who Katie Mann was hitting on.

Not far from Carolyn and Billy I spotted Laddy Taylor in the crowd but could not ascertain if he was with a date or on his own. He was far enough from his stepmother to prevent him from engaging her in fisticuffs, but the night was young.

Judging from the din, the Smart Set appeared to be enjoying a night out. They were garbed in the suggested casual attire: shorts, sneakers, polo shirts, tees with naughty words in block letters and jeans worn low enough to reveal the brand of underwear beneath the denim—a fad I wish would go the way of long-playing records and telephones anchored to a wire.

My near-six-foot frame looked splendid in a pair of trim madras slacks (I believe the relaxed look is for those who have something to hide) and a blue Ralph Lauren button-down. For contrast, I added a white-on-white ascot to the outfit and shod my size eleven hoofs in a pair of canvas docksiders—sans socks, *naturellement*. My underwear will be revealed on a need-to-know basis.

"I guess you're wondering why I gathered you all here tonight," Hayes continued, to laughs, catcalls and applause. "Well, wonder no longer, for the moment of truth has arrived. You will be the first of whom I hope will be many to enter the maze of Le Maze and search for the goal.

"To make your quest more interesting I am going to ask the ladies to pick a name out of this bonnet"—Hayes pointed to a woman's straw bonnet resting on the rim of the platform next to a man's top hat—"and the gentlemen to pick a name from this hat. Those with matching names will be partnered to search for the goal."

Feet shifted and necks craned to size up the possibilities.

"By matching," Hayes explained, "I mean a lady who picks, let's say, Bonnie, will have to find the man who has selected Clyde."

This got a smattering of nervous laughs, giggles and moans.

"Before we begin," Hayes went on, still holding the room's rapt attention, "I would like to introduce you all to the little woman whom I have loved, admired and looked up to since the day we met."

The silence that followed was embarrassing until one brave soul let out an insidious snicker. A moment later the entire room was rocking with laughter, led by Hayes himself who egged everyone on like a maestro sans baton. As the laughter subsided the lights began to dim, slowly, until the great room was dark and eerily still.

A spotlight came on and moved to the foot of the curved marble stairway that descended gracefully to the great room and rose to the upper floor and a balcony where, decades ago, an orchestra once played to the waltzing couples below. The spotlight mounted the stairs, crossed to the balcony, hesitated, and then illuminated Venus de Milo in all her glory. The crowd gave a collective gasp before breaking into unbridled applause.

Marlena Marvel, looking ten feet tall, had to be fifty-plus, but thanks to artfully applied theatrical makeup, appeared to be as ageless and armless as the ancient statue. Her skin was alabaster white and some device had been attached to her waist to make her appear both naked and modest. There was a demure smile on her lips and only her famous red hair broke from a detailed imitation of the original Venus. Forgive the analogy, but she stood as still as a statue with only her shiny black eyes reflecting a glimmer of life behind the facade. It was amazin'.

The spotlight faded as the house lights came on. The audience, shaking their heads and exclaiming over the presentation, hardly had a chance to digest what they had seen before Hayes was beckoning to them to come forth and pick a partner for the search for the goal. "Marlena will join us as soon as she screws her arms back on." He worked the crowd he now held firmly in the palm of his hand with all the finesse of a true carny pitch man.

In the "His" and "Hers" queues I noticed Mr. and Mrs. Vance Tremaine. His family money was so old it died, forcing Vance to marry Penny Brightworth, whose money was so new it squeaked. Mr. Brightworth was a fast-food czar who catered lavishly to his only daughter, whom he called Bright Penny. Vance's smart pals called the match dollar wise and penny foolish. Vance had an eye for young ladies and it was said he had cheated on Penny on their honeymoon. The more callous said he actually did it at his own wedding reception when he went missing from the bridal table for fifteen minutes before being spotted coming out of a utility closet with one of the waitresses.

This has long bothered poor Penny. She once asked her friend and mentor, the formidable dowager Emily Fairhust, "Can a man do it in fifteen minutes?" To which Emily responded, "My dear, he's your husband, you tell me."

A group of Vance's prep school buddies once pasted a bumper sticker to the rear of his Rolls that advised KEEP IT IN YOUR PANTS, VANCE.

Also on line, much to Penny's annoyance and Vance's delight, was the beautiful and nubile Elizabeth "Fitz" Fitzwilliams. Vance had been after the young Fitz for years, to no avail, and Penny had gone to great lengths to keep the two as far apart as aeons in history. When the fates brought them together Penny kept a vigilant eye on both and, should nature call, Penny had been known to cajole Fitz into accompanying her to the loo, refusing to leave them alone for even five minutes, fearing Vance might attempt to break his record.

If Fitz picked Bonnie and Vance picked Clyde, Penny would pick the knife thrower. Come to think of it, what would happen if Carolyn picked Bonnie and Laddy Taylor picked Clyde?

With Fitz was Joe Gallo, a young man who used to be tight with my Georgia. Once a caddie at one of our more prestigious clubs, Joe, who aspired to join the fourth estate as a reporter, had got himself a position as news gatherer for our local television station, which is how he must have made Lolly's list of notables. How Joe got Fitz I wouldn't know.

Also among us were a couple who appear on the channel Gallo labors for with their own morning show, unoriginally titled *Breakfast with Mack and Marge*. It's a television version of the old radio shows that featured celebrated couples who were supposed to be at their breakfast table chatting about their wonderful evenings nightclubbing after the theater or rubbing shoulders at a society ball. These revelations greatly delighted their audience comprised primarily of the secretaries, wives, waitresses and telephone operators who would never see the inside of a nightclub, theater or ballroom.

Mack and Marge work on a set at the studio in West Palm that features a divan for the couple and a few easy chairs for guests. A coffee table holds an urn, cups and saucers so Marge can play mother. After commenting on the weather and making a few public announcements they introduce their esteemed guest. Authors, gardeners, decorators, antiquers and politicians lead the list. My mother, who is a serious gardener, boasting six million varieties of begonias under her care, has been earmarked for an appearance but to date has managed to postpone her debut indefinitely. Mother is at an age where senior moments come without warning, but is cognizant enough of her malady not to tempt the fates on live TV. Amen.

Most recently, Mack had hired a helicopter to fly him and a cameraman over the Amazin' Maze of Matthew Hayes, giving viewers a bird's-eye view of the phenomena. The clip was run on the evening news.

People were now waving white adhesive labels in the air and shouting, "Rhett looking for Scarlett."

"Cathy looking for Heathcliff."

"Cleopatra looking for Caesar or Antony."

"Petruchio here, where's Katharina?"

I heard Vance shout, "Romeo," and head straight for Fitz only to be waylaid by Juliet, a matron of sixty years and three chins. Penny beamed at the coupling.

I picked Adam and went in search of Eve. I ran into Fitz

who gave me a peck on the cheek and announced that she was Delilah. I told her we were in the same church but different pews. Joe gave me an affectionate hug (he's of Italian descent, don't-you-know) and lamented that he was Gatsby, not Samson.

I approached Carolyn Taylor and said, "Adam." She shook her head and answered, "Daisy." I told her where to find Gatsby. Poor Billy had chosen Theseus and looked perplexed. I told him to seek out Phaedra. Clearly, the Greek classics are not these boys' long suit.

Someone tapped my shoulder and I turned to find my Eve in the person of Marge Macurdy. "This is serendipity," Marge exclaimed at the sight of the ADAM label now plastered to the breast pocket of my shirt.

"Serendipitist? Do you think we'll be called upon to be fruitful and multiply?"

"I certainly hope not, Mr. McNally. It didn't work the first time so why beat a dead horse."

"Then I doubt if you'll share even a candied apple with me."

She laughed and looked as pretty as any not-so-recent college grad had a right to look. Marge Macurdy had a head of chestnut curls and true brown eyes, and didn't try to conceal the freckles the sun brings out, but rather flaunted them with a bright toothpaste smile and a lot of attitude. This was my kind of woman.

"If we're going to search for the goal as a team, I think you should call me Archy."

"I'll call you anything you want if you'll agree to appear on my show. I'm determined to snare a McNally, mother or son."

"A discreet inquirer on television would be an oxymoron."

"Don't worry. I won't ask you to drop your fig leaf," Marge insisted.

At that moment the air resonated with the trademark call of a man who taxies around the jungle on exceptionally strong vines, clad in the forerunner of the thong.

"That's Mack looking for Jane," Marge said, wincing. "I begged him not to do it."

Here I will narrate events exactly as I would record them in my journal in the near future and relate them to the police before the night was over.

As the guests found their mates, some with joy, others with polite fortitude, a young woman descended the marble staircase. She wore a black dress with white collar and cuffs, sensible shoes and a ridiculous frilly cap atop her hair which was pulled back from her face and knotted into a bun. So loudly did her manner and dress proclaim her profession that she could have come from a theatrical agency rather than a domestic employment agency. I was immediately reminded of the ungainly maid in a French farce.

She made her way through the crowd, apologizing for the intrusion which no one seemed to notice, and went straight for the dais where Hayes stood. He got down on one knee and presented her with his ear. The message was obviously very brief, for just moments later Hayes was back on his feet and the maid was scurrying up the stairs.

Once more begging our attention Hayes announced, "Marlena is afflicted with the petite headache and will join us for our buffet dinner after one lucky couple has gained the goal."

I whispered to Marge, "Given her size it's amazin' she can have a petite anything," and got a playful poke in the ribs.

"A final word," Hayes boomed, "and we'll be off. In the goal the winners will find two envelopes resting upon a sundial. Each envelope contains ten gift certificates, *pour l'homme et la femme,* redeemable at ten premier Worth Avenue shops."

This got a roar of approval and thunderous applause— and the hunt was on.

I noticed that Lolly did not choose to partake in the contest, preferring to chat with the catering staff as they began to remove the carny attractions to make room for the buffet tables. On those rare occasions when Lolly does not clean his plate he has been known to take home the chef in lieu of a doggy bag.

As we marched out of the house led by Tarzan (Mack Macurdy) and Jane (Penny Tremaine, of all people), the organ grinder serenaded us with "Three Blind Mice." The entrance to the maze was outlined with a string of blinking colored lights and, like Noah's crew, we entered the labyrinth two by two. The couple preceding Marge and me turned right, so we hung a left.

The hedge (privet, I would guess) was some ten feet tall and about half as thick. The paths were cleverly outlined with tiny white lights running along the ground, much like the illuminated center aisle of a movie theater.

I have already recounted the scene as we began our quest for the goal. After a half hour, the laughter began to turn to frustration and even anger. Marge and I arrived at our starting point three times when we thought we were on the opposite side of the maze.

Tired of head-on collisions, many couples began to hunt in groups of four, six and eight, trotting along like the linked cars of a runaway train. It was remarkable, and frightening, how soon many became disoriented and light-headed. One's phobia can become alarmingly claustro in a maze.

"With any luck we'll come to the entrance again, and if we do I'm getting out," Marge griped. Naturally, we never saw it after that.

We did see poor Juliet who had lost her Romeo and was seeking him, not the goal. Other couples who did not think to join hands had been separated in the dark and now roamed in groups, clogging the pathways. The organ grinder was someplace within the maze still grinding out "Three Blind Mice" until it began grinding on our nerves, abetted by our host running up and down the aisles, laughing, teasing and goading us on.

"The next time that shrimp cuts us off," Marge threatened, "I'm going to step on him."

We had been in the maze over an hour, and just when I feared the hunt would turn into a stampede, Tarzan let out a formidable yodel which could mean only one thing.

"Mack's found it," Marge cried. "He said he would, and he did."

Floodlights mounted on poles at the end of each passage came on and Hayes began collecting people like a little Pied Piper. In the light I noticed that the reason for Hayes's remarkable navigational skills was a map of the grid, which he consulted at every right angle.

The goal was approximately ten by ten feet and only a lucky few of us, Marge and I included, could fit within its confines. Others crowded the entrance to peek in. Mack and Penny, all smiles, waved their envelopes at the crowd, as Hayes mounted the sundial to congratulate the winners and ask them, "Can you lead us back to the house?"

"Ask him, he found it," Penny said, indicating her partner.

"Never," Mack stated. "That would be like winning the lottery two consecutive times."

"Then allow me," Hayes boasted, leaping off the garden ornament with the dexterity of one long used to plummeting from a perch. People cleared the entrance as Hayes, taking Mack and Penny by the hand like a child walking his parents, began the procession out of the maze and towards the house. The organ grinder belted out "Hail, Hail, The Gang's All Here" and, like people finally freed from an elevator stuck between floors, voices were raised in thanksgiving to the rousing Gilbert and Sullivan refrain.

"I told you I would do it," Mack called to his wife.

"He did," Marge said in awe, "he really did."

"Have you seen Vance?" a concerned Penny called to us.

"Everyone got all tangled up in the confusion," Marge called back, "he could be anyplace."

Penny stumbled and was rescued by Mack.

"Tangled in the crowd?" I chastised Marge. "You're a bitch, Ms. Macurdy."

"Serves her right," Marge answered. "Penny Tremaine needs Worth Avenue gift certificates like I need a hole in the head."

"It was your husband that got 'em for her," I reminded her.

"And for that I'm going to have a headache for the next ten years," she vowed.

Poor Mack. To the victor go the spoils—but not always.

Tired and giddy, we staggered out of the maze and into the house where an enticing buffet had been set up with servers behind each course and portable bars scattered about the great room. The party atmosphere now restored, everyone headed for the booze, all talking of their trials and travails in the Amazin' Maze of Matthew Hayes.

The guests were getting their drinks, the catering staff was fussing over the buffet, the boys and girls were once again bussing their trays of champagne and our host was underfoot here, there and everywhere. The clatter and chatter rose to a crescendo until it was suddenly silenced by the mother of all screams.

Everyone looked up to see the maid standing on the balcony, her cap askew, her arms flailing the air, her voice raised in anguish as she reported to her employer below, "Mr. Hayes, Mr. Hayes, Madame has disappeared."

3

IN RETROSPECT, I BELIEVE WE ALL ASSUMED THE BAL-
cony scene was part of the evening's entertainment.
Hayes was a master showman and con artist whose skill
was keeping the chumps amused as he picked their pockets. You know, the old razzle-dazzle, from whence comes
the cliché, three-ring circus. If none of your acts can stand
on their own, present them all at once and the audience will
be convinced they're seeing the greatest show on earth.

Hayes even had the *cojones* to feature his wife in one of
the rings, which had to be an all-time Palm Beach first. In a
town where wives are prized for either their waist size or
their purse size, Hayes had committed the ultimate faux
pas by exhibiting his wife as a nude statue. The word *common* comes to mind.

All eyes shifted from the balcony to the sight of Hayes
climbing the marble staircase. The combination of his
short legs and the graceful rise of the steps made it impos-

sible for him to take them two at a time, giving his climb the appearance of a gerbil on a treadmill. I could hear snorts and nervous laughs emanating from the crowd.

"Do you think she'll now appear as the invisible woman?" I quipped.

"To appear invisible is a contradiction of terms," Marge noted brilliantly.

"Nobody likes a smart-ass," her husband reminded her.

Mack Macurdy, born John Macurdy, is a redheaded Irishman with dark eyes and an infectious grin, with a body that announced his college-football-playing past. Our housekeeper, Ursi Olson, who is Lolly Spindrift's unpublished counterpart, told me that Mack Macurdy enjoys a loyal female following who are more interested in Mack than the hot topics of his show. Macurdy is irritatingly aware of his appeal both on and off the tube, making him a bit too full of bluster and blarney for my taste, but then I'm not married to the guy.

It had occurred to me earlier that Mack had found the goal because he knew where to look. By this I mean that he had flown over it in that helicopter, but the result of his snooping was soon made public on his televised show and the evening news. As I recall it was impossible to distinguish individual pathways from the helicopter's altitude, and even if they had been discernable to the naked eye from up there it would have been impossible to commit the layout to memory. Still, Macurdy had boasted to his wife that he would make the goal—and he did. Curious?

The crowd began to drift off into groups, all gabbing about the show that had just been enacted by the master of the house and the upstairs maid. People like to be among friends when in strange surroundings and Le Maze was proving most strange in a town where the norm was anything but.

Joe Gallo and Fitz joined us and, need I add, they were followed by Vance and Penny Tremaine. I could see Carolyn Taylor and Billy Gilbert with a group but could not pick out Laddy Taylor. When Hayes finally reached the balcony he took the hysterical maid by the elbow and led her off to the second-floor hall and oblivion. People continued to storm the bars but, while awaiting the fate of Marlena, no one dared approach the buffet except Lolly, who sampled the crabmeat.

"Do you think we have a news-breaking story here?" Joe mused aloud, hoping for the worst.

"Only if Marlena can't screw her arms back in," Vance said, garnering a look from Penny not unlike that of a mother gazing proudly upon her precocious two-year-old. Vance sought Fitz's approval and got only a blank stare. It has been my experience that the more beautiful the woman, the more blank the stare.

As the wait for Hayes's return grew longer, the natives grew restless—and a little tipsy. I was reminded of my school days when the teacher would leave the classroom and we would sit like good little boys and girls for a prescribed number of minutes. Should the teacher exceed the limit, all hell would break loose.

People had begun attacking the buffet and making party sounds when Hayes reappeared at the top of the staircase with the teary-eyed maid in hand. Together they began their slow descent. A guilty silence now reigned, and the chow hounds tried to hide the proof of their gourmandism.

About midway down Hayes paused and stated clearly and simply, "Marlena has disappeared," as if he didn't believe it. He looked stunned and disheveled, having shed his tux jacket and cummerbund. If this were an act, it was worthy of a Barrymore. The maid clutched a handkerchief, covering her mouth with it every few seconds to stifle her sobs.

"We've searched the house, Tilly and me," he went on. "Bedrooms, baths, closets, even the attic. Marlena is gone."

Gone where? Out of the house, presumably. There was, of course, a front door. We had gone out back, to the maze, via a series of French doors that lined the west side of the great room. The doors gave to a terrace and steps leading to the maze which took up a huge hunk of the property behind the house. Also, there had to be a kitchen door for the staff and deliveries. Marlena had many routes of escape but, as we would soon learn, none was possible for her to access between the time we had seen her as Venus and the time we had all returned to the house.

Hayes and Tilly (as in the Toiler?) completed their descent and moved among the guests who made way for the couple in a silence born either of respect for Hayes's loss or doubt as to his sincerity. Having bought Lolly's expertise in crashing Palm Beach society, Hayes now approached the gossip columnist for either guidance or a refund.

Everyone, including the catering staff, watched the whispered exchange between Lolly and Hayes as if the two were deciding if we should all be detained on suspicion of carting off Marlena Marvel. (Who had the strength to cart the likes of Marlena was in itself a mystery.) When the two, and Tilly, turned to look at me I felt the icy fickle finger of fate run down my spine.

"You're on, McNally," Marge stage-whispered loud enough for everyone to hear.

Hayes beckoned and I approached, fixing Lolly Spin-

drift with a look that would have shamed an honorable
man. It bounced off Lolly like a speeding bullet off Super-
man's chest.

"Lolly tells me this is your type of gig, Mr. McNulty,"
Hayes began with all the social grace of a charging bull.

"The name is McNally, and I am a private investigator."

"I want to hire you to investigate Marlena's disappearance."

"Your wife has been gone for a little over an hour, Mr.
Hayes. That can hardly be termed missing."

"So where did she go?" he asked, looking up at me with
his cobalt eyes.

I wanted to shout, *She's your wife, you tell me,* but
thought the less said, the soonest mended, and the soonest
we could all go home. "Where did you last see Mrs.
Hayes?" I asked Tilly.

Tilly looked surprised at being consulted and we had to
wait for her to regain her composure before answering.
When she did speak her voice was clear, if a bit shaky, and
her story most explicit. "During the presentation I drew
Madame's bath, as usual. Madame must bathe to remove
the makeup," she added.

"After her bath, Madame complained of a headache and
said she would lie down until the buffet supper was served.
She told me to inform Mr. Hayes of this and I did."

"Yes," Hayes blurted, "she did just that. Came right
down here and told me Marlena was resting and would join
the party after the hunt for the goal."

Nodding, Tilly continued, "I saw that Madame was resting comfortably on her chaise lounge which Mr. Hayes
purchased from the previous owners."

"That's not important, Tilly," Hayes noted with obvious
annoyance.

"Yes, sir. I went to my room and rested until I heard the party returning from the maze. I went immediately to tell Madame it was time to get dressed for the supper show."

"It's not a supper show here," Hayes cut in. "Our carnival days are over. It's a dinner party."

"Yes, sir," Tilly said, looking miffed but determined to have her say. "Madame was not on her chaise lounge. I looked in her dressing room, her bathroom, even the closet. No Madame. Then I began to look in all the bedrooms on the floor, there are seven of them, including mine. And the guest baths. There are seven of those too. Each room has its own . . ."

"That's not important, Tilly," Hayes once again admonished the poor girl.

Tilly began crying. "Then I got worried and ran on the balcony and called down to Mr. Hayes. Madame has disappeared. Madame . . ."

"She did just that," Hayes said, cutting off a reprisal of the scene. "I imagine you all heard her." Then he picked up the remarkable story. "I went upstairs and we looked for Marlena. I mean we looked everyplace, including the closets and attic, even though that wasn't necessary."

"What do you mean it wasn't necessary, Mr. Hayes?" I questioned.

"I mean the door to the attic was locked from the outside, the key still in the lock. If Marlena went in, how could she have locked it from outside?"

"The lower level," I suggested, more for something to say than because it held any hope of containing Marlena.

"To get to the lower level, or the front door or the kitchen door or any door, she would have to come down those stairs and into this room, which was filled with the catering staff from the minute we left it to go to the maze," Hayes said, gesticulating like a puppet on a string.

"I never left this room," Lolly corroborated. "And no one came down those steps."

"She's disappeared into thin air," Tilly concluded, unnecessarily.

"What should we do, Mr. McNally?" Hayes asked, and I told him.

"Call the police, Mr. Hayes. Right now."

"You think it's necessary?"

"I don't think, Mr. Hayes, I know. The police are better equipped to handle something like this. They'll search the house and the grounds and if they don't find her they'll put out an APB and start to canvass the island."

"But Marlena wouldn't just walk out without saying a word. That's crazy," the little man shouted.

"But obviously she did," I retorted.

"But how?" he cried.

S. Holmes tells us that once you have ruled out the impossible, go for the improbable. "She could have gone via an upstairs window," I said, "and may be just outside in need of help."

Tilly screamed her scream and raced to the French doors. I immediately grabbed Hayes and told him to call the police before going off on any wild-goose chases. Then I addressed our audience who had been watching the show with unwavering interest, observing that most of them still wore their name tags. In light of what was happening the name tags looked more foolish than festive, like party hats on New Year's Day morning.

"Mr. Hayes is calling the police," I told them, as if they hadn't been listening. "I don't think anyone should leave until the police arrive and take statements. If you get restless you can search the house and if there are any flashlights in the utility closet have a look around the grounds—but not alone. No one should go out alone."

Stepping forward, Laddy Taylor volunteered, "I'll lead a search through the house." Now where did he emerge from? I wondered. Had he left the room and returned, or had I just not noticed him when we came in from our hunt for the goal? "Fitz and I will lead a group outside," Joe Gallo called out.

"I'm with you," Vance quickly volunteered.

"And me," Penny joined in.

"Marge and I will lead a group," Mack Macurdy said. "Joe and I will see about flashlights and anyone caring to join us just fall in behind when we leave. We'll take separate routes to cover the grounds faster."

And all three rings were in full swing.

THE POLICE ARRIVED IN THE PERSON OF LIEUTENANT Oscar Eberhart, with whom I have crossed paths while doing my job of protecting the good names of Palm Beach's bad people. He came with a retinue of four officers, including Sergeant Al Rogoff, a personal friend and colleague of yrs. truly. Al and I do not make a display of our relationship when in public and on occasions such as this merely nod in greeting.

"Do you ever miss a party in this town, McNally?" was how Eberhart greeted me.

"Do you ever miss a chance to crash a party on the Boulevard, Lieutenant?" Eberhart is far from subtle in his aspirations to a more lofty social status in this town. I'm sure that if the call had come from any location other than the prestigious Ocean Boulevard, he would have dispatched a patrol car to see what was amiss.

"I was invited by . . ."

"Me," Hayes said, suddenly popping up before us like a jack-in-the-box. "I'm Matthew Hayes. My wife's disappeared. We've looked everyplace. People are searching the grounds and . . ."

"Into thin air, she went," Tilly cried, "just like that. Poof! Into thin air."

Eberhart looked down at Hayes and, fearing he would laugh, I took him aside and told him to take Al and the other men into the hall and I would join them there.

"What the hell is going on?" Hayes complained.

"I know Lieutenant Eberhart and his men," I said, "and I think it would be best if just one of us explained what is going on."

"I'll come with you," Hayes insisted.

"If you don't mind, Mr. Hayes," Eberhart said, "I'd like to learn what happened from an objective observer like Mr. McNally. You're a bit distraught right now, but I will get to you directly."

"You hired me, remember?" I added to bolster Eberhart's point. "Now let me do my job and you do yours. Get everyone together, including the catering crew, and have them wait here until the police have been brought up to date."

Given a mandate to command, Hayes forgot the police and happily mounted his drum, barking orders. Old habits die hard.

In the hall, the boys were, as I had feared, having a laugh. "Is that the Amazin' Matthew Hayes?" Eberhart exclaimed. "He's two feet high."

"Quiet, he'll hear you," I lectured. "His wife has flown the coop."

"So I gathered. What do you know about it, McNally?"

I told my story, beginning at the beginning, when Marlena appeared as Venus, and ending at the end, when Tilly went ballistic on the balcony and all the stops along the way.

"It's impossible," Eberhart concluded. "She's got to be up there."

"But she isn't," I told him. "Hayes and the maid said they checked upstairs but to be sure I got a group of the guests to double-check. Laddy Taylor is leading the pack."

"Him?" Eberhart cried. "That's the guy who's been after us to investigate his father's death. The old man had a heart condition for years and died of an angina attack. Junior wants us to question his stepmother, for cripes' sake."

"Laddy Taylor is not happy with daddy's will, but wayward sons seldom are. He's out to disenfranchise Carolyn Taylor, who's also here tonight."

"With Laddy Taylor?"

"No, Lieutenant, with her new beau. A lad who used to belong to Lolly Spindrift but Lolly gave him to the widow for comfort and solace."

Eberhart whistled through his teeth, green with envy.

"Excuse me," Al Rogoff intervened, "but this Hayes guy is a con artist and publicity hound. Has it occurred to either of you that this is a hoax?"

Finally, an intelligent word from a man who is long on the commodity. "I have, Sergeant, which is why I connived an independent search of the house. However, that doesn't mean much because some of these mansions contain secret nooks and crannies like hidden closets along the back stairs where the master of the house could hide, if necessary, when on his way to the servant's quarters for a bit of hanky-panky with the parlor maid."

Eberhart whistled through his teeth, greener than ever.

"What's this goal thing?" one of the patrolman asked.

"An enclosed area, except for the entrance, in the center of the maze," I told him. "The purpose of a maze is to hunt for it. It's called making the goal."

"Okay. Now let's all go hunt for Mrs. Hayes," Eberhart ordered. Having gotten all the facts, and not sure what he was getting himself into, Eberhart led us back to the great room where all were assembled—silent, morose and irritable. After introducing himself, Eberhart informed the group, "Mr. McNally has filled us in, but before I begin a formal investigation I want to know what the search parties have found."

"They've found nothing," Hayes called out from the dais where he was sitting, not standing, with Tilly and Lolly.

"We searched the house," Laddy Taylor claimed. "From the attic to the lower level and both were locked from the outside but we looked anyway. Nothing."

"And nothing outside, Lieutenant," Mack Macurdy offered.

"Did you search the maze?" Eberhart asked.

Hayes jumped onto the drum and hawked, "Why the hell should they look there? We were all over the maze. How could she have gotten in it? How could she have gotten downstairs without being seen?"

"He doesn't want us to search the maze," Al Rogoff, who was standing behind me, whispered in my ear.

I glanced at Eberhart and he gave me a nod.

"You searched the attic, Mr. Hayes, when you told us yourself that it would have been impossible for Mrs. Hayes to enter it and leave the door locked from the outside," I called to him.

"So what the hell does that prove?" he bellowed right back.

"It doesn't prove a thing," I said, "but that the lieutenant wants to be just as thorough in his investigation as you were with yours."

Eberhart immediately backed me up with, "Everything about your wife's disappearance is a mystery, to say the least. You said it was impossible for her to leave the second floor without being seen, but she did. Now you tell us it's impossible for her to be hiding in the maze, but she may well be. How do you get out back?"

Hayes leaped off the drum like a performing monkey and raced to the French doors. He opened one and stepped onto the terrace, followed by Eberhart, the officers and me. Our audience soon began opening the other doors and cautiously inching their way onto the terrace. Hayes scooted onto the lawn and then to the entrance of the maze where he fiddled with something hidden in one of the hedges. A moment later the floodlights came on and we were looking across the top of the maze, a sea of greenery for as far as the eye could see.

It was, besides awesome, a tad eerie.

"Some piece of work," Eberhart mumbled, starting for the entrance.

"It's a fool's errand," Hayes groused.

"Then fools we'll be," Eberhart said, sounding as excited as a kid entering the house of horrors at a theme park. "Can you take us straight to the goal?"

Hayes got out his map of the grid. "Follow me, if you must."

Eberhart turned to his men. "You all spread out and check the pathways, and don't follow us."

"I wish you luck," I called to Al as he and the others entered the maze.

Eberhart and I followed Hayes who sped through the aisles like a mouse who had mastered the labyrinth and knew just where to find his reward. Along the way we crossed paths with the meandering officers several times. I gave Al a wink and he gave me the finger.

Hayes finally came to a halt by a cut in the hedge. "The goal," he announced, stepping back to allow Eberhart and me to enter.

In the artificial light the sundial's face appeared to be grinning at us. Lying at its base was Marlena Marvel. She appeared to be quite dead.

4

"IMPOSSIBLE," LIEUTENANT EBERHART SAID FOR THE tenth time—but who's counting?

We were sitting in the kitchen of Le Maze at a refectory table whose provenance was questionable but if pressed I would guess Grand Rapids. The catering crew swarmed about us wrapping and packing the aborted buffet goodies. I believe it is customary for the staff to divvy up any leftovers for their own consumption and, were this indeed the case, tonight's boys and girls were in for a feast of epicurean proportions.

There was the crabmeat Lolly was so rudely interrupted from devouring, lobster tails nestled in artificial shells, whole slabs of filet mignon waiting to be sliced, deviled eggs and sturgeon eggs commonly known as caviar. The peeled shrimp, oysters and clams on the half shell were residing atop crushed ice while the baked goods awaited on hot plates amid a profusion of salads, side dishes, sauces and exotic dips. That salsa and stuffed celery sticks were not on the menu attests to the fine quality of the presentation.

The lieutenant was grilling me as we both picked at the smorgasbord the waiters were carrying from the great room to the kitchen table before it disappeared into silver foil, plastic wrap and Ziploc bags in sizes small, medium, large and humongous. The latter could hold a leftover baby T. rex. In fiction the police do not drink while on duty but O. Eberhart had obviously never curled up with H. Poirot so didn't know he should have refused the champagne I confiscated from a tray that held a dozen glasses of the bubbly. A very nice Moët, I believe.

"The chopped liver is delicious," Eberhart observed, licking his lips.

"Pâté de foie gras," I corrected.

"What's that?"

"The chopped liver, Lieutenant. Actually it's the bloated liver of a goose that's been force-fed till its stomach explodes."

With that, he surrendered the pâté for wrapping. "I wish you hadn't told me that, McNally."

"Try the roe, Lieutenant," I recommended.

He glanced at the offerings whizzing by like the fare on a lazy Susan and helped himself. "I'd rather have the caviar."

"Whatever your heart and stomach desire, Lieutenant." If Oscar was going to rise socially I would strongly recommend he begin by *Mastering the Art of French Cooking* (à la Julia Child) before breaking bread with his betters.

Lest I give the impression that Oscar Eberhart is an oaf, let me state for the record that he is a superb police officer who plays by the rules but is not averse to stretching a point if it hastens the cause of justice and keeps the citizens of Palm Beach out of harm's way. Like his sergeant, Al Rogoff, Oscar hides his street smarts behind a facade of tough talk (in Al's case the talk would cause a grammarian to swoon), both men coming off as dullards much to the chagrin of many a con artist who foolishly underrated the pair.

Al, a big bear of a lug, is a closet intellectual and a devotee of classical music and dance who is grateful to attend the opera or ballet seated in the family circle or standing room if necessary. Oscar, slim and dapper, would suffer through *Aida* only if he were allowed to do so from the royal box at Covent Garden. These men are as essential to my chosen profession as water is to a fish and I strive to keep in their good graces, cooperating rather than competing, when, as often happens, we share a common cause.

WHEN WE RETURNED TO THE HOUSE FROM OUR ASTONishing find in the goal, Tilly came rushing to her boss who took her hand and, on tiptoe, whispered into her ear. Tilly responded to the news with her signature scream before fainting dead away. Those who had started to pick at the buffet now tried to ditch their plates as the guests began to close in on me, the policemen, Matthew Hayes and the now prostrate Tilly. Lieutenant Eberhart immediately took charge, ordering one of the patrolmen to carry Tilly upstairs, telling Hayes to go with them. He told Al to get on the horn to headquarters after calling for an ambulance.

Finally, he mounted the drum with the two remaining officers flanking it. "We've found Mrs. Hayes," he announced to the now stunned guests.

"Where?" someone shouted.

"Is she dead?" came another cry.

"She's been hurt," was all Eberhart would admit to at this juncture. "An ambulance is on the way and more help from police headquarters. I would like you all to remain here, in this room, until further notice, and that includes the waitstaff. If there's anyone in the kitchen I want the person in charge to bring them all in here."

People began shouting questions at Eberhart, all of which he answered with a shrug, making it clear that for the moment the briefing was over. Not getting anything out of Eberhart they began consulting each other, raising a din as they queued up at the portable bars for liquid libations. If it was going to be a long night there was no reason to see it through dry and sober. No one complained of being detained. In fact, if asked to leave they would have done so with great reluctance. Police reinforcements and an ambulance were all this crowd needed to transform speculation into fact. They were witnesses to what tomorrow would be the talk of the town and, given Matthew Hayes's renown, however dubious, perhaps the talk of the nation.

When the sirens could be heard roaring up Ocean Boulevard I spotted Joe Gallo talking on his cell phone, no doubt in communication with his network, with Marge, Mack and Fitz at his side. Eberhart sent one of the patrolmen outside to meet the squad cars and ambulance with orders to direct them up the driveway and round back to the maze. Eberhart went out the French doors, leaving Al and his cohort to prevent the crowd from doing likewise. I noted the lieutenant was still holding the map to the grid which he had confiscated from Hayes.

The crowd got as close to the doors as they could and

raised an excited clamor when Eberhart threw the switch, lighting the scene out back like a movie set. As if an imaginary director had called for action, two medics hauling a stretcher flew past followed by a doctor toting a familiar black bag and a dozen men in uniform and civilian dress carrying the paraphernalia of scene-of-the-crime specialists. All followed Eberhart into the maze.

"She's dead, right?" Gallo was now standing beside me, phone glued to his ear.

"I can't tell you anything more than you heard from the lieutenant. He'll make another announcement when they get her out of the maze."

"She's dead," Gallo announced into the phone's tiny speaker. "They found her in the maze."

Well, everyone had seen them enter the maze so I hadn't jumped the gun on Oscar. The sounds coming to us from the front of the house, mostly irate car horns, told me Ocean Boulevard was now backed up for miles in both directions: the rubbernecks most likely coming to a dead halt before the congregating squad cars with their foreboding red, blue and yellow warning lights. Thanks to the public relations spin Hayes had put on his home and wondrous maze, all out there knew whose villa was under siege this evening. Why, not who, was the question.

If a camera crew from the local network was also out there, Joe Gallo could very well be hooked up to them, giving a blow-by-blow from the inside as they broadcast the scene from without. The rookie news gatherer was in the right place at the right time for a leap up the ladder of media muckraking. Fitz was gazing upon her date with pride and awe as Mack Macurdy tried to wrestle the phone from Joe with little success. Marge, looking amused, gave me a wink before running her hand, like a blade, across her neck. I responded with a slight but unmistakable nod, thinking that upon such mundane gestures trusting relationships are founded.

It was an hour before the medics exited the maze with their burden. The body on the stretcher with a blanket drawn over its face was the proverbial picture worth a thousand words.

When Eberhart returned, he mounted the convenient drum and told everyone, including the waitstaff, that they were to give their name and address to the officers now posted in the entrance hall with pads and pens at the ready, and then they were free to go. They were cautioned not to leave town without confiding their destination to the Palm Beach police and advised to be prepared to give statements regarding their movements this evening to the police when called upon.

Coincidentally, at the end of the short spiel the maze lights were extinguished, turning the glass doors into a black wall, bringing down the curtain on the first act of what was now clearly an official investigation into a suspicious death. Eberhart's announcement, short and to the point, did not invite questions.

I silently agreed with him that it was not necessary to take statements here and now as it was approaching midnight and would take till morning to complete the task. I also felt, not without a tad of pride, that the lieutenant knew he had an objective observer on the scene he could pump for facts that would facilitate interviews if they were deemed necessary.

The crowd lingered, as I thought they would, forming groups, whispering, shaking their heads and, on more than one pair of lips one could read the words, "In the maze? But how?"

I saw Carolyn and Billy make for the exit but they were waylaid by Laddy Taylor. A few words were exchanged between Carolyn and her stepson before she rudely sidestepped him, taking Billy with her. Laddy started after her, thought better of it and stopped abruptly, glaring with pure hatred at the departing couple. I hoped father and I had seen the last of Laddy Taylor but that, alas, was not to be the case.

Seeing that the exodus was moving along in orderly fashion, Eberhart and I went to the kitchen which was approached via a set of swinging doors at the rear of the dining room and down a short flight of spiral stairs that continued to the lower level and servants' quarters. There were no back stairs. The reason for the trip was to question the caterers assigned to the kitchen since their arrival and not to feed our faces. Our good intentions notwithstanding, we decided it was the best place to talk privately and so sat at the aforementioned table where I fed Oscar the facts as well as a cold supper.

The kitchen crew, two men and one woman, swore that only the actors had entered the kitchen, leaving the house from the kitchen door that led to the driveway and delivery area.

Oscar shot me a puzzled look and I began my précis of the evening by describing the carnival attractions Hayes had treated us to before presenting his wife as Venus, followed by the search for the goal.

"What time did they leave?" Oscar asked the man who was acting as spokesperson for the trio.

"Couldn't say, exactly," he answered. "We got here at

seven and were told to begin setting out the buffet upstairs when the actors left, not at any specific time."

"Let's sit, Lieutenant," I interrupted, "and I'll tell you the what and when of this remarkable evening at Le Maze."

HAVING SAMPLED MOST OF THE HORS D'OEUVRES, A kind waiter sliced us a few choice pieces of the filet and a baguette to go with it. The bread and meat had cooled but we made no fuss. Noblesse oblige, don't-you-know.

Oscar pocketed the notebook he had been scribbling on as I spoke and said, "Do you think they're all done upstairs?"

A glance at Mickey's hands told me the new day was an hour old. "I should hope so, and it looks like the crew in here is also ready to call it quits." I stood up. "After you, Lieutenant."

A man had been posted to stand vigil at the entrance to the maze and another at the front door. The big house was strangely quiet now when a few short hours ago it had re-sounded with the excited rumble of some fifty partygoers and the fatuous music of an organ grinder.

Except for the last of the caterers who had just finished sweeping the great room, it was empty save for the sparse furnishings and the huge, garish carnival posters lining the walls. The giant images of Marlena Marvel looking down on a deserted fairway were macabre to say the least.

Hayes was waiting for us in the solarium, a room com-mon folks call a screened-in porch, with Al Rogoff in charge. "The maid took something to calm her," Al told us as we entered. "She's snoring and I couldn't rouse her. Sorry, Lieutenant."

"A barbiturate," Hayes snapped. Either the guy was in-capable of polite conversation or he had been a professional barker for so long he couldn't distinguish between making a simple statement and hawking snake oil for thinning hair. Seated on an ornate divan he looked the size of a schoolboy done up in tux pants and a frilly shirt. Hair disheveled and eyes weepy, he was the embodiment of the grieving widower or a reasonable facsimile thereof.

Hayes had remarkably good skin that was so clean-shaven one wondered if he was devoid of facial hair, again bringing to mind a boy rather than a man who was at least sixty years old. With that baby-doll complexion and those brilliant blue eyes I would say Matthew Hayes was quite the successful Romeo in his day and perhaps still was.

"Nothing illegal," Hayes went on. "In our business the drug is a staple of the medicine cabinet like peroxide and Band-Aids." Explaining the peculiarities of his profession to the police was not a novelty for the master of Le Maze. "What happened to Marlena?" he suddenly blurted.

"If you mean how did she die, we don't know, Mr. Hayes. There are no marks on her body . . ."

"How did she get in the maze?" He rudely cut Oscar short.

Taking charge of the interview, Oscar lectured, "I'll ask the questions, Mr. Hayes. Your job is to answer them. Is that clear?"

Hayes gave a shrug, leaned back on his divan causing his feet to rise above the floor, and sulked.

"You put on a show here tonight, is that right?" Oscar began, taking the notebook from his jacket pocket.

"That's what I do, Lieutenant. Put on shows. I thought this town could do with a good swift kick in the arse to get them off their high horses."

The man was cantankerous and uncouth. The former can be forgiven, but not the latter.

"Who are the actors you hired for this show?"

"They're not actors," Hayes protested. "They're carny folks, down here on tour. I hired them for the evening."

"How many of them?"

"A dozen, give or take. If you think they hurt Marlena you're barking up the wrong tree. They left right after their gig."

"What time was that?" Oscar went on.

"I told them to quit at nine. Then I presented Marlena. Didn't McNally tell you all this?"

"Indulge me," Oscar insisted.

"I started the crowd picking names to match up for the search for the goal. You know about that?" Oscar nodded and Hayes continued. "Then Tilly came down and told me Marlena was feeling poorly and wanted to rest. She would come down for the buffet after we got back from the maze."

"Tilly is your maid?" Oscar put in.

"Matilda Thompson," Hayes said. "She's been with us for a few years. Hired as Marlena's assistant and stayed on after we sold the carnival and came here."

Oscar was consulting his notes as Hayes talked and I could discern no discrepancies between my version of the night's events and what Hayes was expounding.

"We were in the maze about an hour, wouldn't you say, McNally?" Hayes now turned to me.

"A little more than an hour," I said. "It would have been after ten when we came back in."

"That's when Tilly called down to say Marlena was gone. Just like that—gone. I went up and searched all the rooms on the second floor, including the attic which was locked from the outside, so how could she be up there?" Hayes sounded as if he were on the brink of hysteria. "And why would she be up there?"

"Calm down, Mr. Hayes," Oscar advised. "I don't know any of the answers right now and I'm not insensitive to your loss, I'm just doing my duty. It's best to get the facts when they're still fresh than later when our imaginations or wishful thinking color the picture."

Somewhat mollified, Hayes told how search parties were sent to scour the house and grounds, "I hired McNally on the spot and he told me to call you which I did because you're here, right?"

The lieutenant glared at me and I could hear Al Rogoff suppress a chuckle. "You didn't tell me you were working for Mr. Hayes," Oscar griped.

"It was a very informal hiring, Lieutenant," I offered in defense of my omission.

Hayes quickly jumped in with, "What do you need to make it formal, McNally? A down payment?" And I added acerbity to Hayes's other endearing qualities.

"We can discuss it at a more appropriate time, Mr. Hayes," I stated with what dignity I still possessed.

"So," Oscar said, summing up, "the maid left Mrs. Hayes resting in her room and went to her own room for a break. When she returns an hour later to rouse Mrs. Hayes, she finds that Mrs. Hayes is not where she left her. In fact, Mrs. Hayes has disappeared.

"You were all in the maze and the caterers were in the great room and the kitchen. No one could come down the stairs from the upper floor without being seen, and no one was seen coming down."

"So how did Marlena get in the maze?" Hayes demanded once again.

Al Rogoff, whose ability to suffer fools had reached its limit, bravely said what we all knew to be the truth: "She either walked there alive, or was carried there dead."

5

I DIVIDE MY TIME BETWEEN THE FAMILY MANSE ON Ocean Boulevard and a humble cottage in Juno. The amenities at Chez McNally include my beloved parents; our housekeeper-cook, Ursi Olson, whose culinary skills are a savory blend of haute cuisine and down-home scrumptious; her husband, Jamie, our houseman of few words and many hats; and last in order but not in rank, Hobo, the family canine. My digs are on the third floor beneath a leaky mansard roof.

The Juno cottage contains Georgia O'Hara, whom I affectionately call Georgy girl, or just plain Georgy. She is a green-eyed blonde state trooper who is short on the domestic arts and long on sex appeal. If I ever find an accommodating genie in a bottle, I will ask him to grant me Ursi Olson in Georgy girl's body. But askin' ain't gettin', as the mammy of that other green-eyed O'Hara girl so wisely lectured, leaving me no choice but to commute between the two.

Of late I find myself spending more time in the cottage than the manse. It began, I remember, by bringing in a change of shorts and socks, plus a toothbrush and razor, in order to start the day without telltale signs of having camped out, so to speak. But how *tempus fugit* when you're having fun. Now, I seem to have half my wardrobe there, commandeering the lion's share of drawer and closet space, both of which were rather sparse to begin with. It's cozy, to say the least.

That both Connie Garcia and I have taken up with partners some decade younger than ourselves I ascribe more to kismet than the ruthless game of brinkmanship too often engaged in by parted lovers. Connie and I enjoyed a long, open relationship wherein I was allowed to cheat and she wasn't. Being an unabashed chauvinist I found the arrangement smashing, as our English cousins call having fun.

When Connie began talking about her biological clock and playing Golden Oldies like *Apple Blossom Time* by the sisters Andrew whenever I came to dinner, I began to cheat in earnest. It was then that I tripped over a corpse in a tacky motel and got on Lieutenant Georgia O'Hara's most wanted list. Needless to say, I surrendered.

Connie, visiting one of her five thousand cousins in Miami, attached herself to the gyrating hips of Alejandro Gomez y Zapata on a conga line and appears to be having trouble letting go. As a clever tunesmith put it, *The music stopped, but they kept on dancing.* That I have found solace in a pretty, younger woman is, I feel, commendable. That Connie takes comfort in the arms of a handsome, younger man, I find appalling, and tell her so every chance I get. But that's kismet, not sour grapes.

The Juno cottage is actually the guest house of a decaying antebellum mansion, Georgy's landlady being Annabel Lee Hudson, an ancient recluse who came of age during the last big conflict and saw a German spy behind every palm tree. When that war ended she scarcely had a moment's peace before the atom bomb and the red menace replaced the Germans in her nightmares. When Russia gave up sharing in favor of competing, Annabel Lee got some shuteye.

Then along came the terrorists to keep her on constant vigil behind her beaded curtains, scrutinizing the long driveway leading to the cottage, ready to sound the alarm should anyone in a turban drive past. Annabel Lee has grown used to my red Miata and, of course, the caravan of fast-food delivery vans that are Georgy girl's supply line.

Gaining entrance with my very own key I saw that Georgy had left a light on for me in the parlor, or had forgotten to switch off the lamp before retiring. I closed it and felt my way to the bedroom which, given the size of the cottage, is impossible to miss, and began undressing in the dark. I have always slept in half pajamas, the top actually, but Georgy has bought me a nightshirt that is a T-shirt that comes to the knees. I find it rather comfortable except for the fact that the gesture is more the offering of a wife than a lover. This scares me.

Georgy sleeps in a variety of pastel-colored shorty nightgowns with her blonde hair in two pigtails. The overall effect is rather startling and the reason I keep transporting more and more of my belongings from manse to cottage. Tonight's frilly gown was pink and I saw it stir as I put on my nightshirt and took down my briefs.

"You always take off your shorts after you put on your nightshirt," Georgy observed.

"If I knew you were watching I would have reversed the process. I thought you were asleep."

"I heard your car come up the drive," she said, raising her lovely head from the pillow and modestly bringing the bedsheet to her chin. Georgy is so fair she seems to glow in the dark like an apparition that might fade with the dawn, but I knew the morning sun would only serve to make the dream a reality. "How was the party?"

"Not bad until the hostess dropped dead."

"You're kidding?" Georgy said, moving to sit up.

"I wish I were," I told her, "and so, I'm sure, would the hostess."

Wide awake now, she asked, "Accident?"

"The jury is still out. Why don't you go back to bed and I'll tell you about it in the morning."

Glancing at the night table clock, she reminded me, "It is morning, and you know I won't sleep until you tell me what happened."

"I have to get a bicarb. My tummy is talking to me."

Georgy propped herself up by placing my pillow over hers for support. "Your tummy is telling you that less is better. The bicarb is in the bathroom."

As I made my way to the bathroom I recalled Matthew Hayes telling us that barbiturates were the staple of the carnival's medicine cabinet. Thanks to Georgy girl's idea of food, bicarbonate of soda is our staple of choice. I dare not say this aloud as besides her beauty, Lieutenant O'Hara is also the Annie Oakely of the firing range.

I dropped two tablets into a glass of water and as I waited for them to self-destruct, I called out, "I only picked."

"You mean you picked the plate clean."

I didn't have the nerve to tell her it was a table I had picked clean. I drank the lemon-flavored brew and hoped for the best. Georgy had switched on the bedside lamp, looking like a child in her pigtails waiting to hear a fairy tale with a happy ending. I sat on the bed and told her about a party with a deadly ending. I had repeated the story so often, and rehashed it in my mind so many times, I could recite it by rote and did.

When done, Georgy opened her mouth to speak and I put my finger over her lips. "Don't say it," I ordered.

"Impossible." She said it anyway.

"Then I was witness to a miracle," I said, going to the closet and feeling shirt pockets until I hit on a pack of English Ovals, the only brand of cigarettes I used to smoke. I am down to two, maybe three, a day and felt the need for one now, thinking I would have another the next time I witnessed a miracle.

"Time of death?" Georgy grilled.

"Georgy girl, we won't know that until the medical examiner performs the PM, but you know time of death is not an exacting science with parameters of give or take some several hours."

"I also know that Eberhart asked the doc for a ballpark estimate and the doc gave it to him because they always do."

"Okay," I said, lighting up, "based on a career of examining fresh corpses, the doc guessed she had been dead some two to four hours."

"And that was when?"

"It had to be after eleven by then, maybe closer to midnight."

"You saw her as Venus at nine." The little girl in pigtails was now the policewoman in pursuit of the facts. "That makes the time of death shortly thereafter or approximately three hours before the doc saw her. Good for the doc and *cherchez* la maid."

I removed an eyebrow tweezer from a glass coaster and declared it an ashtray. "Lieutenant, we don't even know the cause of death as yet."

"If she had checked out via natural causes she would have been found on that chaise lounge and not in that ridiculous maze . . ." Georgy almost leaped out of the bed. *"The Lady from Shanghai,"* she announced with glee.

I am a Hollywood buff who can hold his own in the World Series of trivia games, but Georgy girl is a true connoisseur of celluloid. I speak of the industry's output from inception to the middle of the last century when they stopped making movies and began making something called "films." Connie would tolerate an evening with Fred and Ginger only to placate her biological clock while Georgy likes nothing better than to pop some corn and sing along with Nelson and Jeannette.

I am familiar with Orson Welles's cult film noir, *The Lady from Shanghai,* mostly because he turned his stunning redhead wife into a stunning blonde for the film.

Georgy now reminded me that the film's final sequence took place in a mirror-maze with . . . "The good guy and the bad guy shooting it out and hitting mirror images of each other. So many broken mirrors everyone connected with the movie had a zillion years of bad luck."

"Interesting, but what's the point?" I asked, happily puffing away.

"Mirror images. Nothing is what it seems. That's the point."

"Go to sleep, Georgy."

"Look, McNally, if she wasn't found on her chaise

lounge she was murdered and carried to the maze, or was led to the maze and killed there."

Which was what Al Rogoff had said. Marlena Marvel either walked there alive, or was carried there dead. But why and how was the enigma. Why kill her in one place and carry the body to another place? How could she have gotten from the second floor of the house to the goal of the maze, alive or dead, without being seen by literally dozens of people?

"You saw her on the second-floor balcony at about nine," Georgy reiterated. "Then you all went to the maze."

"Right." My English Oval was near extinction and I wished for another miracle. "We were all over that damn maze. Up and down every pathway and finally inside the goal. Marlena was not there. Believe me."

"And when the party moved out, the caterers moved into the great room which is in full view of the staircase leading to the second floor."

"Right again," I said. "But we found Marlena Marvel, dead, in the goal of the maze—and don't say it . . ."

"I won't say impossible," she assured me.

"You just did." I doused my smoke and got into bed telling her of Joe Gallo's on-the-spot coverage of the crime. "His name will be all over the newspapers and airwaves tomorrow—or today, that is."

"Joe? Was he there?"

"Big as life," I said, "and with Fitz, of all people."

"Who's he?"

"Not he, my dear. She. Elizabeth Fitzwilliams."

"Really? What does she look like?"

I thought a moment, then said, "Like that lady from Shanghai, only better."

Georgy closed the light. "He'll only make a fool of himself," she predicted.

"What's it to you? And may I have my pillow?"

"It's nothing to me." I got the pillow in my face. "Is she rich?"

"Her father is a Wall Street tycoon and she never wears the same dress twice."

"Another Palm Beach brat. Serves him right. She'll break his heart."

"The way he broke your heart, Lieutenant?"

She rolled over to my side of the bed, snuggling up like a kitten wanting to be stroked. "He didn't break my heart. He left it to make room for you."

I took her into my arms and whispered, "What a lovely sentiment. You're a poet, Georgy girl."

"And you're my inspiration. Are you going to work for this Hayes guy?"

"Not if I can help it. He's a cantankerous little runt and a con artist."

"In that case, McNally, *cherchez* la husband."

"Impossible," I said—then bit my tongue.

"AMAZING," WAS FATHER'S TAKE ON THE DEATH OF Marlena Marvel, which made the front pages of the *PB Post* and *Daily News* this morning, as well as in most of the dailies from Jacksonville to Miami, and the tabloid press across the country.

That father did not declare it impossible was testimony to the rigid objectivity he applied to his legal cases in particular and life in general. We were seated in father's office in the executive suite of the McNally Building on Royal Palm Way where his Sergeant at Arms, in the guise of executive secretary Mrs. Trelawney, dotes on the King and harasses his subjects.

Father explained that he was in the den last night reading Dickens, when Ursi disturbed his nightly journey back to the days of horse and carriage, divorceless marriage and a footman behind every diner. Ursi had come from her apartment over the garage where she and Jamie were watching the evening news when the story of trouble at Le Maze preempted the scheduled newscast. (Hayes is famous for his sense of timing.) Knowing I was a guest there, she thought father would be interested in the breaking story.

"Thankfully mother had retired," father said.

I mentioned that mother is a bit forgetful these days. She also suffers from hypertension. For this reason we tend to protect her from the more worrisome aspects of modern life which isn't easy given the modern media's obsession with doom and gloom. Knowing that her favorite son was in a house to which an ambulance and half the Palm Beach police department had been summoned would not help her cause.

Father put on the telly; as I had imagined, a camera crew had been dispatched to Le Maze and was giving viewers live coverage of the chaotic spectacle on Ocean Boulevard.

"It looked like a scene from a movie," father told me. "I tuned in after the arrival of the ambulance but just as someone from inside the house began communicating with the crew outside. He said that Mrs. Hayes was first reported missing, then found dead in that maze. I must say it was very confusing to say the least—and very distressing knowing you were there."

I didn't acknowledge his concern for my safety as I knew it would only embarrass him. We McNallys are not a demonstrative clan. We are there for each other but do so without getting in each other's way. I told him the reporter was Joe Gallo.

"You know him?"

"Quite well," I said. "He and Georgia were once an item, as Lolly Spindrift would put it."

Father tugged on his guardsman mustache, silently saying he would rather not be privy to the more intimate details of my love life, past or present. Prescott McNally is a gentleman who identifies more with the Victorian or Edwardian ages than the new millennium. In his three-piece suit, regimental tie (which he has no right to wear), starched collar, French cuffs with onyx links and pricey brogues, he resembles an actor waiting for his cue to enter the scene as the pompous Mr. Rich with a heart of gold.

I explained, yet again, the events that led to the discovery of Marlena Marvel's body.

"Amazing," father repeated, shaking his head thoughtfully. "And you were a witness to all this?"

"I was, sir, and so were at least fifty other people."

Playing the devil's advocate, which is a lawyer's prerogative, he asked, "Tell me, Archy, if you were in the witness box would you swear you saw this woman posing as Venus at approximately nine last evening?"

Suspecting where this would lead I answered without hesitating, "I would, sir."

"Based on what evidence?" my father, the lawyer, probed.

"Based on previous knowledge that she was famous for portraying the ancient statue and on the many posters on display which depicted her in the role."

"Both circumstantial," he concluded.

"I think you're implying the possibility that someone was impersonating Marlena Marvel."

"Exactly, Archy."

"So, where did the impersonator go after the perform-

ance? Remember, a search party went upstairs to hunt for
Marlena. They searched every room, including the attic,
and found no one. And, no one, except for the maid, came
down those stairs. Whether it was Marlena or an impersonator on that balcony, how did either disappear after the
show?"

Father leaned back in his leather upholstered swivel
chair and looked at the ceiling. "Could the maid be the
impersonator?"

"No, sir. The maid, Tilly, is a few inches taller than
Hayes, who's about five-feet-four in his heels. Marlena is,
or was, a big woman, and the statue, as you may recall, is
totally nude.

"But, for argument's sake, say there was an impersonator and the real Marlena was never upstairs but outside
the house all the while. Okay, but how did she get into the
goal of the maze? We were all over every passage and finally into the goal itself. When we left the maze not everyone came directly back into the house. About a dozen of
the guests stood outside, smoking, directly in front of the
entrance to the maze which remained lit after Hayes had
closed the flood lights inside the labyrinth. The entrance
to the maze was always in full view of the French windows and it's like looking out on a lit stage from inside the
house.

"Minutes later the alarm was sounded and the search
was on. No one could have walked or carried Marlena
through that entrance and to the goal without being seen."

Father tugged on his mustache. Lawyers like to tally the
facts and come up with a logical solution. In the case of
Marlena Marvel's untimely death the facts, as witnessed by
dozens of people, only exacerbated the mystery. "There's

got to be an answer, Archy, unless you believe in magic, and I don't."

"Neither do I, sir."

"Are you going to take the case?"

"Hayes thinks he's hired me, but I don't know if I want to get involved with him and his traveling carnival. Also, these are early days, very early days. We don't know how Marlena Marvel died and we don't know the intimate circumstances of the Hayes household, both of which the police, I'm sure, are now working to learn. I do know that Hayes is a bully and a boor whom I would be more inclined to suspect than work for. When the police complete their investigation he might need a lawyer more than a private investigator."

"Don't give him my card," father cautioned.

Before leaving I said, "Did I mention that both Laddy Taylor and Carolyn Taylor were at the party?"

That piqued his interest even more than the murder. "Really?"

"Lieutenant Eberhart told me that Laddy has been pestering the police to investigate his father's death."

"And what was their response?"

"That Linton Taylor has had a serious heart condition for years and died of a severe angina attack. His doctor found nothing unusual in his death."

"Just what I told him," father said. "I made it perfectly clear that there were no grounds to contest his father's will, especially since he and his father had been estranged for many years."

I described the scene I had witnessed between Laddy and Carolyn at the end of the evening.

"If he continues to harass her, she may have cause to

petition the police to keep him from approaching her," father said.

"I hope it doesn't get nasty."

"It already is, Archy. Hell hath no fury like a disenfranchised heir."

On that ominous note I took my leave only to be stopped by Mrs. Trelawney on the way to the elevator. "This expense report you dropped on my desk," she began, removing her pince-nez and waving the said report in the air.

"What about it, Mrs. Trelawney?"

"The item entitled dinner at Acquario."

"Do you have a problem with it, Mrs. Trelawney?"

"How many people did you feed?"

"We were two."

"Then I have a problem with it and will authorize payment of one half the amount presented, which could feed a family of ten for a year."

"And I will let it be known that you drink in private and have a passion for South American soccer players."

"You're incorrigible, Archy McNally."

"Only when provoked. Also, it may interest you to know the expense was incurred yesterday in pursuit of information regarding Matthew Hayes who is today's headline from coast to coast."

"Are you saying you anticipated that woman's demise?"

"I am saying, Mrs. Trelawney, that I am worth every cent of that expense report, and then some."

"I heard you were there last night. Your name was mentioned on *Breakfast with Mack and Marge*. They were there, too, and the reporter Joe Gallo who was their guest this morning. The three of them talked of nothing else but the party and the maze and the discovery of the body. The show is going to be repeated this evening by popular demand."

It didn't surprise me that Mrs. Trelawney was a fan of *Breakfast with Mack and Marge*. A woman of her ilk was just the charismatic Mack Macurdy's cup of tea. "You watch the show regularly, Mrs. Trelawney?"

"I never miss it," she cooed and almost blushed.

"I'll try to catch the repeat," I said.

"You can catch it sooner if you go to the mailroom," she called after me.

I paused and turned. "Pray elucidate, madame."

"Binky taped the show and is running it off in the mailroom on his VCR. Half the office has been down there when they should be working."

"I don't get it. How did Binky know this morning's show was going to be a blockbuster?"

"Joe Gallo told him, I guess."

"Binky is matey with Joe Gallo?" I exclaimed. "Since when?"

We do not have an electronic security system in the McNally Building but something far more reliable. We are sandwiched between Herb, our security person in the basement garage, who checks our comings and goings, and Mrs. Trelawney on the top floor who monitors our movements when in residence. They work in tandem like the jaws of a vise. Herb is a retired police officer and Mrs. Trelawney claims to be a graduate of a prestigious business academy. I believe she attended the FBI school for spies with a master's from the KGB. However, there are times, like now, when her information is most interesting.

"I assume, since they're neighbors," she explained.

My knees turned to water as they used to say in pulp fiction, a genre sadly missed by discriminating readers.

"Gallo rented the trailer next to Binky's at the Palm Court. Didn't you know that?"

No, I did not know that, but I do know that Sergeant Al Rogoff calls the Palm Court home. Rub-a-dub-dub, three men in a tub—and *give unto me a break!*

6

I STUCK MY HEAD INTO THE MAILROOM AND CAUGHT A show in progress. By this time all the big boys and girls had had their viewing so Binky's audience now consisted of secretaries on their lunch break. Binky had tried to date most of them but I fear his appeal is more to the mother instinct in ladies of Mrs. Trelawney's generation than to the raging hormones of lassies looking for a mate. A sage once wrote that for every man there's a woman but given Binky's record this may prove to be presumptuous, to say the least.

Binky's blond hair is desperately in need of "body," and Binky's pink-and-white body is desperately in need of hair. His brown eyes are woeful, even when he laughs. But perhaps I am being too harsh on one of my best friends. After years of job hunting that was no more successful than his quest for romance, I secured Binky Watrous a position as mail person for McNally & Son where he seems to have found a home. Translation: Mrs. Trelawney adores him.

On Binky's minuscule TV screen the dynamic trio of the moment were reporting, with gusto, the events leading to the discovery of Marlena Marvel's body in the goal of the maze. I must say it was riveting reportage by two pros and a rising star. Joe Gallo's small-screen debut was more than promising and while he wasn't as yet the suave anchorman with trendy tonsure and Savile Row suit, he was the boy-next-door with a bright future. The boy sported jeans and a tee, explaining, "I rushed right over and didn't bother dressing."

Didn't bother? Joey's garb was as calculated as his ambition. The comment got a glare from Mack and a smile from Marge. Poor Mack suddenly looked stodgy in his blazer and summer flannels. Marge, in a white pantsuit with a rainbow ascot at the throat, was the epitome of Palm Beach chic. I knew she was made up for the show (the endearing freckles were not visible) but the makeup artist, no doubt taken by her wholesome good looks, kept the war paint to a minimum and let her smile say it all.

Naturally they ran the footage of Mack's helicopter ride over the maze and, as I had recalled, it was not possible to distinguish the passages that led to the goal, but I did catch a fleeting glimpse of the sundial. I now knew it to be in the goal itself, but one would not know that from Mack's film. Also, the show's director ran a tape of Joe's reportage from inside Le Maze, more to Mack's annoyance and Marge's amusement. Was it all part of their act or were hubby and wife more competitors than helpmates?

Marge kept the hour from being totally maudlin by telling her audience about the fairway side shows and the clever way Hayes had contrived to pair off his guests for their search for the goal, and she gave the ladies (and perhaps the gentlemen) a titillating description of Carolyn's miniskirt and bare midriff.

"The beautiful Elizabeth Fitzwilliams wore a skirt that showed off her lovely legs, topped by her father's dress shirt, tails out, that showed off the rest of Fitz, as she is known locally. And Fitz was our own Joe Gallo's date."

Cut to a big fat close-up of Joey's boyish mug, grinning sheepishly. Oh dear, Georgy girl was going to blow a gasket over this telecast.

My name was mentioned as being present and as having been asked by Matthew Hayes to help find his wife when the maid reported her missing. So much for my desire to keep a low profile in this town.

Mack concluded the show with, "We saw Marlena Marvel in her fascinating portrayal of Venus de Milo only a few short hours before we saw her body being carried from her husband's celebrated maze. How did she die, almost before our very eyes, and how was she transported from her luxurious bedroom, through the dizzying passages of that labyrinth and to its hidden center without being seen by the dozens of guests she and her husband were so lavishly entertaining? These are the questions the police, the nation and you, our loyal viewers, must be asking themselves this morning.

"Marlena Marvel was a woman of a thousand faces, a seer and a healer. What dark forces, beyond our ken, did she summon to assist in her calling and, like Mephistopheles, did she finally have to pay the piper? We hope to have Matthew Hayes himself as our guest in the very near future, as well as Lieutenant Oscar Eberhart of the Palm

Beach police who is in charge of the case, and even Archy McNally, who may well be conducting his own investigation of Marlena Marvel's untimely demise. This show will be repeated at six this evening. Enjoy your day in enchanting Palm Beach."

Not a bad close if you like a cliffhanger, but I didn't appreciate his suggestion that Eberhart and I were in competition to solve the mystery of Marlena's strange death. Also, I hope Mack remembers to send his guest wish list to Santa.

When the show was over the girls turned to leave, chatting not about dark forces but about the cute reporter, then spotted me in the doorway. They smiled politely. After all, I am the CEO's favorite son. "You were there, Mr. McNally," one of them said in passing.

"What name did you pick?" another asked.

"Adam," I said.

"And who was Eve?"

"Marge Macurdy."

For some reason this got a laugh.

Binky was rewinding, no doubt in preparation for the afternoon showing. "Is this a postal holiday, Mr. Watrous?" I demanded.

"With the kind of mail you get, Archy, what difference would it make?"

And what is this? Sassing his betters? "Mrs. Trelawney knows what you're doing here, Binky. Beware the wrath of the Dragon Lady."

"Of course, she knows," he told me. "Mrs. Trelawney and your father were down here for the first show. We need an auditorium that can accommodate the entire staff. That's what I told your father."

My knees yet again turned to water having hardly solidified from the last jolt. "My father is a kind and patient man, Binky, but beware the length of the unemployment line."

Binky pushed some buttons and ejected the cassette. I hate people who are efficient at this sort of thing. I have recently converted from vinyl to tape in an effort to "get with it" as Georgy girl insists I should do. I reminded her of what Shakespeare accomplished with a quill pen but she didn't buy it.

"Joe told me Hayes hired you last night." Binky spoke as he rummaged through the letters, postcards and manila envelopes on his work station.

"You and Joe Gallo are neighbors, I hear."

"Jealous, Archy?"

What cheek! "And why would I be jealous?"

"Maybe you wanted that trailer. The Palm Court is hot right now in case you haven't heard."

"Moi? Moi?" I exploded. *"Moi* rent a trailer in the Palm Court? Why would I trade a home on *the* Boulevard with an ocean view for a glorified railroad car mounted on concrete blocks?"

"You're a snob, Archy."

I had been called incorrigible and a snob and the day was only half over. Who knows what other honors would be bestowed upon my person before the sun set? Binky continued to move the mail around his work station as if in search of two pieces of a jigsaw puzzle that meshed. Also, he was avoiding eye contact when talking and he had not, as yet, begged to assist me should I tackle the Marlena Marvel case. Add to this his surly responses to my civilized queries and I suspect a subtext to this tiresome meeting.

"How did Joe hear about the vacant trailer in the suddenly highly desired Palm Court?"

"It's a long story," he said to an envelope with a foreign stamp.

"I have all day," I encouraged.

"Joe was having a drink with Connie at the Pelican . . ." Binky began.

I should have known. Women and the Pelican, a lethal combination. The Pelican is a social club founded by a group of gentlemen, myself included, who find the more traditional Everglades and Bath and Tennis a tad too supercilious for our taste. The fact that neither of the aforementioned clubs would court our membership was not relevant to our decision to form a more perfect union. And perfect it was until some blockheads suggested we allow women to join our fraternity.

I opposed the movement on the grounds that when dating Connie *and others,* I could take *and others* to the Pelican without fear of running into Connie brandishing a stiletto. I fought a long, tough campaign for keeping women out of the Pelican, except when escorted by a member— and lost. Good Queen Victoria said the women's suffrage movement sounded the death knell of civilization; however, Her Majesty didn't know it would one day get Joe Gallo digs in the Palm Court.

So Connie became a Pelican and I could no longer take the *and others* to my club for a meal. Now I take Georgy to the club and Connie takes Alex to the club when he's in town, which is very often. It was inevitable that we four should one day collide. Introductions were made and Connie and Georgy took an instant dislike to each other and became good friends as women who dislike each other often do. Georgy invited Joe Gallo to join us one evening when Connie and Alex were also there and lo! we are now one big unhappy, extended family.

For those who are keeping score, let me remind you that I am an ex of Connie Garcia's, Joe is an ex of Georgy girl's, leaving Alejandro Gomez y Zapata the only virgin (in the broadest sense of the word) among us. Does it bother me that I am the oldest of this male trio, threatened by a Latino hunk and a Norman Rockwell poster boy? Yes, it does. In fact, if I could evoke Marlena Marvel's dark forces to transport the pair to Oz, I would do so without a moment's hesitation.

So Connie and Joe are at the bar of the Pelican when in walks Binky (whose membership I sponsored), and when Joe mentions that he is a man in search of a residence, Binky tells him about the vacant trailer at the hot Palm Court.

"I assume it's the trailer twixt you and Al Rogoff," I said.

"That's the one." Binky addressed a letter in a priority mail envelope. I wondered how long it had been sitting in the mail room.

"What does Al think of his new neighbor?"

"You know Al. He doesn't say much," Binky told the priority mail.

Al thinks Binky insipid and after last night he will declare Joe Gallo verbose, a word I added to Al's lexicon to replace yenta.

And what was Connie doing at the club with Joe? My guess is she was scouting him out as fodder for her boss lady's insatiable appetite for male pulchritude while pretending to enlighten him on the newsworthiness of Lady

C's latest charity. Connie's job description now includes dangling goodies before her boss in order to keep her eyes off Alejandro Gomez y Zapata. And Lady C has enough *dinero* to buy back Cuba, which makes Connie one nervous señorita—and Archy one happy guy.

From experience I knew the only way to get Binky to tell me what was on his mind was to pretend I didn't want to know. "Well, Binky my boy, a blessing on all three of your households. Now I must be off, as duty calls."

With that he swung around and faced me. "You're going to take the Marlena Marvel case, Archy?"

"I think I'll wait to learn how she died. There's a possibility that there may not be a case here at all."

"If you do take it," he said, "I might not be at liberty to assist you."

All things considered, that might be the best piece of news I had all day, however it was also the most curious. "Are you leaving our employ, Binky?"

"Actually, I'm moonlighting as a stringer for Joe Gallo," he finally confided.

A stringer in the news business is many things. Among them: assistant, gofer, snitch, wannabe and ambulance chaser. Yesterday, Joe Gallo was practically a stringer himself, but since breaking the Marlena Marvel story we have a Lowell Thomas in our midst. Setting priorities, I cautioned, "I hope you remember that anything you see or hear in your position with McNally and Son is considered confidential and must never leave the confines of this building."

"I know that, Archy," Binky protested.

"Just make sure you don't forget it," I lectured. "I take it Joe Gallo wants to further his career by solving the Marlena Marvel case. Yes?"

"He was in on it from the start," Binky reminded me.

"So were dozens of others," I reminded him. "If I get involved in this brouhaha, and it's a big if, may I know why you would rather string for a novice like Joe Gallo than a pro, which I am?"

"It's a matter of compensation, Archy. Joe is talking ready cash for services rendered."

"And, like someone else I could mention, thirty pieces of silver bought your loyalty. Shame on you, Binky Watrous."

"I knew you would have an attitude over this," he countered.

"Attitude? Not at all. I wish you well in your new career path, Binky, but I also wish that you and Joe would keep your noses out of the Marvel case and leave it to the police. It's their job as it's Joe's job to report the news, not make it."

"Joe has some very original ideas about what happened," Binky said with an enthusiasm for his new leader once reserved for me. Such is the power of ready cash, a commodity I lack.

"And may I know what Joe Gallo thinks of all this, Binky, or are you sworn to secrecy?"

"He's going public on the ten o'clock news tonight," Binky proudly announced, "so it won't be secret for long." Here Binky took a deep breath, squared his rather bony shoulders and exhaled the word, "Levitation."

Good grief. "You mean up, up and away like the man in tights and a cape?"

"Marlena Marvel was a mystic, Archy. She read the cabala and practiced the black arts."

A witch hunt. I might have known. And it was Mack Macurdy, not Joe Gallo, who was behind this proposed media blitz which accounted for Mack's dark forces finale to today's show. Before this was over Mack would have every medium, seer and kook in southern Florida on the show and garner national publicity for his efforts. There's nothing the public likes better than a magic show as it beats having to exercise the cerebral cortex any day of the week. Hence the resident clairvoyant and daily horoscope column in all our tabloids.

Joe Gallo had jumped on the bandwagon because Macurdy was on to a good thing and Joey boy was no fool. As for solving the mystery of the death of Marlena Marvel and all that implied, Mack's bizarre input could yet prove a double-edged blade. One, it would keep the amateurs out of Eberhart's hair or, two, it could rile the public into a state of panic as did the flying saucer craze of some years back. What Palm Beach did not need was to play host to the next convention of witches and warlocks. There are those in this town who would say that would be like carrying coals to Newcastle.

"And just where did Joe get all this scintillating information on the life and times and reading habits of the late Marlena Marvel?"

"The Internet," Binky said as if I should have known and, in retrospect, I guess I should have. "The carnival has a web site that gives her bio as well as her cures, predictions and daily horoscope forecasts. She was deep, Archy."

"She was a carny lady. A charlatan, a quack and a swindler and somebody beat her at her own game."

"So how did she get from the house to the maze, Archy? Tell me that."

"I don't know nor do I profess to know, Binky my boy. How did she die is the question. By her own hand or that of another? If the latter, who done it? The answers will lead you through the maze and to the goal. Again, I strongly suggest that you and Joe keep out of this. If there's a murderer about, be he of flesh and blood or atmospheric vapor, don't court his attention.

"I also suggest you deliver that priority envelope to the addressee before it gathers moss."

He picked it up, looked at it and handed it to me.

Priority mail for me? This had to be an all-time first. As Binky had so blatantly put it, my mail is nothing to write home about, if you'll excuse the pun. I cradled it in the open palms of my hands, gingerly, much like a father being presented with his firstborn.

"You think it's a letter bomb?" Binky speculated.

"Who would want to blow me to smithereens?"

"You've helped a lot of people in this town, Archy, and no good deed goes unpunished."

"And from whence comes that bit of misanthropic gibberish?"

"From you, Archy."

"Oh!"

7

"ALIENS," SIMON PETTIBONE OFFERED ALONG WITH the perfectly drawn lagers he placed before Al Rogoff and me. "That's the concerted opinion of today's lunch crowd, Archy. Too bad you missed it, but you can still get in on the pool if you're feeling lucky, unless your connection to the case disqualifies you. On Wall Street they call it insider trading."

"What's the entry fee, Mr. Pettibone?"

"A C-note, Archy. Like always, I'm the bank."

In fact, Simon Pettibone was a closeted investment banker whose Wall Street smarts got him the sobriquet D.J. (for Dow Jones) Pettibone. He is also the Pelican club's bartender, majordomo and father confessor. An African-American of regal bearing, he and his family are the nuts and bolts of the Pelican, with lovely daughter Priscilla as waitress, son Leroy the chef and Mrs. Pettibone our den mother.

We Pelicans are famous for our pools that go from the sublime—sporting events—to the ridiculous—the number of inches between the hem of Priscilla's miniskirt and her knees which draws estimates that prove the imagination is far more ingenious than the eye. Most of Palm Beach and vicinity had got the details of last night's gala-cum-tragedy from the Macurdys' show. Between the show and the morning papers, the circumstances of Marlena Marvel's death were the talk of a town whose citizens thrive on dividends from gilt-edged securities and scandal. It was, in short, fodder for a Pelican pool to guess who done it.

"Aliens?" Al Rogoff scoffed.

"Correct, Sergeant," Mr. Pettibone told him, polishing a glass and gazing into it as if it were a crystal ball. "According to the boys who lunch, the wee people beamed this unfortunate woman up to their waiting saucer for her annual checkup that went awry as happens more often than your local GP cares to admit, then beamed her back down to the center of that maze doohickey thinking it was a cemetery."

In answer, Al drank from his pilsner goblet and licked the foam from his upper lip.

"Do you go along with aliens, Mr. Pettibone?" I probed.

"Not at all, Archy. Given the lady's arcane leanings, I suspect Voodoo. You take a chicken, wring its neck . . ."

I raised my hand to silence him. "We await lunch, Mr. Pettibone."

With a toothy smile and a sly wink he retreated to the far end of the bar and delved into the arcane postulations of *The Wall Street Journal.*

Knowing that Al worked last night and wouldn't report back for duty until this evening, I had invited him for a late lunch at the Pelican. Aside from a few stragglers in the dining room lingering over their coffee, the clapboard dwelling that houses the Pelican was quiet and even Priscilla had vanished to the Pettibones' apartment upstairs or, more likely, to catch a few rays on the beach in her itsy-bitsy bikini designed to drive innocent men to wrack and ruin.

"If you think the alien connection is goofy," I said to Al, "wait till you hear what your new neighbor is about to impart to his listeners."

"Joe Gallo?" Al mused. "Nice kid but a little verbose, if you know what I mean. I saw him at the party last night but I didn't know he was broadcasting live until this morning. Did you catch the Macurdy show?"

I said I hadn't but mentioned that Binky gave the entire staff at McNally & Son a taped viewing this morning. "Gallo is going to stress the occult, Al, and play it for all it's worth."

"I know," he answered. "I talked to the palace this morning and they're already getting crank calls thanks to Mack Macurdy's close that linked the Marvel dame to dark forces."

The palace is Al's name for Palm Beach police headquarters on South County and Australian Avenue that resembles a Palm Beach villa, replete with acres of barrel clay tiled mansard roof, making it worthy of Al's sobriquet.

"And you may as well know," I warned, "that Joe has talked Binky into joining him in the witch hunt which I'm sure is being masterminded by Mack Macurdy."

Al laughed. "It'll keep the two from trick-or-treating all over the Palm Court come Halloween."

Leave it to Al Rogoff to cut to the source of Mack's ignoble scheme. Halloween was indeed fast approaching, a fact I'm sure influenced Mack's decision to play up the dark forces angle. Matthew Hayes would admire Mack's timing—or was the amazin' one the puppeteer who had the media dancing to his artful manipulations? I never knew a case to have so many questions the morning after the night before.

"You gonna take the case, Archy?"

"Everyone is asking me that. I don't know, Al. Hayes hired me on the spot to find his wife last night, but that was before your gang found her dead in the maze. The guy is a flake, so who knows if he'll even remember who I am today."

"How come Binky is deserting you for Joe Gallo?"

"It's a question of compensation, of all things."

"You mean you ain't never given him a dime for services rendered, right, pal?"

"No, Al, I ain't never, but I bought him many an expensive lunch and dinner."

"Hint, hint," Al teased, downing the rest of his beer.

"I got Binky out of my back pocket, Sergeant, but he and his new sidekick will nestle right into yours in search of classified information."

Al told me what they were likely to find in his back pocket but prudence prevents me from putting it in print. However, he did add, "You know my doormat that tells visitors to GO AWAY in big black letters?"

"I do, Al."

"Well, since Joe took the trailer next door I've added a second line to the message."

"What's that?"

"BOTH OF YOU."

With that Leroy arrived with our repast. Mr. Pettibone had set us up at the bar and due to our tardiness we simply ordered the day's lunch special which was fish and chips.

This is the granddaddy of fast food, invented in England where it is served to go wrapped in the London *Times,* or *The Mail,* or the daily of your choice. Leroy's came on a plate and the cod was sparingly breaded and sautéed rather than fried. There is a difference. The chips (french fries to Americans) were of the shoestring variety, prepared from scratch and rendered neither soggy nor brittle, but crisp.

Two monkey dishes containing coleslaw and horseradish, which is a root vegetable of all things, accompanied the meal as well as a fat kosher dill for each of us. Not bad for latecomers to the feast.

"You in on the pool, Archy?" Leroy questioned.

"I may be disqualified, Leroy, on the grounds of inside trading, according to your father. Did you take a plunge?"

"I did," Leroy confessed.

"Aliens?" Al asked, drowning his chips in ketchup.

"No way," said our chef.

"Demons?" I speculated.

Leroy shook his head. "A rope ladder," he prophesied. "You know what I mean. You've seen them advertised in magazines. You hook it on the windowsill, roll it out and climb down in case of fire. That's how she got out, Sergeant. Dig around and you'll find the ditched rope ladder."

Not bad, I was thinking. I had suggested last night that Marlena went out the window but I was thinking more of a free fall than a portable fire escape. At any rate, it beat being beamed up to a flying saucer.

"How did she get in the maze?" Al asked him. "There were people standing outside the entrance."

"Those people, Sergeant, were puffin' and chattin' and so busy looking at each other an elephant could have tramped by and they wouldn't have noticed."

Leroy certainly knew the Palm Beach Smart Set. When deprived of a mirror they did tend to gaze upon their companions, looking for flaws.

"She got to that goal thing because she knew the secret," Leroy declared. "Lordy, her husband done built the zigzag cabbage patch. Right, Archy?"

"He did, Leroy. But why did she climb down a ladder and go to the goal?" I asked, rather impressed with Leroy's theory. "And how did she die there?"

Leroy summed it up in two words. "Carny folks. She goes down that rope ladder, he says she's disappeared. The search is on and they find her in the center of that maze. How did she get there? Magic, of course. It's like the three-card-monte scam. How did the pea get under that middle shell when you saw it go into the one on the left? Carny folks, Archy."

Al listened to every word but did not pause in his noshing to do so. "So how did she die?" he wanted to know.

"Ain't figured that out as yet," Leroy said with a shrug. "But the pool has two parts. Who did her in and how did she get into that maze. I think I'll take half the prize as nobody thought of a rope ladder."

When Leroy departed I intoned, "Not bad, Sergeant, you must admit. A rope ladder could be the answer."

"Sorry, pal, but it ain't."

Sensing I was about to learn something not yet known to the public at large I cautiously asked why.

"She was dead when she was dumped in the maze."

"Is that a fact, Al?"

"I told you I talked to the palace this morning. I wanted to see if they needed me to come in early but they were covered. It'll be on tonight's news so I ain't telling no tales out of school. The PM showed that she was moved after death."

"But how?" a little voice inside my head kept asking. How? Then came the jackpot query. "How did she die, Al?"

"Digitalis poisoning," came the jackpot answer.

I aborted the delivery of a crispy chip from plate to mouth. "Say again?"

"You heard right," Al said. "Digitalis poisoning, ingested orally."

"Isn't that a medication taken by heart patients?"

Al nodded. "So they tell me, and before you ask, she wasn't on any medication for her heart. In fact she was in good shape for a dame her age."

"I don't get it," I groaned.

"You ain't alone, so don't get puffed over it."

I signaled Mr. Pettibone for refills. He pulled our beers and served them with the utmost discretion. A good bartender knows when to prattle, when to listen, and when to disappear. Mr. Pettibone, a master of the craft, always knew which of the three was required and acted accordingly.

"You made a thorough search of the house last night." It was pure rhetoric but one had to start someplace.

"We were there till daybreak," Al said, "and found nothing for our pains. Eberhart posted a man at the entrance to that maze all night and as we speak the boys are raking those paths with a fine-tooth comb."

"What about the attic? Hayes claimed the door was locked from the outside when he looked up there but we only have his word, and the maid's, for that. It seems to me that up is the only way anyone could have gone without being seen. No one could have come down those steps, I'll swear to that to my dying day."

"The attic held what you would expect from the owners of a traveling carnival, Archy. Props, costumes and a dozen steamer trunks full of more of the same. There's even a wooden Indian up there, remember them?

"There were barbells that looked like they weighed a ton but Pete, our rookie, picked it up with one hand. Decks of cards that were all the ace of spades, mirrors that distorted images, jackets with hidden pockets, magic wands, and one of those boxes you put a pretty dame in and saw her in half. It had a pair of wooden legs sticking out of one end and a bald head sticking out of the other end. The ankles of the legs opened and inside was a tiny battery-operated motor. You know why, pal?"

"Press something and the toes wiggle like they belonged to the lady being sawed in half."

"Give the guy a cigar. And there was even a trunk full of Marlena's tonic for men, guaranteed to put lead in grand-pop's pencil."

Unable to resist, I quipped, "I always wondered where Viagra got its start."

"There was everything you'd expect to find in Hayes's attic but no human being or escape hatch anyplace up there except the windows." Al finished his spiel as well as his lunch. The man eats like Smokey the Bear and in many ways he resembles the cartoon omnivorous mammal.

"Back to the rope ladder," I sighed.

"Forget the rope ladder, pal. Can you see anybody carrying that big lady down one? And who was up there to do it? The maid? She's like two inches taller than her boss who's a glorified midget." Al shook his head. "Everything connected with this crowd is pure hoke. Pick a card, any card, and you'll always pick the ace of spades. Someone poisoned the lady and carried her down to that confounded maze."

"Eberhart is treating it as murder?"

"Archy, suicides don't roam around after the fact. They are always found *in situ.*"

"Forget how she was moved from bedroom to maze," I advised. "That's the ruse, the smoke screen, the hocus-pocus, engineered to keep us all from working to discover why Marlena Marvel was killed which would lead us to who done it. In short, Sergeant, keep your eye upon the doughnut and not upon the hole."

Al gave this careful consideration before answering, "You think Leroy got one of them glazed doughnuts for dessert?"

"MIRRORS," URSI UTTERED THE MOMENT SHE SAW ME peeking into the kitchen for a sneak preview of the evening's bill of fare. "They do it with mirrors."

The magnificent bouquet wafting out of the oven door as she opened it for inspection told me this prodigal son's fatted calf was to be a rib roast. Ursi spooned the juices emanating from the meat and lovingly poured them over the quartered potatoes and sliced onions surrounding the ribs. I had picked a good night to touch base with those I loved.

"Have the good people of Palm Beach nothing better to do with their time than speculate and postulate on the death of Marlena Marvel?" I scolded.

"Of course not, Archy," Ursi readily admitted as she darted from refrigerator to cupboard to chopping block. "And why not? First that maze and now a suspicious death inside the creepy thing. Why, it's replaced Carolyn Taylor versus Laddy Taylor as dinner table conversation in better homes all over the island."

Should you be wondering why our Ursi is privy to dinner conversations in better homes, it is because Ursi and Jamie are the unofficial heads of the nonexistent domestic confederation of Palm Beach. With a communication system that would dazzle the Pentagon, the chefs and butlers, the parlor maids and au pairs, the chauffeurs and valets, report to the Olsons every nuance of the life and times of those they serve.

And how right Ursi was. Her comment made me realize that I had not thought of Carolyn and Laddy since reporting their encounter at Le Maze to father earlier in the day. "How do they work the mirrors, Ursi?"

"Well, how should I know that?" she snapped. "But Felicity, she's the laundress over at the Stuart house, has a brother who ran away from home to join a traveling carnival, and it was him that told her they used mirrors to make you think you were seeing one thing when all the time you were seeing something else. Makes me dizzy to think about it."

Watching Ursi organizing dinner made me dizzy but I didn't let on. *Seeing one thing when all the time you were seeing something else* stuck in my craw. Obviously they (whoever they are) had us all hoodwinked last night. What had we seen that wasn't there or what had we not seen that was there? Believe nothing of what you read and one half of what you see I have always thought to be sound advice, but which half of what we saw last night was real and which wasn't? It was more than intriguing, it was unsettling to those of us who believed in a logical universe.

"Jamie and I were watching the late news last night when the story broke," Ursi said, breaking eggs for what would later prove to be coffee soufflé for our dessert. "It was thrilling, and knowing you were there I ran right down and told Mr. McNally what was happening. He tuned right in and that reporter fellow started broadcasting from inside the house. What was it like, Archy?"

"Not as exciting as Joe Gallo would have you all believe, I'm sure. If you watched the Macurdy show this morning you know as much as we who were there."

"I never miss *Breakfast with Mack and Marge,* Archy," she said with that look women get when they're smitten— or when they're beating eggs for a coffee soufflé.

Mack certainly had the mature ladies of Palm Beach eating out of his hand and he wasn't about to relinquish the position to young Joey Gallo. The battle of the newscasters was off and running and the odds are twelve to seven that tomorrow morn Mack appears in jeans and tee with dear Marge laughing her cute head off.

"Your mother knows about last night, Archy," Ursi went on. "Impossible to keep it from her what with everyone talking about it and her attending a meeting of the garden club this afternoon. She learned you were there so I'm glad you decided to bed down here tonight and show her that you're all in one piece."

In fact, it was just the reason I had come home to roost. I called Georgy to tell her I would not make it to Juno this evening and she informed me that it was just as well as she had to appear at the local high school to give the incipient drivers a lecture on defensive driving. She told me every member of the football team, basketball team, tennis team and swimming team had signed up to attend. You see, last semester, in order to make the meeting more informal and relaxed, Georgy had foregone her uniform in favor of shorts and rugby shirt. Word of mouth had ensured tonight's SRO audience but how many of those poor teen athletes would come away with a sound knowledge of defensive driving? Oh, Georgy!

I STILL HAD ENOUGH OF MY WARDROBE LEFT AT HOME to dress properly for the McNally happy hour. I stuck with the jeans I had worn all day and replaced my lavender polo with a white dress shirt, a black, hand-knotted bow tie that drooped in the western fashion, and a linen jacket in lime green. Rather natty for a catch-as-catch-can endeavor.

Mother insisted on seeing the Macurdy show rerun on the grounds that she was the only person in Palm Beach who had not seen it. We gathered in the den where father mixed our stand-up martinis in his silver cocktail shaker, poured them into two crystal stem glasses of impeccable quality, and added a green olive to each before serving. It was all much ado about very little as father's martinis are as dry as a rain forest in August. Mother, wisely, drinks only sauterne.

The show was mercifully devoid of commercials, making it shorter than the original but not any less engrossing for having seen it before. Like any clever puzzle it could be watched by those seeking a solution countless times in search of clues that had escaped them previously.

Mack reported the facts, Marge filled in the background and the tape of Joe's live coverage made for a show that proved, yet again, that truth is not only stranger than fiction, it is also far more entertaining. After Mack's original close, a new one had been added with Mack stating, "We have learned from Lieutenant Oscar Eberhart that Marlena Marvel died of digitalis poisoning, taken orally, and the case is now officially classified a suspicious death. Digitalis is a heart medication. Marlena Marvel did not suffer from any heart ailment, nor did anyone in her household, and no traces of the medication have been found in Le Maze, the Ocean Boulevard mansion currently occupied by Matthew Hayes and his late wife, who was known professionally as Marlena Marvel.

"How did a lethal dose of digitalis find its way into Le Maze and into a drink ingested by Marlena? Digitalis is derived from the dried leaves of the foxglove plant, an herb that, for centuries, has been a staple of witchcraft pharmacology.

"Please stay tuned for the evening news and the latest details of the Marlena Marvel mystery. This is Mack Macurdy hoping you will join my wife, Marge, and me for breakfast tomorrow morning."

With a press of the remote, father banished Mack Macurdy from our den. "Enough of that," he said.

"I'm so confused," mother complained, her cheeks flushed. "Is he saying this is the work of witches?"

Mother's hypertension was clearly aggravated by the excitement and nonsense being stirred up by Mack Macurdy and was most certainly not what she needed while relaxing with her glass of wine. Father was now annoyed and glaring at me because he had no one else upon whom to vent his ire over television in general and Mack Macurdy in particular.

"He's muckraking, mother, and there just isn't any polite way of saying it. It's now a case of suspicious death and that's as much as the police, or anyone, knows at this point, but that doesn't garner viewers so Macurdy is luring his listeners with claptrap."

"You were there, Archy. What do you think happened?" she persisted.

"I think, like the police, that someone died suspiciously last night and an investigation is underway."

"They said this man, Matthew Hayes, hired you last night. Is that true?"

"Mother, he hired me when his wife went missing. As we now know, she was found. I think that ends my participation in the case. Besides, I may be out of town and unavailable."

As intended, that got her mind off murder and witchcraft or, more likely, she allowed me to spare her the details of Palm Beach's latest scandal. Mother is aware that father and I try to shield her from the seamier side of modern life and indulges us in our efforts. Madelaine McNally, despite her recent failings, is still a vital, intelligent woman and for that I am ever grateful.

Even father raised one bushy eyebrow at my news which I have tried many times to emulate, but simply can't.

"You're going on a trip, Archy?" Mother exclaimed, hoping it would be a honeymoon cruise on some love boat out of Fort Lauderdale.

"New York for a long weekend is what I have in mind," I told my amazed audience. "Edward Brandt, who goes under the professional name of Rick Brandt, performed in a revival of *Death of a Salesman* at our local theater which was seen by a producer from New York. It seems the man was impressed with Rick's performance as Willy Loman's son and offered him a role in an off-Broadway show he was mounting. Rick, or Todd as he then called himself, was a waitperson at the Pelican on busy Saturday nights and he's sent me two tickets to the opening via priority mail."

"How exciting," mother said. "I like a success story." Then, rather timidly, she asked, "Will you be taking Georgia?"

Since Connie and I came to a parting of the ways and I took up with Georgy girl, mother is a tad skittish over who might be my significant other of the moment. My parents have met Georgy and were very taken with her, especially father who is keen on shapely blondes.

"If she can get away, that is just what I had in mind," I said.

Father wanted to know if I planned to stay at the Yale Club. He is a member, having graduated from that university as well as its law school. I attended Yale but, alas, got the boot for reasons that are none of your business.

This led to a discussion of the many benefits of staying at the club with mother recalling the happy times she and father had enjoyed there when visiting the Big Apple. "Why, it's our New York apartment," mother noted. "Of course you'll stay there, Archy. Take a suite and charge it to father's account."

Father raised one eyebrow.

URSI'S RIB ROAST, WITH OVEN-ROASTED POTATOES AND balsamic-glazed pearl onions, was superb. With it came asparagus, which I always think is so elegant, served at room temperature and garnished with a drizzle of olive oil and a smattering of lemon zest. The bread was Ursi's own sourdough loaf and the starter was a Caesar salad—chopped hearts of romaine lettuce tossed with plenty of freshly grated Parmesan and creamy dressing with a hint of garlic and topped with anchovies, then nestled within individual lettuce leaves.

The lord of the manor decanted a rare vintage Bordeaux St.-Èmilion poured into stemware that explodes if subjected to a dishwasher. Also not destined for the dishwasher was mother's gold leaf Limoges father referred to as our "everyday" china. What comes out on special occasions? Don't ask.

At my love nest in Juno we dine on ovenproof stoneware which is impervious to dishwashers, however, the Juno cottage does not boast such a convenience. Such are the anomalies of life.

The finish was the coffee soufflé concocted with Starbucks's best beans and presented with a dish of freshly baked *tuiles*. Home is where the stomach is and Juno is where the heart is and never the twain shall meet.

Mother retired early, leaving father and me to our port and tobacco, a tradition of a bygone era father observes and I go along with because I'm a good son—and I like a good port. I opted for an English Oval, my first of the day, and father made a show of clipping the end of a very expensive-looking cigar before lighting it. I poured the port.

Father opened the conversation with, "Laddy Taylor called just before I left the office. He wants me to execute an order to exhume his father's body."

"On what grounds, sir?"

"That Carolyn Taylor poisoned her husband with the digitalis he was taking for his heart condition."

"Oh!"

8

I HEARD FATHER'S LEXUS PULL OUT OF OUR DRIVEWAY just as I came out of the shower. I've often wondered if he revs the engine when leaving in the morning to wake me or to warn the drivers on the A1A that a man obsessed with getting to the office before nine is about to merge with those not in training for the Daytona 500.

I gave my attire extra attention as the previous evening father had requested I attend his conclave with Laddy Taylor, which was to take place at three this afternoon. After hearing Laddy's startling accusation against Carolyn coming on the heels of the PM findings on Marlena Marvel's death, father thought I should be part of the encounter and I fully agreed.

As I was to sit in on a high-profile meeting in the executive suite I decided to dress up rather than down, ergo I selected a tan gabardine single-breasted suit that I hadn't worn in years. I took a deep breath and managed to get the zipper zipped, the fly button buttoned and a red, white and blue mesh belt (which wasn't necessary) through the loops and buckled before exhaling. I felt slightly dizzy but such are the forfeitures of dressing up—not to mention forego- ing my daily two-mile swim while making whoopie in Juno.

A yellow silk shirt by Armani, no tie, and a pair of ankle-high boots completed the picture of a man to be reckoned with.

In the kitchen Ursi was clearing away the breakfast dishes and Jamie sat at the table sipping coffee and leafing through his morning paper.

"You missed Mack and Marge," Ursi couldn't wait to tell me. "And what a show it was. Witch Hazel and Count Zemo were the guests."

"Witch Hazel," I gasped. "Are you sure you weren't watching a commercial?"

"No, Archy. Witch Hazel is a famous clairvoyant. She reads the tarot, tea leaves and palms on selected cruise lines all over the Caribbean. She studied in Haiti where the zombies come from and Mr. Macurdy was lucky to get her on such short notice."

I could not believe what I was hearing. Macurdy wasn't only playing this angle for all it was worth, he was chewing the scenery in the process.

"And what did Ms. Hazel have to say about Marlena Marvel?" I foolishly asked.

"She knew her, Archy," Ursi said with awe. "Witch Hazel knew Marlena Marvel."

And why not? They were in the same line of business, competing for the patronage of the suckers whose numbers are legion. "Did their paths cross in Tiffany's while shopping for crystal balls?"

"No," Ursi said, setting me up with a place mat, napkin and silverware before pouring out a glass of fresh squeezed orange juice. "They knew each other three thousand years ago in Egypt. It seems they were both concubines to a pharaoh who might have been a woman disguised as a man."

"Besides preposterous, Ursi, it sounds rather risqué. I hope you don't believe any of this."

"Oh, it's all in fun, Archy, and such a diversion from the dreary guests Mack and Marge have had on lately. But you have to admit these clairvoyants' predictions come true sometimes and it's enough to give you the gooseflesh."

Sometimes the weather forecaster's predictions come true, but it's never given me the gooseflesh.

"Witch Hazel thinks Marlena was working on a new recipe," Ursi carried on, "and went too heavy on the foxglove which we all now know is where the heart medicine comes from. Imagine doctors prescribing a witches' brew for a bad heart."

And right there was the crux of why Mack Macurdy should be stopped from foisting this nonsense on the public. He had cleverly equated digitalis with foxglove with witchery in the minds of the gullible and unsuspecting. Not only would the police be getting crank calls, so would doctors and, no doubt, the clergy. I wondered what Marge thought of all this.

"So how did she get in that maze?" Jamie said, not looking up from his paper.

Speaking without being addressed was so unusual for our Jamie that both Ursi and I turned to stare at him. How

Ursi got him to say "I do" is one of the more perplexing
unsolved mysteries of our age.

"What's your take on all this, Jamie?" I asked him.

"The papers say she died of this digitalis poisoning and
was moved after she expired, so someone carried her to
that maze."

"I'm with you, Jamie," I told him.

"Well, gentlemen, tell me how it was done with a houseful of people and no one seeing her moved?" Ursi said in
triumph. "And Count Zemo, who's an astrologer for one of
those tabloids, cast Marlena's horoscope for the day she
died and it said she was to expect the unexpected."

"As she didn't expect to drop dead I guess you have to
hand it to Count Zemo. Now, Ursi, do you think I can have
a cup of java and breakfast *without* Mack and Marge?"

"What would you like, Archy?"

In my gabardine girdle I thought it best to go easy on
the victuals. "I think one scrambled egg and a slice of dry
rye toast."

"You feeling sick, Archy?" Ursi inquired.

"I'm trying to lose a few pounds so I can fit into my
suit," I admitted.

"Which suit is that, Archy?"

"The one I'm wearing."

BEFORE LEAVING I STOPPED TO VISIT WITH MOTHER IN
the greenhouse which is more an ICU for her begonias than
a botanical incubator. I so enjoy seeing her in this setting
where the morning sun, filtered through the tinted glass,
casts her in an angelic glow. Here, going about her work in
straw bonnet, apron and gardening gloves, her smiling face
reflects a serenity her medication can't duplicate.

She tried to brush a smudge from her cheek as I bent to kiss it and only succeeded in making it worse. "Oh, what a lovely shirt, Archy. Yellow is my favorite color, you know."

I also know that any color I choose to wear suddenly becomes her favorite hue. "I hope you're not paying any attention to the nonsense Ursi tells me is being beamed into unsuspecting homes this lovely morning. Remember what I said last night about Mr. Mack Macurdy."

With a wave of her gloved hand, she boasted, "I've lived long enough to know when my leg is being pulled. I grew up when we all had our own personal fortune teller called a Ouija board. It said I was going to marry a prince."

"Well, you certainly married a man who thinks he's one," I teased.

She laughed and pretended to chide me for poking fun at father. "I'm glad you're taking this for what it's worth," I said. "The mystery of poor Marlena Marvel will soon be resolved with nary a ghost nor goblin figuring in the final solution."

Putting down her miniature hoe she looked up at me and said, "You know, Archy, we mustn't think all things can be explained scientifically, either now or in the future. We've all had experiences that defy the laws of logic. My mother and grandmother talked of strange occurrences in their lives they credited to divine intervention. Miracles are the foundation of most religions, remember, so don't stick your nose in the air at all things mystic because you might end up tripping over a sleeping gnome and falling flat on your face."

The woman I had come to reassure at a time of mass hysteria had summed it all up in a few well-chosen words. Keep an open mind, and in matters of faith always hedge your bets. "I will remember that, Mother, but I doubt if a gnome carried Marlena from her bedroom to the maze. She was a very large lady."

"Will you be involved?" she asked yet again.

"I honestly don't know, Mother, but let's hope the police have it all wrapped up before the day is over. I understand they're giving this top priority, so keep your fingers crossed—or shouldn't I say that?"

"It can't hurt," she maintained.

When I bent to kiss the smudge, she wanted to know if I had made my plane reservations for the trip north.

"I don't think I'll book a flight, Mother."

"Then how will you get there?"

"I thought a broomstick built for two would be just the thing."

"Off with you, Archy McNally, and do bring Georgia to dinner before too long—and Connie, too, I think—Oh, I'm so confused."

"François Marie Arouet, otherwise known as Voltaire, said we should all tend to our own gardens, Mother."

"As you can see, that's just what I'm doing."

I GAVE HERB A BEEP AS I DROVE THE MIATA INTO THE underground garage of the McNally Building, parked, and took the elevator directly to my office. The monster's little red eye blinked in greeting as I entered the converted utility closet that has my name on the door. For years I avoided getting hooked up to what is called voice mail which, by the bye, I believe is a contradiction of terms. Mail is something you read, not something you listen to. A tag I find more suitable for the red-eyed monster is squawk box.

Mrs. Trelawney flatly refused to continue to take my messages when I was out of the office which, being a high-priced snoop, is most of any working day. To make her point she had the temerity to disconnect the link that transferred my calls to her on the third ring. Being cut off from the outside world I acquiesced to her demands, grudgingly, and joined the twenty-first century.

Now, when I press the button, an electronic voice from Hades announces, "You have four messages."

Click. "Archy, it's Georgy. What is going on down there? Joe's name is in all the papers and his puss is all over the television. Your fancy party ends up a Murder One case and Joe's playing show-and-tell on the evening news. Last night he did a duet with a foxglove plant and said it was what witches used to garnish the goulash like it was oregano. That Fitz girl got her picture in our local rag with the caption saying she stood by Mr. Gallo throughout his history-making broadcast. I'll bet she did. Call me. I'll be at the Juno barrack all day doing paperwork—and oiling my revolver. I'll expect you for dinner tonight. It's roast chicken with a foxglove salad."

I found a bottle of extra-strength aspirin in my top desk drawer, opened it, removed two tablets and took them straight.

Click. "It's Connie. Lady Cynthia Horowitz requests the honor of your presence for cocktails this evening at six. It's a command performance, so be there. Lady C has flipped her lid over the Marlena Marvel uproar and wants to get all the facts straight from the horse's mouth. Get that look off your face, Archy, it's better than being called upon when that animal's other end is evoked. You know Lady C never gets up before noon but today she had the housekeeper, Mrs. Marsden, bring in her café au lait at eight, practically dawn around here, so she could watch the Macurdys' show.

"Did you see it? What a hoot. The only thing Mack left

out was little Eva running barefoot over the ice with blood-hounds snapping at her derrière. But it gave Lady C the brilliant idea of giving a Halloween party and inviting everyone who was at Le Maze the other night, especially Joe Gallo, if you please—or even if you don't please. She's going to have Witch Hazel tell fortunes and Count Zemo cast horoscopes. Costumes are de rigueur and Madame plans to be Venus de Milo if she can figure out what to do with her arms. Do you think Alex and I should come as Frankenstein and his bride? Alex is so tall, and his shoulders are so broad, he would hardly need any padding. But what a shame to disguise his lovely face.

"Are you working for Hayes? Madame wants to invite him and the maid, Tilly—what a name! Is Hayes really three feet high? He can come as a Munchkin. Ha-ha. Call me."

I discarded the bottle of extra-strength aspirin and rummaged through my desk drawers for something more potent—like arsenic.

Click. "Adam? This is Eve, a lady on the verge of a nervous breakdown. Did you see the show this morning? Well, if you think it was the pits tune in tomorrow for an interview with a woman who claims she was healed by Marlena, another who claims she was poisoned by Marlena and a man who claims he was Marlena's lover when she was Molly Malone in Des Moines. They're crawling out of the woodwork and Mack is booking them without bothering to screen them first. Our producer is delighted because our ratings have soared and there's talk that we might be picked up for national syndication.

"Witch Hazel brought a flask to the set which I'm sure was filled with booze, and proceeded to lace her coffee with it every time she was off camera. She was practically comatose before the hour ended and people called asking if she had gone into a trance. Count Zemo couldn't keep his hand off my knee and suggested he read my horoscope in his motel room this evening. Mack keeps calling Hayes, begging him to appear on the show, and has offered the maid, Tilly, a fortune for one appearance—and you and Eberhart are on his hit list.

"Help! Can we have a quiet drink this evening? I need a shoulder, but your rib will do."

I forgot the arsenic in anticipation of a tête-à-tête with Palm Beach's newest star. What a gal. In the midst of chaos she's able to keep her sense of humor and share it with one in need. I was still smiling when . . .

Click. "Matthew Hayes here. I hired you but I don't remember firing you. So where were you all day yesterday when the police were all over my house and maze, looking for clues? Did they find anything? How the hell should I know. They don't tell me anything, they just ask foolish questions like I know the answers when I know as much as they do, which is zilch.

"Have you talked to them? Will they level with you? In my dealings with the police I've always found that a well-greased palm keeps them from working my side of the street. You have my permission to spread the wealth but don't go hog wild. My pockets are deep, but they don't reach China. I'm a grieving widower but no one in this sunbaked paradise shows any respect for my plight. I'd like to see you at your earliest convenience which, according to my schedule, is noon today."

The pipsqueak. The nerd. The contemptuous braggart. Grease palms? Matthew Hayes was a sleazebag and if I went to work for him it would be for one reason only—to prove he knows more about his wife's death than he's fessing up to.

POP! A thousand-watt bulb lit up in the balloon over my head and—by Jupiter, I would do it. I would swallow my pride and do it. For the first time in my career I would take on a client for the sole purpose of exposing him as an iniquitous fabulist.

Unethical? When you're tiptoeing through the trash you're bound to get your feet dirty, and I had no choice. What better place to learn the secret of the maze than in Le Maze itself, and Matthew Hayes has just opened the door to his nemesis. The sire would remind me that one is considered innocent until proven guilty and I would abide by that dictum, giving Hayes every chance to recant any complicity in the crime.

I wouldn't grovel to his offensive demands but I would bend just enough to have him believe he had nailed his mark. Nor would I be the first McNally to play the fool and have the last laugh. My grandfather, Freddy McNally, was a clown with the Minsky circuit who bought Florida acreage for peanuts and sold it for gold.

This decision had me feeling full of P and V and raring to go. The game is afoot, as a predecessor used to say, and I was off and running sans my Watson who has forsaken me for financial gain. Not to worry, I had Georgy girl and her well-oiled revolver.

Prioritizing my time, the first thing I did was call the damsel in distress. Thanks to the number of times I had called Marge to decline her offers on mother's behalf, her number was in my Rolo.

"This is Zemo's brother Count Dracula, inviting you to indulge in a bloody Mary with me this very evening."

"Archy? Thank goodness. I thought it was another kook who knew Marlena and was willing to tell all for a modest honorarium. Are you free this evening?"

"How about the Four Seasons for a drink at six? You'll have to take a rain check for dinner."

"A drink and some sane talk would be fine. I'm not putting you out, I hope?"

"Not at all. The only thing I had going was a date with an Egyptian mummy but she got tied up."

"Ugh!" Marge responded.

"Sorry. Does hubby know you'll be clinking glasses with a handsome young man this evening, or should I beware Tarzan on the prowl?"

"Mack is so wrapped up in his sudden success he couldn't care if I were dating a blond surfer from South Beach. He's having dinner with our director and producer. I declined on the grounds that enough is enough. I've got three calls waiting, Archy. Six at Four Seasons."

Had she implied that a blond surfer from South Beach would be more a threat to Mack than me? My ego was bruised, but it would heal.

Next, I called Georgy. "Don't hold dinner for me and keep the foxglove chilled. I'll be late."

"Why?" she questioned.

"I have a date for drinks with a lovely lady at the popular Four Seasons. That's why."

"Oh, Archy, be serious."

Always tell the truth when you don't want others to know what you're up to because the truth is the last thing they'll believe.

Again stating the facts, I said, "I'm taking the Marlena Marvel case for her husband."

"I thought you didn't like him."

"I don't, but it's got so much play in the press and on television I think I should jump on the bandwagon. It can only enhance my already impressive reputation."

"Meaning there's more to it than you want to repeat on the phone."

"You are so bright, Georgy girl."

"Are you going to work with Joe?"

"Joe, my dear, has teamed up with Binky Watrous," I informed her.

She was still laughing when I hung up.

The next damsel on my prioritized list was Consuela Garcia.

"Lady Cynthia's residence."

"The horse's mouth is calling to tender his regrets. I have a sore throat and I've better things to do than listen to her blab about her Halloween party where she will parade around in her seventy-five-year-old birthday suit. I also have a suggestion as to where she can put her arms, but decorum expurgates the thought."

"Madame will not like it, Archy."

"Then Madame will have to lump it."

"Are you working for Hayes?"

"That's for me to know, and you to find out."

"You're having a hissy fit, Archy."

"If I am it's because you took Joe Gallo to the club for drinks, thereby getting him a trailer at the Palm Court. Al Rogoff is not thrilled."

"Then Al Rogoff can lump it. What's it to you, Archy?"

"You were scrutinizing that poor boy on behalf of your lady boss. Admit it, Connie."

"Don't be silly," she said, knowing how silly that sounded.

"You are a dealer in human flesh, Consuela Garcia, and should go to the party as the bride of Simon Legree."

"That's rich, coming from a robber of cradles."

"People in glass houses . . ."

"I must go, Archy. Good day."

"Before you do," I persisted, "can you tell me what Alex was doing with Carolyn Taylor at a marina in Miami?"

"That's for me to know, and you to find out."

Showing restraint, I calmly hung up the phone, sat at my desk, buried my head in my arms and cried.

9

As I turned into Hayes's driveway I passed Mack Macurdy, in a black Jaguar, pulling out. I assume he was making a pest of himself trying to enlist Hayes and Tilly for a stint on his show. I wondered how long Hayes could resist hamming it up for a live TV presentation, and I imagined Tilly was already spending the loot Mack was dangling before her like a carrot egging on a donkey.

If I had anything to do with this case I would discourage either of them from appearing on television or making statements to anyone but the police. This would also spare the public Hayes's crocodile tears and Tilly's histrionics. These are the perks I give, gratis, to the citizenry of Palm Beach, for which I am never thanked.

Tilly opened the door and gave me a reverent curtsey. In all my years of being greeted by housekeepers and butlers in this town it was the first time one reacted as if I were a prince making house calls. Le Maze was so full of theatrics one didn't know where the show ended and reality began.

"Mr. Hayes is in the den," Tilly informed me.

On close observation, and in less chaotic circumstances, I noted that Matilda Thompson was a pretty little thing with a figure and gams the shapeless maid's dress and sturdy oxford shoes diminished but could not entirely hide. What other duties did she perform for the carnival besides lady-in-waiting to Marlena? Salome dropping her seven veils for gawking teenagers at two bits a pop? Or did she step into the magician's box and get sawed in half?

I gave her the standard line for calling upon a house in mourning. "How is he holding up?"

She responded with the standard comeback, "As well as can be expected, sir."

The niceties observed, I got down to business. "Were they a happy couple, Tilly?"

"Oh, yes, sir. Very happy. Mr. Hayes is distraught over his loss. How could such a thing happen when we were all . . ."

"I was here, Tilly, remember?" I cut her off before she could tell her story which no doubt would include the chaise lounge Mr. Hayes had purchased from the previous owners of Le Maze. "I don't know how it happened, but it certainly did happen."

"Yes, sir."

She led me to the den, tapped on the door, removed a piece of paper from the pocket of her uniform, shoved it into my jacket pocket and, purposely avoiding my astonished gaze, opened the door to announce me. My flabber was gasted but I composed myself for my entrance only to be admonished by the little man himself. Rising from his overstuffed divan, he accused, "You're late."

"According to your schedule, I may be, according to

mine, I'm not, and the only schedule I adhere to is mine. *Comprende*, Mr. Hayes?"

He glared up at me, was about to speak but changed his mind and laughed instead. "If you had let me get away with that I would have thrown you out," he said.

"Before this association is over, Mr. Hayes, you may yet find it necessary to show me to the door."

"So," he cajoled, "we have an association."

"Only if your schedule doesn't conflict with mine and if you pay your bill when presented and not gasp at my outrageous fee."

He gave me that amazin' glare, shrugged, and waved to a club chair that did not match, in fabric or color, the divan. But then it would be hard to find one that could match what appeared to be a piece designed especially for the waiting room of a high-end bordello.

"Okay, okay," he barked, "get off your high horse and have a seat. I expect to be cheated and if you came cheap you wouldn't be worth the breath to blow you away."

I took my seat. "I won't cheat you, Mr. Hayes, nor will I grease palms. I don't work that way and neither do the Palm Beach police."

He sat on the edge of the divan so that his feet touched the floor. "Spare me the sermon. I know what you and everyone in this town thinks of me. Brassy and trashy and out with the garbage. They came to my carnival but they won't invite the carny man to break bread in their homes."

"Then why did you come here, Mr. Hayes?"

"Why not? I have the money for it. I wanted to retire down here but Ringling and Barnum had already staked a claim on the West Coast so I came east and bought this mansion in a town where I would stick out like a sore thumb and rattle a few beads. It's what I do, Mr. McNally. Rattle sacred beads."

The note Tilly had slipped me was rattling for attention and I had all to do to keep my hand out of that pocket. Le Maze was taking on all the characteristics of a house in a gothic novel. Thanks to the various search parties I knew the attic did not hold the master's mad wife, nor did the basement contain comfy hiding places for those who shun the sun. What it did harbor was two carny pros who might just be leading me up the garden path which, in this case, was a maze. Archy, you're in a stew and surrounded by cannibals.

Having confessed to his reason, inane as it was, for coming here and being dubbed *persona non grata* for his pains, Hayes sank back onto his divan and dropped his chin to his chest like a naughty boy seeking sympathy. Dye the gray hair black, exhibit him with clever lighting and you would peg him for a preppy. His body was remarkably trim due I'm sure to genetics rather than any conscious effort to keep the belly flat and the skin taut.

Today he wore jeans and a sweatshirt with a Ferris wheel logo manufactured, I guessed, especially for his carnival and available on the fairway. (Fool that I am, I suddenly wanted one.) His black shoes appeared to be the same ones he had worn with his tux and I suspected they were the only shoes he wore in public. In my father's day they were called "elevator shoes," with the heel built up both within and without, adding a good two inches to the wearers' stature. Deception was Matthew Hayes's forte, from head to heel.

"What happened to Mrs. Hayes?" I asked, hoping the question would remind him of the reason for my presence.

"Someone poisoned her and she died. Haven't you heard?"

"Let's cut the rhetoric, Mr. Hayes, and see if we can't begin to make some sense of what happened here the other night. For that I'll need your cooperation, not snide comments. That is if you want to learn what happened to your wife or just bask in the publicity."

He leaned forward and put his hands on his knees to signal his displeasure. "You're a saucy bastard, McNally."

"And you're a calculating one, Mr. Hayes. Shall we go on with this or do you want to show me the door?"

He shrugged as if in resignation and said, "You think I'm a cold and calculating S.O.B. because I'm not prostrate with grief and bawling over what happened. Well, you're wrong, Mr. McNally. I'm sick over what happened to Marlena and I'm scared out of my wits. But I'm carny, born and bred, and we don't wear our hearts on our sleeves, as the saying goes. That's for the suckers.

"I wasn't born in a trunk, but in a tent on the night the carny was packing it in, one step ahead of the sheriff. Carny folks are all family so they dug in and paced with my father. When the law showed up, the sheriff and two deputies, they brought them to our tent to witness my coming into the world like they were the three wise men. Now I ask you, would anyone serve papers on a scene like that? Of course not. My father gave them a shot of the bathtub gin they had come to arrest us for selling and we all lived happily ever after.

"So you see, Mr. McNally, I was on the game from the moment I was born."

Nice story, but how much of it was true? "Why are you scared, Mr. Hayes?"

"Why? Because if they got Marlena, they'll get me next, that's why I hired you."

"Who are they?"

"I don't know, Archy, I swear I don't know. I pulled a lot of scams in this big country and made a lot of enemies. Now one of them is coming after me. Between us, Archy, I made a lot of husbands angry and more than one took a buckshot to my rear. I figure one of them got Marlena to make his point."

I noted how he suddenly dropped my given name as he made his appeal. I was also aware of the effectiveness of this maneuver. Could I believe him? Dare I believe him?

"What do you know about digitalis, Mr. Hayes?"

"I've heard of it. Who hasn't? But it was never prescribed by a doc for me, or Marlena. How it got into her tea, I'll never know."

"Tea?" I questioned. "When did she take tea?"

"Right after her gig, like always. I mean after she did her turn as Venus. Tilly always brewed her a pot of tea after a performance and Marlena took it while she soaked in the tub. She had to bathe, you know, to get off the greasepaint."

This got better all the time. If Marlena took the lethal dose of digitalis while soaking in the tub, someone had to not only haul her out of the tub, but dry and dress her before carrying her to the maze—with a houseful of people running amok all over the place. I'll believe it when a snowstorm snarls traffic on the Dixie Highway. (Bite your tongue, Archy.)

Remembering the note, I asked, "Can you trust Tilly?"

"With my wallet," Hayes answered, revealing his priorities. "She's a good kid. Not too bright but she's been with us for over two years. She was an aspiring actress we found slinging hash in a diner trying to make enough in tips to get her bus fare to New York. Marlena told her we were headed east and Tilly joined the tour. Between us, she was a star attraction in the stag tent. She did Cleopatra with a garden snake that passed for an asp. Not bad, and she got half the box office every performance."

There was a hell of a lot transpiring "between us" on this initial interview and I added one more. "Between us, Mr. Hayes, are you and Tilly strictly boss and employee, no hanky-panky and exploding buckshots?"

He raised his hand, high. "On my word of honor, Archy."

I almost laughed in his face.

"Have the police leveled with you?" he wanted to know.

"I haven't talked to them since the night Marlena died." It wasn't really a lie as I don't consider my personal talks with Al Rogoff official banter with the PB men in blue. "I take it they haven't said anything to you that might help our cause."

"Not a thing. They searched the house and the maze all day yesterday, questioned Tilly and me, but never said what they found or what they were thinking."

Because they didn't find anything and were thinking that they were being bamboozled but couldn't figure out how. I know, because I was feeling the same way. "These people who you claim may be out to get you, do you think they're carny folks?"

"They could be," he answered. "There were plenty I duped and cheated and fired over the years. I don't play favorites, Archy. Now I'm settled down with big bucks and a plan to make more in Palm Beach, and maybe someone doesn't like it. Could be carny folks."

"There were carny people here the night of the party. They supposedly left before we started our hunt for the goal. Did they all leave?"

"If they didn't, where are they hiding? Behind the wallpaper?"

Good point.

It was time to make the final pitch and I did so without preamble. "How was it done, Mr. Hayes? You know all the tricks of your trade. Share this one with me, and the police, to avenge your wife and perhaps save your life in the process."

"You're wrong," he bellowed, waving his arms and fidgeting in his seat. "I don't know all the tricks. That's a sucker's conceit. Anyone who says he knows it all drops his guard and when you drop your guard you're dead. Don't ever forget that, Archy. If there's a sucker born every minute, there's a new scam being concocted every thirty seconds to keep up with the demand.

"Did you ever see a performing magician hold a piece of string, about a foot long, in his hands and ask someone in the audience to come forward and, handing him a scissors, have the person cut the string in half? The magician now holds two pieces of string, one dangling from each hand. He clasps them between the palms of his hands, pretending to pray, opens his hands and, presto, he is holding one piece of string, about a foot long.

"A theater full of people, far more than were gathered in this house the night Marlena died, and all of them have been hoodwinked by the oldest trick in the magic trade. All of them will swear the string was cut in two and magically rejoined in the illusionist's mitts. Do you know how it's done, Archy?"

"No, sir. I don't."

"But you know it's a trick."

I nodded. "Conceded. I know it's a trick."

"Well, I don't know how Marlena was poisoned in her bath and carried to the goal of the maze. But, like you, I know it was a trick."

Very clever. He just confirmed what the police and I already knew but did so in the form of a parable. While other little boys were reading the adventures of Huck and Tom, little Matthew was reading Elmer Gantry. But, I bear witness, Matthew Hayes was beguiling. If I sat here any longer he would make a convert of this skeptic.

"So we can rule out magic," I offered.

He laughed. "You've been listening to that Macurdy fellow. A lot of hogwash but don't write him off. He's latched on to a good thing and is making the most of it. I would do the same."

"Did Marlena believe in the supernatural?"

He seemed to mull this over before answering, "Yes and no. Look, I taught Marlena everything she knew about the carny business. You know how we teamed up. Everyone does. It's no secret. I showed her the ropes. Fortune-telling, healing, lucky charms, contacting beloved ones on the other side. Marlena was good at it. A natural, you might say. And like all naturals, I think she was beginning to believe her own hype. No surprise. Film stars, athletes, politicians—sooner or later they all believe the lies planted by their press agents.

"Let's say Marlena thought she had the gift."

"Could she have been fooling around with digitalis? Experimenting with it as a potential restorative? A kind of medically endorsed snake oil."

I got the shrug. "Could be, but so what? If she was using herself as a guinea pig who carried her out of the house and to the maze? Her medium?"

It always boiled down to the same thing. How did Marlena Marvel get from the house to the maze? The razzle-dazzle. The illusion. "Find her murderer," I thought aloud, "and we'll know how it was done."

"That's your job, Archy." He rose to signal the end of the meeting.

"One question before I go. Who, besides you, had a map of the maze, showing the way to the goal, or had access to it?"

"I had the only one, which the police have confiscated. Only the architect of the maze knew the secret and he gave me the map. I doubt if even the men who did the planting could figure it out. Of course Marlena had access to my copy."

But that's not how she got to the goal of the maze.

"A final piece of advice." I spoke as we left the den and made for the front door. Tilly was nowhere in sight. "I would not appear on the Macurdy show if I were you. Nor should your maid, if she's asked."

"Why not?" he snapped.

"It would not help your reputation as a publicity hound and it would cast doubts as to the depth of your sorrow. Not to mention that everything you say can, and will, be held against you. Keep a stiff upper lip, Mr. Hayes, but keep it shut."

"There's a limit to what I'll take from you, Archy, and if I want your advice, I'll ask for it."

"Meaning you'll go on the show?"

"Meaning I haven't made up my mind." We arrived at the front door and he put his hand on the big brass knob. "What's your next move, Mr. Detective?"

"I haven't the foggiest idea, Mr. Hayes."

"Try to learn what the police are thinking. That guy, Eberhart, is your pal, right?"

"He's an acquaintance, Mr. Hayes. I'll stay in touch."

"You want a retainer?"

"Check your mail. It comes with a self-addressed return envelope."

He opened the door and bowed me out.

I walked very slowly to the Miata, the note in my pocket feeling like a piece of the family silver I had pinched from my unsuspecting host. When on official business I always drive with the top up as a young man racing around Palm Beach in a convertible suggests frivolity. It also serves as a cover when I want to read a clandestine note passed to me by the help and not be viewed doing so from an upstairs window.

I got in the car and even fastened the seat belt before extracting the treasure from my pocket.

"When you read this, I'll be browsing in the bookstore on South County Road."

Matthew Hayes had best keep a watchful eye on his wallet.

10

THE CLASSIC BOOKSHOP IS A PALM BEACH FAVORITE with locals as well as our winter visitors and this afternoon it was bustling with patrons in search of a good read. The Classic bills itself as a Full Service Bookstore and is true to its word. Autographed first editions, book signings and interviews with authors are just some of the reasons the shop is such a popular community gathering place.

Its logo appears in bold black letters over the canopy that shades the large display window, and two palm trees flank the storefront. Entering, I nodded to several acquaintances before spotting a woman, all in black, whom I suspected was my date. She was browsing in the mystery section which I thought was rather germane to the events that brought us here. And, how clever of her to have picked the Classic for our rendezvous. Owing to the shop's popularity it was a venue that would cause the least amount of speculation should we be observed, as opposed to a corner table in a tacky saloon.

Not wearing a hat I couldn't tip it, but I did perform a slight bow. "Fancy meeting you here."

"Thank you for coming, Mr. McNally." She was indeed all in black, from shoes to slacks to blouse with décolletage that showed a hint of black bra. The dark glasses completed a picture of someone striving for anonymity and failing miserably. In Palm Beach on a sunny fall afternoon, she stood out like a giraffe frolicking with penguins.

"Thank you for asking," I said. "I take it you have something you'd like to impart that you did not want Mr. Hayes to hear. Yes?"

Examining the paperback titles, she replied, "Someone visited with Madame the night of the gala. The night Madame died."

This was certainly a revelation. "And who was the caller?"

"Mrs. Taylor," she muttered through pursed lips.

"Carolyn Taylor?" I questioned, unable to mask my astonishment.

"Yes, her." Tilly continued to look at the spines of the shelved paperbacks and not at me. It was most distracting. We were also blocking the aisle to the annoyance of the browsers.

I touched Tilly's elbow and gently moved her toward the rear of the shop. "Carolyn Taylor called on Marlena the night of the party? By invitation? They knew each other?"

"I don't know if she was invited upstairs, but they knew each other. Since we came here Madame has met with Mrs. Taylor many times. I drove Madame to luncheonettes and coffee shops in West Palm and Lake Worth where Mrs. Taylor would be waiting. They talked over coffee and sandwiches. I was never invited in so I don't know what they talked about."

My astonishment turned to disbelief. "Did Mr. Hayes know Mrs. Taylor was friendly with his wife? Did he know they were meeting clandestinely?"

Tilly shook her head. "I don't believe he knew."

Not being able to see her eyes went a long way in reinforcing my distrust in her story. "But if Mrs. Taylor came to the house, he must have seen her."

"She came to the house the night of the party, just like everyone who was invited. Remember when the lights went out before the presentation, then the spotlight came on and moved up the stairs to the balcony where Marlena was standing? We rehearsed that several times the night before the gala. I was on the balcony, in a corner where I was hidden from view, but close to the stairs.

"Just when the spotlight illuminated Madame I saw Mrs. Taylor on the second-floor landing. She ran into the upstairs hall. When the presentation was over and the light faded, I quickly led Madame off the balcony and to her bedroom. Mrs. Taylor was not there."

"You mean Mrs. Taylor went back downstairs, to the party?"

"I don't know where she went. I only know that she was not in Madame's bedroom when we got there."

"Did you tell Madame what you had seen?"

"No," she answered. "Madame and Mrs. Taylor were so secretive about their relationship I thought it best not to mention the incident. Perhaps Mrs. Taylor had arranged to bring something for Madame that was not my business to know."

My, my, wasn't Tilly the most circumspect of ladies-in-waiting.

Carolyn was with us, downstairs, when the lights came back on and people began queuing up to draw names out of the hats. But was she there from the time the lights came back on or did she arrive moments later? I honestly didn't know. Hayes was talking, people were milling about, I couldn't swear who was or wasn't present at that exact moment.

Tilly's news was so startling I was having a difficult time taking it all in. Also, we had to keep walking, pretending interest in the books on display without hampering the efforts of more serious shoppers. Perhaps the Classic wasn't the ideal place for this meeting but now that we were here I had no choice but to make do.

Carolyn Taylor and Marlena Marvel were friends who met regularly at off-beat coffee shops in the surrounding area, but never in Palm Beach proper? It was possible, as all things that are not impossible are possible. But was it likely? Of course not.

Carolyn could have mounted the stairs when the lights went out. Sticking close to the wall she would have gone undetected by the meandering spotlight. Marlena was highlighted for a minute, perhaps two. During that time Carolyn could have come back down or, when the spot faded and before the lights came back on, she could have done it. In fact, there was so much confusion at the time, she could have made it down unseen even if the lights came on before she reached the last step. Possible, yes. Likely, no.

Most curious of all, why was Tilly telling me this? So I asked her, "Why haven't you told this to the police or Mr. Hayes?"

"I don't want to get involved with the police," she stated vehemently.

Probably because you might have to give them your real name. Could I believe anything this woman said?

"And Mr. Hayes? Surely you're not concerned about getting involved with him, as you already are."

"I am loyal to Madame, Mr. McNally. If she didn't want Mr. Hayes to know about her relationship with Mrs. Taylor, it is not my place to tell him. Also, I do not want Mrs. Taylor to get in trouble for something that may be easily explained."

Her altruism did not warm my heart. "So why are you telling me?"

She heaved a sigh and began to sniffle. Unable to see behind the dark glasses I could not tell if this sudden display of emotion was real or feigned. "I am so confused, Mr. McNally," she sobbed, "and I don't know what to do so I turn to you for guidance. Mr. Hayes says you are most respected in Palm Beach for your—what is the word? Discretion?"

Between her outfit and now obvious distress, we were being anything but discreet in the Classic Bookshop. I again took her by the elbow, but this time I guided her out of the shop. In the bright light of day she looked even more bizarre. "Have you told anyone else the story of Mrs. Taylor being on the second floor the night of the party?" I questioned.

"Yes, sir."

"Who?"

"I will not tell you," she brazenly informed me. Or should that be she did *not* inform me?

"Out of loyalty, I presume."

"Yes, sir."

People strolled by in shorts and sandals giving us the eye. *Check out the tall dude in a tan gabardine suit that looks a bit snug about the waist and the little woman in widow's weeds.*

"You know, Tilly, I will have to report this to the police and to my client, who is your boss. Both of whom you do not want to tell yourself."

"I did what I had to do, Mr. McNally, and you must do what you have to do."

"Translation. I force your hand, the story gets out, and your loyalty is never breached."

She shrugged. "I did my duty."

"After a fashion, I would say."

"Goodbye, Mr. McNally."

She turned to leave but I stopped her with a gentle tap on the shoulder. "One more thing, Tilly. Mr. Hayes told me you made tea for Marlena after the presentation. Is that right?"

"It is," she said. "I always serve her hot tea which she takes in her bath following the show."

"Where did you brew it? Downstairs, in the kitchen?"

"No. We keep an electric perk in the bedroom. I boiled the water in it and poured from it to make the tea."

"And was the perk filled and ready to be turned on when Marlena was performing?"

"It was."

"So anyone who happened to be on the second floor that night could have tampered with the tea water. Isn't that what you're trying to tell me?"

Tilly shook her head violently, sobbed and fled.

I GOT BACK TO THE MCNALLY BUILDING ONLY A FEW minutes before Mrs. Trelawney announced the arrival of Laddy Taylor. This precluded me from briefing the sire on my meetings with Matthew Hayes and Tilly. So eager was

Laddy to accuse his stepmother of a heinous crime he was some ten minutes early for his three o'clock appointment.

Father and I stood as Laddy rudely brushed past Mrs. Trelawney and entered the inner sanctum, brandishing a newspaper. "Digitalis poisoning," he said by way of greeting, "isn't that enough reason to request and be granted an order to exhume my father's body?"

Father responded with all the zeal of an English butler putting a bourgeois intruder in his place. Motioning to a visitor's chair, he invited, "Won't you have a seat, Mr. Taylor?"

Taking the hint, Laddy calmed down and sat down.

"You know my son, Archy?" father introduced me.

Laddy looked at me, nodded, and put the newspaper on father's desk. "You've seen this?" he said.

Laddy Taylor has got to be getting on to forty, give or take, and is of average height. He is beginning to show the signs of one who has gone through life in the fast lane, pausing only to refuel at pit stops along the way. He has the beginning of a paunch, his hair is thinning and his clothes are strictly off the rack. One could see why his disinheritance had him grabbing at straws to keep from descending any lower.

"If you're referring to the fact that Mrs. Hayes, or Marlena Marvel as she was known, died of digitalis poisoning, I have seen it as has all of Palm Beach and most of the United States," father said, his fingers ever so slightly pushing the newspaper back toward Laddy Taylor.

"You called me yesterday, as soon as the news was made public," father continued, "and demanded we use the information as a basis for requesting permission to exhume the late Mr. Taylor's body. I fail to see the connection between the cause of Mrs. Hayes's demise and ordering a writ of exhumation."

"Then let me fill you in, sir," Laddy boomed, leaning forward in a most belligerent manner. "My father was on a digitalis regimen due to his heart condition. Now we know that Marlena Marvel died of digitalis poisoning shortly after she was visited by Carolyn the night of the murder."

Taken by surprise, father blinked, but I immediately put in an appearance. "How do you know Mrs. Taylor visited Mrs. Hayes that night?" I asked.

Laddy finally acknowledged my existence by turning his attention from father to me. His reply was short and curt. "Someone told me."

"The maid, Tilly?"

For a moment I thought I had caught him off guard, but he rallied and snapped, "She told you?"

So Laddy was the other person Tilly had confided in but refused to reveal his name. Why? And was Laddy disturbed by the fact that Tilly had talked to me behind his back, as it were? I felt as if I were once again in the Amazin' Maze of Matthew Hayes, alone, and without a map to the goal—or the exit.

Father and I have worked together long enough for him to immediately realize that I was privy to certain facts I had yet to pass on to him. He gently stroked his mustache, watched and listened.

"You and Tilly are acquainted," I stated.

"We are," Laddy admitted, "not that it's any of your business, and my relationship with Tilly has nothing to do with the reason I'm here."

"I beg your pardon, Mr. Taylor, but I think it's the only reason you're here," I countered. "I have been employed by Mr. Hayes to make inquiries into his wife's death which you just termed a murder, but I believe the police have yet to determine that.

"In my capacity as Mr. Hayes's investigator, Tilly told me of Mrs. Taylor's alleged visit to Mrs. Hayes's bedroom that night and, as you just said, Tilly also told you. Hence, your rather intimate relationship with Tilly and what she revealed to you has brought you here, asking for an exhumation of your father's body. The connection, sir, is very clear."

"What do you mean by alleged?" he asked in a manner that was more a challenge than a question he wanted answered.

"Just what the word implies," I told him. "Tilly says she saw Mrs. Taylor on the second floor the night of the party, just before Mrs. Hayes appeared as Venus. There are no witnesses to corroborate Tilly's allegation but there are fifty or more people, myself included, who would swear that Carolyn Taylor was on the first floor at that time and never left it."

"Why would Tilly lie?" Laddy shot back.

"I don't know, sir, but seeing as she confides in you, perhaps you can tell me."

He bristled, something Laddy Taylor does very well and very often, and put me down by turning to father. "I didn't come here to be interrogated."

"No," father said, "you came here to hire me to beg a writ of exhumation on your behalf and I fail to see any plausible reason for doing so."

Laddy sighed and rolled his eyes skyward in a rather insulting manner to convey the fact that he was dealing with fools who needed to be enlightened, if not spanked. Father began tugging on his mustache, a sure sign that he would not suffer Laddy Taylor another five minutes.

"Let me explain," Laddy began condescendingly. "Marlena Marvel was a witch doctor. A quack. She told fortunes and administered to the sick, mostly women in need of a friend. Excuse my language, gentlemen, but she was an abortionist. In trendy Palm Beach you may not know it but there are places in this country where women still resort to the likes of Marlena Marvel when in trouble. To visit a legal clinic in the so-called Bible Belt would get her branded with Hawthorne's scarlet letter. Carolyn and Marlena were meeting secretly since Hayes rented the house here and, given her age and sophistication, dear Carolyn is not in need of Marlena's specialty."

"Are you saying . . ." father began but did not finish.

"I'm saying that Marlena Marvel was a student of the black arts and knew very well the lethal effects of foxglove and its uses in modern medicine—a medicine readily available to Carolyn. Marlena told Carolyn how to poison my father, slowly to avoid detection, and then Carolyn gave Marlena a dose of her own medicine to keep her quiet. It's as plain as the mustache on your face."

With that last remark, Laddy lost any hope of being represented by McNally & Son in his efforts to dig up dear old dad. The sire looked so offended at the rather impudent mention of his beloved whiskers, I doubt if he would represent Laddy Taylor in protesting a traffic violation summons.

"I suppose Tilly told you about the meetings between Carolyn Taylor and Marlena Marvel," I quickly got in before father called Mrs. Trelawney to escort Laddy out of the building. Besides legal secretary, spy and informer, Mrs. Trelawney is also our Sergeant at Arms.

Laddy once again hit on me. "Why do you keep harping

on my association with Tilly which I told you is none of your business?"

"I harp on it because everything you know about Carolyn and her alleged dealings with Marlena Marvel has come to you by way of Tilly. How long have you two been exchanging confidences?"

"I don't have to answer that," he said contentiously.

"Then don't," I assured him.

Perhaps thinking that he had gone too far in antagonizing those he sought for help, he relented somewhat, shrugged and said in a more kindly manner, "Okay. I'm upset. My father was murdered and I won't let Carolyn get away with it. I met Tilly when I came back here. She had come to Palm Beach a few weeks earlier with Marlena and Matthew Hayes. We met in a bar. I forget which one, not that it makes any difference. I hadn't been back here in years so Tilly and I were like the new kids on the block. We hit it off."

And became bosom buddies, I reflected, whispering confidences into each other's ears. Was one of those confidences the late Mr. Taylor's net worth?

Sensing that I wanted to get information out of Laddy Taylor before showing him the door, father again sat quietly and listened, fighting the urge to stroke his mustache. A reformed smoker, more or less, I commiserated with his misery in suppressing a comforting habit.

"Why did you come back, Mr. Taylor? It's common knowledge that you and your father have been estranged for years," I probed, hoping to learn as much as I could while he was in a conciliatory mood.

"My father and I never got along, if you must know. The family money was all from my mother and he doled it out as if it were coming out of his pocket. Mother let him run the house and the bank account. Like most tyrants, he was a charmer. When my mother died I left home for good."

"Your mother left you nothing?" I questioned.

He raised his arms as if surrendering to the inevitable. "I was a wild kid. Got kicked out of several colleges before they gave up on me." He fidgeted in his chair as if in search of a more comfortable position. "I was into drugs, big time. I mean I did nothing halfway. My mother was afraid to leave me any cash, fearing it would go to the dealers, and maybe she was right. She said she would change her will, leaving me a good trust fund, when I straightened out.

"So I straightened out, but she died before she had a chance to do it. My father got it all and refused to honor her promise. Then he married Carolyn, who's my age, in case you haven't noticed and the two of them were living high off my mother's money which is rightfully mine."

Whether it was rightfully his or not was a moot question. It was left, legally, to his father to do with as he wished and he didn't wish to share it with his *enfant terrible,* as the rich call their miscreant offspring.

"Why did you choose to return at this particular time?" I asked once again.

"Carolyn wrote and told me he was dying—and we know how she knew that."

"She was in touch with you?" I questioned, not hiding my surprise.

"I have a business mail drop. Letters sent there are forwarded to me. I'm on the road a lot but keep them informed of my whereabouts."

I waited, but any clues as to where his travels took him, and why, were not forthcoming. "So you came back," I said, encouraging him to continue.

"Yeah. I came back and found my father dying and my stepmother consorting with a rent boy."

Rent boy? The Victorian term for a male hustler impressed father enough to make him ask, "You know for a fact that Mrs. Taylor was seeing this young man before your father died?"

"Everyone in town knew," Laddy said.

Father looked at me for verification as it is my job to be cognizant of the local gossip, especially among the noblesse of our village. I responded with a quick shake of the head to signal my ignorance. Until Lolly told me that Carolyn Taylor was seeing Billy Gilbert I had not heard a thing about their liaison.

Thinking it was time to rain on Laddy's parade and send him on his way, I expounded, "Mr. Taylor, to recapitulate, the maid, Tilly, told you she saw Mrs. Taylor on the second floor the night of the party. The night Mrs. Hayes died. From that you concluded that Mrs. Taylor poisoned Mrs. Hayes."

"It's not just that," he cut in. "Carolyn and Marlena Marvel were seeing each other regularly. They were in cahoots."

I held up a hand to deter him from going any further. "Please, sir, let me finish. You are saying that Carolyn Taylor somehow managed to sneak upstairs that night, spike Mrs. Hayes's tea water which Tilly, I'm sure you know, had prepared, and return to the party without anyone noticing her movements.

"She then came with us to the maze to search for the goal. This I know for a fact because I saw her and I know who partnered her. Joe Gallo, in fact. Now, according to you, Mrs. Taylor left Gallo, found her way out of the maze and returned to the house where the caterers were setting up the buffet under the watchful eye of Lolly Spindrift; she climbed the stairs once more, removed Mrs. Hayes's body from the tub where she was soaking with her cup of tainted tea; she carried the body downstairs and through the great room where the caterers and Lolly waved at Mrs. Taylor lugging Mrs. Hayes's corpse and didn't even offer to help her.

"Undaunted, she carried her burden into the maze where we were all running about in search of the goal; she somehow found the goal and deposited Mrs. Hayes therein. I guess we didn't notice the body when we all gathered in the goal, or did Mrs. Taylor wait for us to leave before making her deposit and then once again rejoin the party?"

Laddy did not care for my summation. "She did it," he shouted. "I don't know how, but she did it."

Now father joined the harangue. "Mr. Taylor, if your father's body is exhumed, what do you think will be found?"

"Digitalis, of course," Laddy answered.

Father nodded. "But of course they would. Your father was taking digitalis for his heart. He had been taking it for years. The surprise would be if they didn't find traces of the drug in his body."

Laddy Taylor slumped in his seat and buried his face in his hand. When he looked up there were tears in his eyes. "So she gets away with it," he mumbled. "She gets away with my mother's money—and murder."

11

LADDY TAYLOR, WHO HAD ENTERED FATHER'S OFFICE with all the ardor of an avenging angel, left with his wings clipped and his faith in tatters. He thanked father in the manner of a condemned man forgiving the executioner before putting his own head on the block. He even remembered to give me a polite nod on his way to the door, leaving in his wake an eerie silence, not unlike a schoolroom minutes after the three o'clock bell has tolled.

Father, once again in command of his mustache, stroked it thoughtfully as he asked, "And what are we to make of all that?"

"Besides the fact that Laddy Taylor's theatrical range is as daunting as all the Barrymores rolled into one, I think we can safely assume that both he and his lady friend, Matilda Thompson, want us to bring Carolyn Taylor's alleged escapade the night of the party to the attention of the police."

"Finger-pointing by proxy," father noted. "Now tell me what you were about this morning. It's clear you talked to this Matilda Thompson and did I hear you say you were investigating Mrs. Hayes's death on behalf of her husband?"

"Correct on both counts, sir." This was followed by a critique of my interviews with Hayes and Tilly.

"She slipped you a note?" father commented. "She could just as easily have asked you to meet her in the bookshop. They certainly do have a flair for drama, but are they writers as well as actors, I wonder?"

"And directors?" I added.

"I begin to smell a red herring, Archy."

"In fact," I answered, "the aroma is so strong you have to wonder if it isn't being laid on to keep us from seeing the shark for the herrings. Tilly didn't confide in her boss because, she says, she's being faithful to her Madame who didn't want Hayes to know about her relationship with Carolyn Taylor. She didn't go to the police because she doesn't want to cast aspersions on Mrs. Taylor. But she tells Laddy and me."

Father leaned back in his executive chair which tilts as well as rotates in a full circle should the need arise. "I believe she told Laddy and he told her to pass it on to you, Archy."

"Mrs. Taylor's visit to Marlena, if true, plays right into Laddy's hand as did the announcement that Marlena died of digitalis poisoning. He called you instead of the police because he's been hurling accusations against Carolyn Taylor all over town and the police are beginning to treat him like the boy who cried wolf. But if a prestigious law firm and its investigative arm raises the alarm, that would have Lieutenant Eberhart and Co. snapping at poor Carolyn Taylor's shapely ankles."

Father, who is not above noticing a shapely ankle, nodded in agreement of either my statement or the comeliness of Carolyn's ankles. He expressed my thoughts when he said he didn't believe that Laddy wasn't cognizant of the foolishness of exhuming his father's body and having it examined for digitalis when the man had been taking the drug for years. What Laddy hoped to accomplish by today's visit was to impress upon us his stepmother's ingenious plotting and the fact that she would get away with murder if not brought to justice by the good offices of McNally & Son.

"If she was so clever as to poison her husband with his own medication, why was she so foolish as to eliminate her accomplice with the same drug?" father reflected aloud.

"Which brings us to the meandering corpse." I said.

"Beg pardon, Archy."

"Don't you see, sir, how Marlena was killed pales in the light of her body being moved from the house to the goal of the maze with a houseful of guests in both places at the time she was transported. And let's not forget that the guests included all the likely suspects as well as this discreet inquirer."

"That red herring, Archy?"

"If so, it's the size of a whale."

"How does Matthew Hayes impress you after your first formal meeting with him? You said the other day he was a bully and a boor you would be more inclined to suspect than work for. Have you changed your mind?"

"No, sir, I have not."

"Then why are you working for him?" father questioned.

"To prove that I'm right."

Father started, squared his shoulders, and glared at me across the vast expanse of his executive desk. "Unethical, to say the least," he lectured.

"Perhaps," I said, and proceeded to expound on the rationale of my decision, assuring him that I was not out to railroad Hayes.

"But give him enough rope, et cetera," father said with that tinge of sarcasm in the delivery that told me I could proceed, but with caution. "You will tell the police and Mr. Hayes what the maid had to report," he concluded.

"Not immediately, sir."

Father arched an eyebrow. He could tolerate one ethical lapse, with cause, but never two. What I had to do, quickly, was appeal to his lawyer's penchant for fair play.

"The maid says Carolyn Taylor was upstairs the night of the party, presumably within access to the pot of water being boiled for Marlena's tea. And let's not forget that we don't know for a fact that the tea water was poisoned. The police have not yet said how Marlena ingested the digitalis, nor will they until they have talked to all the possible suspects whose number is legion. As you heard me telling our visitor, there are no witnesses to back the maid's allegation. I reserve the right to apprise Mrs. Taylor of this accusation and hear what she has to say before going to the police and having them confront her.

"I don't buy the maid's reasons for not going to the police or her boss with her amazing story, and see no reason to play the messenger boy. After seeing Mrs. Taylor I will, of course, tell the police what Tilly says she saw and let them take it from there."

Father nodded thoughtfully as I spoke and when I was done he waited an excruciating few moments before giving me a verbal pat on the back. "Very good, Archy. I should have thought of it myself. Also, it would be a fine opportunity to introduce the widow Taylor to the advantages of coming to us for legal counsel."

Dear old dad. Let it never be said that he missed an opportunity to present himself to a rich Palm Beach widow in need. But I don't complain. I brag. If his intent is financial gain it is well deserved, for our clients profit in direct proportion to our earnings. Prescott McNally is a true Renaissance man posing as a Victorian and his son, Archy, is not just another pretty face—but you know that.

As if summing up a brief, the sire stated, "And, as we speak, Hayes is ignorant of all this? Strange, I would say."

I agreed with a nod. "And stranger still if you knew the man. To succeed in his chosen profession he had to stay one step ahead of his customers—and the law. That his wife went gallivanting with the likes of Carolyn Taylor without his knowing is a bit too much to swallow."

"I understand," father said, "Hayes and his wife had a successful business partnership, but have you learned anything of their relationship when they weren't in the limelight?"

This was more than the obvious query for a domestic murder case. Father's lifelong love affair with mother prompts him to question how others have fared in the marital sweepstakes. I have long used my parents' relationship as a deterrent to tying my own knot, refusing to settle for anything less idyllic than the blissful merger of Prescott and Madelaine McNally.

That this is a cop-out does not escape my attention for they, like all newlyweds, had no way of knowing if their union would survive the long haul. In short, you can't win if you don't play the game.

"Tilly, who was Marlena's personal maid, told me the partnership was a roaring success both on and off the fairway, but our resident snoop, Lolly Spindrift, believes Hayes had an eye for the ladies and a low tolerance for marital fidelity.

"Hayes, whom I thought was rather crass regarding his wife's fate, told me he was a tough carny man who didn't wear his heart on his sleeve, but that didn't make his loss any easier to bear. I should mention here that Hayes brought up the possibility of revenge being the catalyst in his wife's murder. He admitted to picking many a pocket in his long career, not to mention the pint-sized Romeo's propensity for cuckoldry. Matthew Hayes sleeps with one eye open."

"More braggadocio than substance, Archy?" father wondered aloud.

"No doubt, sir, but I believe a good deal of his story with one exception."

"That being?"

"That he doesn't know how his wife was moved from the house to the goal of the maze. When it comes to the art of illusion, little Matthew Hayes is the Grand Master of the cult."

"Then why is he keeping it a secret?" father wanted to know.

"For two reasons I can think of, sir. One, there's honor among thieves and he doesn't want to give away trade secrets. Two, he's the architect of the scam."

"And a murderer in cahoots with the maid who could be his paramour." Father, as you can see, is a quick study. "But where does Laddy Taylor fit into the scenario?"

"A discontent with a big mouth who wants to make Carolyn Taylor the heavy, taking the suspicion from Hayes and Tilly. In short, a living red herring and the answer to Hayes's prayer."

Father gave this some thought, rocking gently in his captain's chair and pushing a pencil with a razor-sharp point across his desk. "It makes sense, but logic is not the long suit of this case, so *caveat emptor,* Archy. And let's not forget those dark forces," he concluded with a twinkle in his blue eyes.

"Mack Macurdy," I stated. "He should be censored. There's been nothing like it since the flying saucer craze and Al Rogoff tells me the police are getting crank calls from the hopeless and helpless who are always among us. They now fear candy laced with foxglove will be the goody of choice for the trick-or-treaters."

Father nodded. "A nuisance, to be sure, but being a by-product of freedom of speech, one we must abide with thanks, as well as caution."

Bless the man. Like Nathan Hale, his fellow Eli, Prescott McNally's only regret is that he has but one life to give in defense of our Bill of Rights. He makes me proud and that's as good as it gets. I stood up to leave as I spoke. "A sudden thought, sir. What would happen if Carolyn Taylor were guilty of poisoning her husband?"

"She would go to jail, of course."

"And her inheritance?" I questioned.

"Surely you know, Archy. One can't profit from a crime. The court would confiscate everything left to her by Linton Taylor."

"And the millions would go to . . ."

Father looked up at me with the slightest trace of a smile on his lips. "Linton Taylor's next of kin."

"Who is his son, Laddy Taylor."

After a significant pause the sire said, "Keep me posted, Archy."

"LIKE THE MONTH OF MARCH," MRS. TRELAWNEY SAID as I passed her desk on the way to the elevator.

"You speak of the weather, Mrs. Trelawney? I believe it's October."

"I speak of our visitor, Linton Taylor Jr. He came in like a lion and went out like a lamb. What did you do to him in there?"

"Your boss explained the facts of life to Laddy, which preclude digging up dear old dad."

Mrs. Trelawney shook her head of polyester gray hair and removed her pince-nez. "Ghoulish, I call it. Since that woman's mysterious death this town has become obsessed with the macabre."

"And for that you can thank your pin-up boy, Mack Macurdy. Are you going to have Count Zemo cast your horoscope, Mrs. Trelawney? But I caution you, dear lady. You will have to give him your birth year, as well as your birth date. And don't lie, Mrs. Trelawney, because Witch Hazel will rat on you. She was around three thousand years ago and might recall attending your first birthday party."

Mrs. Trelawney replaced her pince-nez and glanced at her lapel watch. "They say men approaching the midlife crisis stage babble incessantly and lust after young women—blondes mostly—and wear clothes they have obviously outgrown. If you keep sucking in your tummy, you're liable to turn blue.

"And, I'm preparing a memo giving new guidelines for expense account reports. Documentation will be necessary for all amounts in excess of one dollar, and 'miscellaneous' items will be automatically deleted by accounting. Good day, Archy."

Fearing further retribution for my little jest, I rang for the elevator and thought I heard the executive secretary chuckle behind my back. Spoilsport, I thought, as I sucked in my tummy. In the elevator I opened my belt a notch. It didn't help.

I found Binky and his mail cart in my office, leaving just enough room for me to slither around them and commandeer my desk. "Well, what do you hear from the other side?" I asked.

"Joe is hearing from a lot of women on this side, Archy. The network is getting calls asking when he's going to appear again and Macurdy flatly refuses to have him back on the show."

So there's trouble in paradise. The dynamic duo of the dark forces are squaring off after only one day of teaming up to scare the bejesus out of Palm Beach and vicinity. If there's one thing an old peacock can't tolerate, it's a young peacock. I bet Marge is laughing her head off, but I doubt if my Georgy girl will be amused by Mr. Gallo's instant fan club.

Why does my fair lady get so roiled up over the escapades of her ex? I don't begrudge Connie her relationship with the handsome Alejandro Gomez y Zapata. What I begrudge is the fact that it seems to be working.

"Fitz was with him last night, when he went on live TV with the foxglove plant. What a gal. She could be a movie star. Then they went back to Joe's place for pizza and beer." Looking around to make sure there was no one else in the office (between us and the cart a mosquito couldn't get in), Binky whispered, "I think she spent the night."

Poor Binky. The beautiful Fitz so near and yet so far. "I hope you didn't snoop," I counseled.

"I glanced out a few times, checking the weather. Joe's lights didn't go out till the wee hours and I never heard her car pull out till this morning."

So Binky was up all night, imagining the worst—or should that be the best? I imagined him pacing his trailer between trips to the window—and Georgy girl oiling her revolver.

"Maybe she walked home," I suggested, "leaving Joe with uneaten pizza crusts, empty cans of beer and one fox-glove plant."

"We got a lot of milage out of that plant," Binky beamed. "The network was bombarded with calls asking where he got it."

"And where did he get it?"

"A nursery in Boca," Binky answered. "The guy specializes in exotic plants. After last night's showing he's going to offer them for sale with a full-page ad in the *Palm Beach Post*."

I certainly hope they don't replace the more traditional garden flora, like mother's begonias. I could just see some clever PB matron breaking off a leaf or two and asking her husband if he'd like a tad bit of mint in his julep. This was indeed getting out of hand and dangerous to boot. The sooner a rational explanation for Marlena's death and *post obitum* movements was announced, the better for our sun-drenched island of swaying palms, purse dogs and conspicuous consumption.

I asked Joe Gallo's stringer, who was my former gofer, what he and the television reporter had come up with in the Marlena Marvel case besides hyping witches, warlocks and the exotic plant industry in Boca.

"What did you come up with?" he shot back.

My, my, aren't we being cagey. One day as a TV stringer and he's giving his betters lip. "I asked you first," I told him.

"They say you're working for Matthew Hayes," Binky more or less accused rather than stated.

"And who are *they?*"

"My information came with the promise of anonymity for my source."

This was too much, and no doubt the end result of watching countless television programs that extol cops, robbers, reporters seeking the truth and lawyers seeking justice. "Reveal your source, Binky Watrous, or I'll tell Joe you're spying on his love life. Do you know the meaning of voyeur, young man?"

The boy blushed from Adam's apple to eyebrows. "I was checking the weather," he blurted.

"At three o'clock in the morning? Come, come, my friend. Who told you I was working for Hayes?"

He began backing his cart out of the office. "I'm running late. Catch you later, Archy."

"Fine, Binky. Bye-bye. I must remember to tell Mrs. Trelawncy you're moonlighting in a field that may be in conflict with the interests of McNally and Son."

"Blackmailer," he shouted.

"Peeping Tom," I called back.

He and his wretched cart came to a halt. "Why do you always win?" he cried.

"Because God is on my side. That's why."

"Then ask God how I know you're working for Hayes."

"That, Binky, is blasphemous."

He slumped over his cart handle. I had worn him to a frazzle and could get him to tell me the exact hour the lights went out in Gallo's trailer. I don't gloat. I love Binky Watrous—especially when he acquiesces to my demands. "Let's have it," I said.

Raising his head he fixed those woeful brown eyes upon me and blew the cover on his informer. "Hayes told Mack and Mack told Joe and Joe told me. Satisfied?"

I was more than satisfied. I was curious. Mack had been to Le Maze before me this morning. In fact, I saw him leave as I pulled into the driveway. If Mack knew I was formally employed by Hayes it meant that Hayes and Mack were in contact after I left. What were they up to?

More curious was Hayes's refusal to take my advice not to appear on Mack's show. Was it because he didn't want to make Mack hostile to his cause, or because he feared what Mack might do if spurned? Whatever the reason, I didn't like it. I didn't like it one iota.

And Mack had made the goal. I mustn't forget that.

"Thank you, Binky, you're a good man."

"If we're sharing, Archy, would you tell me what Hayes told you that might help solve the murder. I guarantee your anonymity."

This boy had the *cojones* of a brass monkey but didn't know it. Ignorance is not only bliss, it's useful. "He told me nothing that helps, Binky, and that's the truth."

"Have you thought of a tunnel?" he muttered, as if he were sharing more than he should.

That pricked up my ears, as they say. "You mean a tunnel going from . . ."

"The house to the goal of the maze," he completed my thought like a child eager to show his cleverness. "This town is full of tunnels, mostly under the A1A leading to the beach," he went on like a locomotive out of control. "Maybe when they were building the maze, Hayes also had them construct a tunnel."

Not bad, I thought. Not bad at all. "But the tunnel would

connect to the lower level. So how did they get her from the second floor to the lower level without being seen?"

"We're not ruling out magic," he stated.

"Ta, ta, Binky."

"Ta, ta, Archy."

12

THE FOUR SEASONS IS ALMOST AS FAR SOUTH ON Ocean Boulevard as you can go before leaving Palm Beach and heading for Manalapan. The car jockey relieved me of the Miata and I entered the long, elegant lobby, two stories of glossy marble. I traverse it thinking I'm on my way to an audience with the last czar in his winter palace.

The bar is called the Living Room, mainly because it's furnished with comfy chairs and little tables, soft rugs and a grand piano that's not just for show. As I entered, the pianist, in black tie, was tinkling out a Cole Porter melody that, like all Porter tunes, was conducive to ordering an old-fashioned while gazing into the eyes of a beautiful woman.

Excuse me if I wax poetic but the Living Room and Cole Porter have that effect on this romantic. Need I add that I was in one of my favorite watering holes?

At the far end of the room, opposite the bar and just beyond the piano, a few steps lead up to a smaller and therefore more intimate area where a fireplace, lit of course, is the focal point. My beautiful lady was seated in a corner awaiting her date.

"You're the tops, you're a Berlin ballad," I sang as I took the chair opposite Marge Macurdy.

She laughed, showing off a set of pearly teeth in a beguiling freckled face. She wore a hat, which was yellow, peaked, and resembled a baseball cap, of all things. It sat jauntily on her curly head. Her yellow dress featured a shawl collar and vee neckline that, for Palm Beach, was very modest. (See-through dresses are suddenly the rage. Ugh!)

"I bet you know all the lyrics," she teased.

Given that lead-in I proceeded to prove that I did.

"Hush," she warned. "People are looking. It'll be rumored tomorrow that I was serenaded in a faulty tenor by a man who was not my husband."

I forgot that Marge was probably recognized the moment she walked into the Four Seasons. One of the drawbacks of escorting a celebrity, major or minor, is that you are scrutinized from head to toe by the hoi polloi, all hoping that you will do something either naughty or nutty. I think I was veering toward the latter.

"I take umbrage at the word faulty."

"Really? I thought I was being kind," Marge explained.

Sassy? Yes, this was my kind of woman, but why speculate on what might be when she's got a hubby and I have a very enchanting significant other?

"You haven't ordered?" I noted, glancing at our empty table.

"I haven't been asked, but here she is now," Marge said.

A pretty young thing was hovering over us, pen and order form in hand. "What's your pleasure, please?" she asked in an unmistakable British accent.

"You're a long way from London," I said.

"I'm even a longer way from Sydney," she informed me.

Marge grinned and I groused, "So I was mistaken. It happens, but not often."

"You're a breath of fresh air, Archy, and right now I could use all the fresh air I can get," Marge kindly soothed my slightly damaged ego.

"That bad?" I asked.

She nodded stoically. "But a martini would help ease the pain."

"Two Ketel One martinis, straight up with a twist, and some nibbles, please."

As Sydney departed a woman and young man came up the steps and took the table directly across from Marge and me. She was elderly, flawlessly coiffed and affected a rather disagreeably haughty air. The young man was in jeans and a polo shirt. He looked petulant.

Sotto voce I mumbled, "The original odd couple."

Marge put a finger to her lips and whispered the woman's name. I was impressed. The lady, whom I certainly knew by name but had never met, was often dubbed the queen of Palm Beach society. That she was taking her libation in a public pub, however chic, was almost unthinkable.

"It's said," Marge informed me in hushed tones, "that she has the most powerful Rolodex in Palm Beach."

I rather liked that unique description of the lady's power in our town. What Marge meant was that with a few phone calls, Queenie could make you, break you, or rustle up a hundred people to subscribe to your charity and pay through the nose for the honor. "And the boy?" I asked.

"Her son and the proverbial *enfant terrible.* He's been

tossed out of all the best schools, all the best clubs and all the low-life bars. She adores him."

What a town. A queen and her errant prince bending their elbows with the proletariat. If the boy was not welcome at Colette, mummy would shun it to make a statement. Blood, you see, is thicker than the waters of café society. And if he was as bad as Marge claimed I wondered how long it would be before Her Highness called upon Archy McNally to bail him out of a mess the mater's money couldn't quell.

Our drinks arrived in crystal glasses, the icy white liquor looking like the nectar of the gods. The nibble tray was respectable, if not overly imaginative. Nuts, mini pretzels, cheese bits and black olives. Recalling the feast Oscar Eberhart and I had consumed at Le Maze did not make the nibbles any more appetizing.

"To Eve," I toasted.

She raised her glass but didn't respond before sipping her drink. When she did speak it was to state, without preamble, the reason she wanted to see me. After all, we had observed the niceties of polite chitchat: small talk and gossip. The arrival of our drinks was a prelude to the more serious business on her agenda. There is nothing like a martini to get the tongue wagging.

Marge opened with, "What's going on, Archy?"

"Strange. That's just what I was going to ask you," I said, "but you seem to know as much, or as little, as I do."

"I know you're working for Hayes."

"A fact you learned from your husband." I then asked what I already know because I wanted to see just where Marge stood in whatever was going on between her husband and Hayes. Was it a duo, or a triangle? "And who told him?"

She didn't hesitate a moment before telling me. "Hayes,

of course. He and Mack were on the phone shortly after you left Le Maze this morning."

"Now it's my turn, Marge. What the hell is going on? Mack and Hayes are suddenly very tight. Why?"

She sipped from her glass before answering, and so did I. I even reached for a wedge of cheese and an olive. I moved the nibble dish to her and she dismissed it with a wave of her hand.

"All I know, Archy, is that Mack is trying to get Hayes to come on the show. He's made several visits to Le Maze for that reason. I told Mack he was chasing rainbows, but now I think Hayes is actually considering doing it."

I may be a sucker for a lovely and clever woman, but I now felt that Marge didn't have a clue as to what her husband was plotting or how he got Hayes to cooperate. "I got the same impression from Hayes," I said. "I advised him not to do the show and he told me to mind my own business."

"That sounds just like the man. May I ask you why you took him on as a client in what has got to be the most bizarre as well as the most sensational murder mystery in Palm Beach history?"

"Bizarre, thanks to Hayes and his Amazin' Maze, and sensational because of the spin given it by *Breakfast with Mack and Marge.*"

"Don't lay that on me, Archy McNally," she protested. "I agreed to having Joe as our sole guest the morning after the night before. His on-the-spot reporting of the crime with us present made it not only plausible but exciting. It was the right thing to do. It was Mack's idea to push the dark forces angle and, naturally, Joe went along with it because he was on a roll and loving every minute of it. You know Joe's been promoted to full-fledged reporter and is right now the network's great white hope."

"I hear he's also the darling of silly ladies who should know better, and Mack is refusing to have him back on the show."

She laughed. "Mack is acting like a diva who wants to shoot the ingenue. My husband, Archy, has an ego the size of an elephant's behind, in case you haven't noticed. He played varsity football at college and had all the girls hot on his trail, including this one. After graduation we went to New York to seek fame and fortune. We both modeled with moderate success until Mack got a small part on a soap. He was written out of the script after two seasons.

"Hal Ingrams, our producer, was pitching the breakfast show to the network down here and, seeing Mack on the soap, asked him to do a pilot. I was brought in to pour the coffee and no one was more surprised than Mack and me when the network bought not only the concept, but us to boot. It's called a package deal."

It's always interesting to know how people get from being one of the bunch to top banana and, more than just coincidentally, luck rather than talent is the impetus. I speculated on the fact that they had known each other since their undergraduate days. No doubt the affair was consummated before they legalized it—if they ever legalized it. In show biz one never knows, and I didn't dare ask.

"I imagine," I offered, "for Mack Macurdy, this is just a stepping stone to the big time. Hence, the dark forces, Witch Hazel, Count Zemo and every and any crowd pleaser he can get into the mix." What I didn't say was that Marlena Marvel's murder was Mack Macurdy's luck factor in his quest for stardom, making him the only one to date with a motive for the crime. But that was too bizarre even for this bizarre case.

At this point I couldn't help noting that the queen was

drinking a Manhattan while the bad boy was belting down a bottled beer without benefit of a glass. Gauche!

"Mack and Joe ran Hayes and Marlena through Nexis and came up with enough material to start the ball rolling," Marge continued. "Mack found that foolish witch and the phony count in an advert in some spiritual publication. After their appearance the kooks started coming to us. It's a nightmare, Archy, and unethical."

"But your ratings have soared," I reminded her.

"Now you sound like Mack. Yes, the ratings are off the charts, but the end doesn't justify the means this time."

"You're getting national attention, which should please you," I said.

"It pleases Mack more. Do you think we can have another martini?"

"I'm sure we can." I gave Sydney the high sign and pointed to our almost depleted glasses. "So you have no idea how or why Mack and Hayes became bosom buddies?"

She gave this a moment's thought and then exclaimed, "Can I hire you, Archy?"

Well, I certainly gave that more than a moment's thought. "If you need help, I'm at your service. Gratis."

The drinks arrived and our waitress removed the old before presenting us with the new. The interval gave us both time to contemplate her strange request and my gallant answer. Let's see: on this day I had taken on a client to prove his guilt, and had just offered my premium services, gratis, to a married woman I found too attractive for my own good. Should I consult Count Zemo to see what else was in store for this Pisces before the dastardly day ended? Georgy girl, I kept remembering, awaited me in Juno with a foxglove salad and a freshly oiled weapon.

Marge and I imbibed before picking up where we had

left off. Feeling my way, I said, "You're concerned about more than Mack's iniquitous media blitz. No?"

She gave a shrug and seemed to relax, as if having come to a decision to share her burden had somehow lightened the load. Or was it the second Ketel One?

"Mack is up to something and I want to know what it is," she explained.

So do I, I told myself. "Does it have anything to do with Marlena Marvel's murder?"

"It has everything to do with the murder, Archy, that's what has me worried, and scared. I can deal with Mack's ego and unscrupulous ambition. I've been doing it for fifteen years. He's always bragged and speculated about making it big on the small screen and is in almost daily touch with our agent in New York to that end. When we got the show down here he hired a public relations firm with offices in New York and Los Angeles to get us press where it matters. They're expensive and so far got us mentioned in several New York and L.A. gossip columns which any press agent could do for half the cost."

Fifteen years? If they left college when they were twenty-one or twenty-two, Marge would be just about my age, plus or minus. Okay, minus. I don't want you to think I'm trying to guess her age when I should have been listening to her tale of woe, because I was doing both. In my line of work you learn to be ambidextrous when absorbing information.

"What's different now?" I questioned.

Marge took a deep breath and expelled, "He's suddenly full of himself. He's acting as if his dreams of fame and fortune are no longer dreams, but fact. It's not just the instant success and national attention we've had because of poor Marlena. It's more than that, Archy, far more."

"Give me a for-instance, Marge."

Her answer, terse and to the point, was testimony to the amount of time her husband's newly found confidence in attaining his goal had occupied her thoughts. She simply spoke aloud what she had been saying to herself the last two days.

"At first, Archy, I was amused with the occult aspect of Mack's reportage. Corny, I admitted to myself and told him, but good for a few laughs and if it helped our ratings that was even better. I was against putting on the silly witch and the astrologer and thought we would return to our own format after their appearance. When Mack started booking the kooks who began calling, I protested but was ignored when Hal, our producer, sided with Mack."

Marge paused long enough to quench her thirst and helped herself to a pretzel at the same time. I took it as a sign that her appetite had returned now that she was confiding in me. I should have been a psychiatrist, but that's another story.

"My first indication that something was askew was when Joe Gallo's audience response proved more than just positive. They say for every person that voices their approval, or disapproval, to the network, there are a few hundred who feel the same way but don't bother calling. Joe got about a dozen calls, all in his favor.

"Mack was furious. I mean furious, Archy. He not only refused to have Joe back on, against Hal's wishes, but said that if they insisted on putting Joe on, he would walk off the show. That's unheard of. Mack has been upstaged before, but he's never threatened to quit a show because of it. He couldn't afford to. Jobs are scarce in this business. If the network gave us the sack, what would we do? But Mack didn't seem to care. It was as if he had that old ace in the hole, what actors dream about when making demands. What I'm saying, Archy, is that he's acting like a star, which he isn't, and being a perfect bitch toward Joe Gallo, a green kid who's unaware of his attractive screen presence."

But not for long, I was thinking. Joe is already making it with Palm Beach's most sought-after young lady, which has to tell him he's got more going for him than all the rich lotharios in a town lousy with rich lotharios.

I interrupted with, "I can see how Mack's vanity has him refusing to be on-screen with Joe, and I understand your concern over losing your job, even if your husband doesn't give a rap for reasons we don't know. But that doesn't say Mack has found the keys to show business heaven. Could be he's just feeling his oats after being a witness to a sensational murder and impressing his audience with the ghostly details. Maybe Mack is just playing a game with his producer and the network."

Marge started shaking her head even before I finished speaking. "I've saved the best for last, Archy."

"Let's have it," I said, raising my glass.

She took a deep breath. "For years Mack has wanted to produce a pilot for a TV detective series. A very sophisticated and urbane detective, to be sure, like Dashiell Hammett's *Thin Man*. What one needs, of course, is backing. A money man who's willing to gamble on the success of the project. This morning, before I called you, our New York agent called. Mack was at Le Maze and I took the call. Andy, our agent, asked to speak to Mack. I told him Mack was out and could I take a message. No, he would call later, but before ringing off Andy said, 'Marge, I want you to know how happy I am that Mack has found an angel for the pilot. It's going to be a smash. Break a leg, honey.' "

"What did you say?" I quickly asked.

"I said thanks, Andy. What else could I say? I don't know what Mack is up to and I didn't want to queer whatever it is. But why is he keeping it a secret from me? Something is rotten in Denmark, Archy."

"And in Palm Beach, unless I'm mistaken. All this has transpired since the night of Hayes's ill-fated party? There was never any mention of a backer for the pilot before this?"

"That's right."

We were silent for a long time, both thinking the same thing, neither of us willing to go public with the astonishing idea. "Matthew Hayes," I finally intoned.

"Who else?" Marge responded.

Who else, indeed? "Hayes told me he admired Mack. I quote, *He's latched on to a good thing and is making the most of it. I would do the same,* unquote."

"So he's going to risk a few million to watch Mack solve crimes in black tie and opera pumps? I don't believe it, Archy."

"Neither do I, my dear."

"Isn't it strange," Marge said, "how we all went to that little man's vulgar party, intent on laughing behind his back, and now it seems the laugh is on us. The moment Marlena Marvel was found in the goal of that overgrown hedgerow all our lives changed, only we didn't know it at the time. Joe Gallo's rise. Mack's great expectations. My trepidation and you hot on the trail. Why are you working for Hayes, Archy?" she asked again.

"Because I want to solve the mystery of the maze, and I think the wee man has the answer. That simple."

"You think he murdered his wife?"

"I think he knows how it was done. More than that I

won't say at this time. Can you tell me how Mack found the goal that fateful night?"

She shook her head. "If I knew, I would tell you. Lord knows I've told you everything else."

"You say this all began when Marlena Marvel turned up dead in the maze. I'll backtrack and say it began when Mack found the goal. Do you understand?"

"Mack knows something," she stated.

"Only he didn't know what he knew until after the murder. What helicopter service did Mack use to photograph the maze?"

"There are two the network employs. Palm Beach Helicopter in Lantana and Ocean Helicopter in West Palm. It would be one of them, I'm sure."

"Is Mack putting the squeeze on Hayes? If so, why?" I asked Mack's wife.

She reached across the table and put her hand, ever so gently, on mine. Her nails were painted a lustrous pink. Funny what one notices at such moments.

"That's what I want you to find out, Archy," she pleaded.

13

I ARRIVED AT THE JUNO COTTAGE JUST IN TIME TO catch the last five minutes of *Casablanca*. Bergman, in her lovely wide-brimmed hat, was kissing Bogart, in his lovely wide-brimmed hat, goodbye, before flying off with Paul Henreid and leaving Bogcy to saunter off into the fog, arm in arm with Claude Rains.

Georgy, in pigtails, slacks and one of my shirts, sleeves rolled to her pretty elbows, was dabbing at her eyes. "It always gets me right here," she said, pointing a thumb at where she imagined her heart resided.

I kissed her cheek and inhaled the tantalizing scent of lavender soap which said Georgy had soaked in a bubble bath in anticipation of joining Bogart and Bergman in Rick's Café-American—no doubt humming the film's nostalgic theme song. Georgy loves to relax in a bubble bath, lavender or jasmine, after a tough day ticketing speeders on Interstate 95. I have, on more than one occasion, joined her in the aromatic and effervescent waters but that, too, is another story—and it beats playing with a rubber duck, let me tell you.

Georgy returned my kiss with ardor, no doubt inspired by Bergman's performance. I did the gentlemanly thing and responded in kind. Not an hour ago I was captivated by the freckled face of Marge Macurdy, but now it was Georgy's impeccable peaches and cream complexion that tickled my fancy. There's a song (by Sigmund Romberg, perhaps?) that was written with me in mind, I'm sure. *When I'm not near the girl I love, I love the girl I'm near.* Go on, call me a cad. See if I care.

"You should give that suit to Goodwill," she noted, eyeing me up and down. "They might find someone it would fit."

"Cute, Georgy girl. Real cute. Living so far from the ocean I have neglected my daily two-mile swims in the surf and have put on a pound or two. I intend to lose them momentarily."

"How? By taking off the suit?"

"For starters, yes."

I left the parlor, went past the galley kitchen and turned left to enter the bedroom. That, plus the bath off the bedroom, constitutes the cottage. I began to get out of my tan gabardine straitjacket and when I was down to my briefs in walks Georgy.

"Don't you believe in knocking?" I scolded.

"Why? It's my house."

"And what am I? Your concubine?"

"Sure. And I'm the pharaoh disguised as a woman." She put her arms around my waist and squeezed. "You're getting love handles."

Feigning indifference, I said, "So you heard about Witch Hazel?"

"Who hasn't?" She pinched me where once a crab had nipped me while I was skinny dipping with Connie. Now how did Connie get into this?

"Let me put on a shirt," I begged, modestly.

"Which shirt?"

"The one you're wearing, that's which shirt."

We laughed, kissed and fell onto the bed where she traded her shirt for my . . .

An hour later I came out of the shower wrapped in a terry robe and found my girl pouring a white Orvieto Classico into two chilled wineglasses. A chicken, roasted and missing a leg and hip joint, sat on the table in the breakfast nook.

"I made it myself," Georgy boasted. "Are you hungry?"

"Starved. Toast some bread and I'll have a chicken breast sandwich with mayo." I picked up the two glasses and handed one to her. "You are lovely," I whispered.

"So are you," she answered.

"But not as lovely as you," I insisted.

"Okay, you win," she surrendered with a resigned shrug.

She put two pieces of rye in the toaster (I have outlawed soggy white bread) and I got a carving knife from the kitchen cupboard and began slicing the bird's breast which glowed a golden brown. It came away white and succulent.

"Did you really roast this?" I questioned.

"Who else. It's the cook's day off."

From the refrig she extracted a salad bowl containing freshly washed and cut iceberg and romaine lettuce, a quartered tomato and thin slices of cucumber. Basic, but for Georgy girl an overwhelming culinary achievement. Before my arrival on the scene her salads were whatever side dish came from a variety of ethnic take-out establishments.

When she began dressing my salad, not with something spooky in a plastic squeeze bottle, but with a mixture of olive oil and red wine vinegar, I almost applauded. A perfectly roasted chicken breast on toasted rye, with mayo, and a fresh salad bowl, no matter how mundane, was the best meal Georgia O'Hara had ever prepared for me—and I told her so.

After our post-*Casablanca* interlude, Georgy had gotten into a white cotton wrap, belted with two patch pockets, that came just to her knees. Handing over my toast she flashed me a silly grin and said, *"Bon appétit."*

With my sandwich, salad and properly chilled wine now in front of me, I wondered if this was domestic bliss. All appetites sated and . . . and what? Rewind *Casablanca* and go to bed? I had wished for an Ursi in Georgy's body and got a chicken breast sandwich and a salad for a response. In my heart of hearts what I wanted was Ursi cooking, Georgy girl in a bubble bath, Connie skinny dipping and Marge Macurdy on the side. Hey, I'm honest, if nothing else.

Could I retract my wish? The gods work in strange ways, and never stranger than when they're deciding the fate of Archy McNally. I finished my glass of wine and poured another. Georgy cut off the bird's remaining leg and daintily began to nibble on it, while I topped off her wineglass.

"Now tell me all about Matthew Hayes, Marlena Marvel, the witches, the ghouls and things that go bump in the dark."

While eating I gave Georgy a recap of my day, includ-

ing why I took on Hayes and my meeting with Marge
Macurdy. Georgy, remember, is an officer of the law, sharp
as a tack and, like Al Rogoff, a professional colleague.
Also, like Al, she is often privy to information that can
help my cause.

"You had drinks with the woman from the TV show at
the Four Seasons?"

Women are really something else, as the saying goes. I
had just given Georgy my take on a murder that had gar-
nered national headlines, a firsthand account of the characters involved, and the astounding effect it was having up
and down our gold coast, and what does she hit on? My
cocktail date with Marge. *Mon Dieu.*

What do women want? Freud lamented. They want to
know who you had cocktails with—and why—that's what
they want, Ziggy.

"Yes. I believe I told you that was why I would be late."

"I didn't catch her name," she said.

"I didn't throw it," I rejoined. "I said I was going to have
drinks with a lovely lady at the Four Seasons. And I did."

"And she ratted on her husband," Georgy pounced, waving the drumstick at me.

"Put that thing down and curb your imagination. She
didn't rat on her husband. She's worried, scared even, and
came to me for help because I'm now officially involved
with Marlena Marvel's murder and so, it seems, is her husband. That's what I do, Georgy, I help people in trouble."

She finished her drumstick, dabbed at her lips with a
napkin and twirled the wine in her glass thoughtfully while
I made myself another sandwich. Like other, more esoteric
things, one is never enough.

"Let's take it from the top," she began. "Hayes's party,

where you all met. Did Macurdy give any indication that he knew Hayes, or had met him before that evening?"

Liberally coating the freshly cut slices of chicken breast with mayo, I responded in the negative by shaking my head.

"But he had hired a chopper to fly over the maze and took along a TV cameraman to record the event for his audience. Why?"

"Because it was the thing to do," I explained. "Everyone was talking about the construction of the maze thanks to Hayes's big mouth and inbred penchant for getting his name in lights. Marge does a five-minute spot during the hour entitled 'What's New in Palm Beach,' and the maze got mentioned, naturally. Being a TV show they needed visuals and Mack came up with the idea to photograph it from the air."

"You call her Marge?" Georgy questioned.

"What should I call her, Nelly?"

"What about Mrs. Macurdy," Georgy offered.

"We got on a first-name basis the night of the party. Didn't I tell you we were paired off to search for the goal? I was Adam and she was Eve."

"Quaint, I'm sure. Did you wear fig leaves?"

"Come off it, Georgy. I'm not amused." (Possibly because I was feeling a smidgen of guilt.)

"Okay. Okay. Just having my little joke," she said. "And this Macurdy found the goal, or made the goal, as they say?"

"He did. But don't think he learned the key to the grid from that helicopter ride. They reran the tape the morning after the murder, when Joe made his TV debut. You can't see much from that distance, and certainly not the passages that lead to the goal. The speed of the copter is also a factor. It passed over the maze so quickly one would be hard-pressed to memorize the layout."

"But he saw something," Georgy persisted. "Something that has him milking Matthew Hayes. You said the mystery begins with Macurdy making the goal. I don't think so, Archy. I think it begins with that helicopter ride."

"I got the names of the two helicopter outfits the network uses when in need. I intend to question the pilot who flew Mack over the maze. He might be able to tell us something."

"Just what I would do," Georgy agreed. "And see the cameraman. Remember, there were three of them, including the pilot, in that chopper."

That was a good point. I had forgotten all about the cameraman. "Even if we do learn Mack's secret, it won't help solve the mystery of how Marlena got from the house to the maze, or who put the digitalis in her tea water." I accentuated the negative.

Georgy poured out more wine for us which finished the bottle. Just as well, it was getting on to midnight and there was much to do in the morning. "Which brings us to Tilly the Toiler and the merry widow, Mrs. Taylor," she pondered. "What about the widow's paramour? Does he figure in this?"

"His name is Billy Gilbert . . ."

"Billy Gilbert," Georgy shrieked. "You remember him, Archy. He was the big, fat character actor who was always being harassed by Laurel and Hardy or the Marx Brothers."

"This Billy Gilbert is young, slim and handsome, and he doesn't figure into anything that I know of. Laddy Taylor thinks Carolyn was seeing Billy before her husband died and as a result hastened the senior Mr. Taylor's death with digitalis, and . . ."

Georgy held up her hand, a gesture learned in state trooper school and used for stopping vehicles. It certainly stopped me. "Easy. You're getting ahead of the story. Indulge me, and let's take it in sequential order. We may come up with an inconsistency."

"Be my guest." I pulled a pack of English Ovals from the pocket of my robe and lit up. My first of the day which would end in five minutes. Were it not for this brainstorming session, I would have had my first tobacco-free day. I had made a pact with myself stating that after my first day without a cigarette, I would give them up forever. Had something deep within my unconscious made me have one before the stroke of midnight? I'm sure it did.

As I succumbed to my waning addiction, Georgy ran through the events I had gone over mentally a dozen times since they transpired.

Marlena appears in the guise of the famous statue of Venus, *sans* arms.

Tilly comes downstairs to tell Hayes that Marlena will rest and join us after the search for the goal.

The guests enter the goal, two by two, and Mack Macurdy makes the goal.

We return to the house and Tilly sounds the alarm. Marlena has disappeared.

We later learn that Tilly had drawn a bath for Marlena after the showing and brewed her a cup of tea. She then left her mistress resting on the chaise lounge and went to her own room. When she returned, Marlena was not there.

The search, the arrival of the police and, finally, finding Marlena Marvel in the goal of the maze, dead.

"And I saw it all," I reminded Georgy.

"Or what you thought you saw," she said. "Something you saw was not what you thought it was and I think that something was Marlena Marvel herself."

"I went over that," I sighed. "If it was an impersonator, where did she disappear to? And forget Tilly. She's barely two inches taller than Hayes, and Marlena towered over him. If Marlena was already in the goal, why didn't we all see her? It always comes down to the fact that a human body left the second floor of that house and turned up in the maze which was teeming with people. Finis." I stubbed out my English Oval a few seconds before the birth of a new day.

"Now this Tilly says she saw Carolyn Taylor on the second floor of the house just before Marlena went on and that the water for Marlena's tea was in the pot, ready to boil," Georgy stated.

"That's what Tilly claims," I said. "She also claims Marlena and Carolyn Taylor had met in secret several times before the death of Linton Taylor. So Laddy, who has been left out of his father's will in favor of Carolyn, is claiming that Marlena, who was some sort of quack healer— read: abortionist—told Carolyn how to get rid of Linton with his own medication, and then Carolyn thanked Marlena by giving her a dose of the same stuff."

"And this Tilly, who fingers Carolyn, is smitten with Laddy Taylor who wants Carolyn fingered," Georgy said. "Add the fact that this Hayes guy, who sounds like a control freak, claims to know nothing, and I would say either everyone is lying, or no one is telling the truth."

She wasn't telling me anything I didn't already know. This conversation had cost me an English Oval and an hour's sleep. However, it did add the cameraman to the list of people I had to see, and laying out the facts as we did put

Georgy in the loop. They say two heads are better than one, whoever *they* are.

"There's something else," I said, stifling a yawn. "Lolly Spindrift told me that Carolyn Taylor and Alex Gomez y Zapata have been seen together on more than one occasion at a marina in Miami."

"Doing what?"

"That's what I'd like to know. I asked Connie and she gave me the brush-off."

"Maybe Connie doesn't know," Georgy speculated.

"Ha!" I laughed. "Connie knows the last time Alex changed his socks. Believe me, I've been there."

"But does it have anything to do with the murder and Mack Macurdy?"

I shrugged. "Who knows? Carolyn is the common denominator in both cases. I have much to ask the lady when I see her, which I hope will be tomorrow."

"Suppose she refuses to tell you anything, or even refuses to see you?" It was Georgy's turn to accentuate the negative.

"It's one of the hazards of the trade, Georgy girl, now let's go to bed."

"First tell me about Joey and that dreadful girl."

"Let's go to bed."

"Tell me what I want to know or you sleep on the couch."

I groaned. "She's not a dreadful girl. She's a member in good standing of Palm Beach's Smart Set and, as such, above reproach. So there."

"How did they meet?"

"Who knows?" I said. "He's a roving reporter, so maybe he roved into her one day. And what's it to you?"

"Nothing, but I worry about him. He's a boy at heart and can't take care of himself," she whimpered.

Recalling Binky's description of Joey's night with Fitz, I would say the boy was doing exceptionally well on his own. "He's an overnight TV star, Georgy, with a growing fan club. Get used to it."

"All that dark forces nonsense and showing off that asinine plant. Do you know where he got the plant, Archy?"

"Binky says it came from a nursery in Boca that deals in rare plants."

"Rare plants, is it?" Georgy cried. "Well, the guy's most profitable crop is a rare plant called cannabis. The police have been on to him for years but he's cagey. It's a wonder Joe didn't go before the camera holding an armful of marijuana. You see what I mean? And now he teams up with Binky Watrous. What next?"

What next? Binky gets a job delivering "rare plants" for the nursery in Boca. I was going meshugah over what Georgy had just told me. And I had better warn Joe before the vice squad joined his witch hunt.

"Binky is okay," I said in defense of my friend. "A little spacy, but loyal, I'll say that for him."

"Spacy? He can't walk and chew gum at the same time."

"That's cruel, Georgy, and unworthy of you. It's Joe you're down on and you're using poor Binky to get at Joe."

"I'm not down on Joe. I just don't want to see him get hurt. Right now he's enjoying his fifteen minutes, but that's all it'll last, fifteen minutes. Then what? And that girl will break his heart."

I couldn't think of a better way to break a heart than by tripping over Fitz. Georgy, of course, was being unreasonable, and I think it was Joe's success that had her nettled,

the same way Connie's success with Alex had me perturbed. You see, when you break up with someone the first
thing you do is wish them well. Then, if they do well, you
shout foul.

"Lighten up, Georgy, and let Joe Gallo go," I counseled.

She got up, came around the table, put her arms around
my neck and kissed the top of my head. "I let him go the day
we met, and maybe I'm a little jealous of his sudden success.
When he was with me he was a caddie, for Pete's sake."

"And you were a rookie, and now you're a lieutenant.
I'm a little jealous of your jealousy of Joe Gallo."

"Don't be. Don't ever be, Archy. Your Georgy girl loves
you."

"Good. Now let's go to bed."

"I thought you would never ask."

IT BEGAN TO RAIN JUST AS WE GOT INTO BED. THE
pitter-patter on the roof above us as we snuggled together
was paregoric as well as seductive. A time for whispering
sweet nothings into a pretty ear. No sweet nothings came to
mind so I did the next best thing.

"Would you like to go to New York for a long weekend?"

"New York? Oh, Archy, I would love it. When? Why?"

"You remember Todd Brandt, whose real name is Ed
Brandt and who now goes under the name of Rick Brandt?
He was a waiter at the Pelican."

"Sure, I do," Georgy said. "The actor. We saw him at the
playhouse in Lake Worth."

"Well, he's got himself a part in an off-Broadway show
and he sent me two ducats to the opening. We can book
into the Yale Club and play tourist."

She was all over me, laughing and threatening to quit

the force if they didn't allow her time off. "But I have time coming," she said. "When, Archy? When?"

"First Saturday in November, I believe."

"Just a few weeks off," she lamented. "Will you be finished with the case?"

"Or the case will have finished me, but either way we're going to New York that weekend."

She giggled, kissed me and cuddled closer. "What should I wear?" was the sweet nothing she whispered in my ear before she withdrew, sat up and jumped out of the bed.

"Where are you going?"

"I forgot to rewind *Casablanca*," she called out in the dark.

I pulled the covers over my head and shuddered.

14

F LAMINGO RUN CAN BE FOUND IN THE FIFTEEN HUN-
dred block of Ocean Boulevard. A prime location in a
hamlet of prime locations, the area is the jewel in the
crown. A few doors down, a dot com billionaire is in the
process of erecting a palace which is rumored to be costing
him ninety million dollars. The landscaping includes trees
of not less than one hundred feet in height, giving the appearance of antiquity so sought after by the *nouveau riche*
which fools no one but the *nouveau* inhabitants of the mansion. Strange how a society that worships youth dotes on
things antique, from furniture to autos to pedigree. Will he
call his new, trying to pass for old, mansion Xanadu? One
hopes not.

Did I mention that he is tunneling under the Boulevard
and building a beach house not a hundred yards, as the
mole crawls, from the villa? The line between sumptuous
and coarse has been breached often in this town but never

with such a blatant disregard for propriety, which means Mr. and Mrs. Dot Com will be lionized socially unless they do something crass, like lose their money.

Flamingo Run, a white stucco villa with a twenty-foot-high center hall and north and south wings, is not hidden by tall trees but fronted by a well-kept lawn and is therefore in full view of those traversing the Boulevard, should they choose to look. The housekeeper answered my ring and I asked if Mrs. Taylor was at home and receiving.

"She's here." The woman, wearing the housekeeper's trademark white uniform and gum-soled white bucks that often had me wondering if these domestics divided their time between housekeeping and nursing, eyed me suspiciously. She took in my summer flannels, fuchsia Lacoste, penny loafers and straw boater with its band of matching fuchsia silk shantung before espying my red Miata in the driveway, and immediately came to the wrong conclusion. "You want Mr. Gilbert?"

"No. I would like to see Mrs. Taylor." I gave her my card. "This is a social call. I'm not selling encyclopedias nor the path to salvation."

She looked at my card, opened the door wider and gestured for me to enter. "I'll give Miz Taylor your card. Please wait here."

I stood, hat in hand, in the entrance hall whose vaulted ceiling was painted sky blue behind billowing white clouds with pink linings. I looked about for a font to bless myself but saw none. There were two settees of museum quality flanking the rather austere hall. The parquet floor, which could be seen on either side of the long narrow oriental rug that ran the length of the hall, was polished to a glossy shine.

The housekeeper returned. "Follow me, please."

I tossed my hat on one of the settees and did as I was told. I was led to the rear terrace where the lady of the house was at table. Carolyn Taylor was in athletic attire: white sweats and sneakers. Her short auburn hair was crowned with a white sailor's hat, the brim turned down roguishly. In short, a typical PB matron taking her elevenses after her morning jog on the beach. Needless to say Mrs. Taylor could pose for a poster proclaiming the benefits of jogging and the good life in sunny Florida. She's slim, tan and lovely to look at.

"Mr. McNally. I've been expecting you," she called as I approached.

"Is that good or bad, Mrs. Taylor?"

"That depends on who you're representing. My stepson or Matthew Hayes—or both."

The PB grapevine, with tentacles reaching as far south as Miami and as far north as the Hamptons, makes telegraphing seem like snail mail. It's said that a bit of gossip uttered at a dinner table and overheard by the serving girl would be common knowledge before the coffee and *petit fours* made their appearance. Thanks to our Ursi, the McNally kitchen is the command post for such domestic transmissions.

"You know I'm working for Matthew Hayes," I stated, not bothering to ask how she knew as the possibilities were endless.

"Well, he did hire you the night poor Marlena was done in," she said, adding, "Sit down, Archy, if I may call you Archy, and have a cuppa."

Like a good boy I again did as I was told and watched as Carolyn poured out a cup of java from a silver urn seated on a hot plate. Cream and sugar were on the table but not a hint of edibles.

"Would you like a sweet roll, or toast?" she asked. "I don't take anything between meals myself."

And judging by her appearance, her meals consisted of fish (mostly sole) and sensible salads. Remembering my own vow to take off a few pounds, I declined the offer with a violent shake of the head. (I would have given my genuine Stork Club ashtray for a sticky roll.)

I added cream to my coffee, shunned the sugar and got down to business. "I understand you knew Marlena Marvel, Mrs. Taylor."

She didn't seem the least bit fazed by this. She poured herself more coffee, added nothing, sipped and looked across the flagstone terrace to the tiled swimming pool where a young man in black short shorts and nothing more was vacuuming the water that glistened invitingly in the early morning sun. Billy Gilbert earning his keep? Whoever would have thunk it?

"You spoke to the maid, Tilly," she said.

"Not really, Mrs. Taylor. Tilly spoke to me."

"And she told you that Marlena and I met on more than one occasion shortly after Marlena arrived in town." I noticed that she didn't ask me to call her Carolyn. "Well, we did."

I waited for her to go on, but she didn't. An awkward silence followed before I said, "Were you a friend of Mrs. Hayes? She and Hayes settled into their house about a month ago, shortly after the maze was completed. When did you meet her?"

"Twenty years ago," she blurted.

Well, ain't that a kick in the kimono. "I seem to have come in in the middle of the movie," I said.

"No, Archy. You came in at the end of the movie as far as Marlena is concerned. Her end, and mine if Laddy has his way. Shall we lay our cards on the table?"

I opened my arms and offered, "I'll show you mine, if you'll show me yours."

I got a vacant stare before she laughed, much to my relief. "Okay. It's no secret that Laddy has been bad-mouthing me to anyone who'll listen. He's claiming that I killed his father, with Marlena's help, and then I killed Marlena."

I nodded. "He's been to see my father about executing an order of exhumation. My father refused to act on his behalf."

Now it was her turn. "Linton cut Laddy out of his will because Laddy had a problem with drugs and, regardless of what he told your father, he never got the monkey off his back. Linton and Laddy's mother did everything they could to help him and he repaid them by forging and cashing checks, pilfering the ready cash they kept in the house, seducing a young Cuban girl they hired to assist the housekeeper and—need I go on?"

"I get the picture, Mrs. Taylor."

Here came the unmistakable sound of water being disturbed. We both turned toward the pool. Billy, sampling the fruits of his labor, had dived into the sparkling clear water. A black pair of short shorts was clearly visible atop a white towel draped across one of the deck chairs. My, my.

When our eyes met again, she said, "You think I'm a dirty old woman."

"Mrs. Taylor, my abiding motto is judge not, lest you be judged. I have been hired by Matthew Hayes to find out who murdered his wife, why, and how it was done. Besides, you're not old."

She laughed, tossing back her head and almost losing her hat. "You're a bastard, Archy McNally."

"But cute, Mrs. Taylor. Yes?"

"Not bad," she conceded, still not telling me to call her by her given name. I guess I wasn't as cute as all that. "Where were we?" she posed.

"Laddy Taylor was seducing the maid and robbing the poor box."

"He left home when his mother died because the poor woman, as mothers will, kept him in cash and clean underwear," she continued. "Over the years that followed, Linton tried to find his son and reconcile with him. He hired a detective agency who traced Laddy and each time they did, sweet Laddy told his father to go . . ."

I could see why the lady preferred sailor hats.

"Linton cut the boy out of his will, for good reason, and now the ungrateful [censored] comes home to claim his right and accuse me. I was a good wife to Linton Taylor, Archy, and made his final years happy. His son made him miserable."

"When did Laddy come back to Palm Beach?"

"About a week ago. Shortly after I notified him that his father had died."

"He told me you contacted him via a mail drop," I said.

"That's true," she answered. "A few years ago he wrote his father for money. What else? He give Linton the postal box number for the mail drop. Linton sent him a sizable check. I used that address and he received my letter."

"He and Tilly certainly got acquainted in record time if he's been here only a week," I pointed out.

Carolyn Taylor saw nothing strange in the instant coupling. "Birds of a feather, Archy. They attract like magnets."

"How did Laddy manage to get invited to Hayes's bash? Surely Tilly didn't put him on the list."

"No. Lolly put him on the list. Marlena told me Hayes had hired Lolly to put together an A list for his amazin' party—excuse the jest. Lolly had written that Laddy was back in town and not knowing who would prevail in our family feud, Laddy or me, he put us both on the list. Dear Lolly takes no risks."

The gathering, trust me, was as far from the Palm Beach A list as A is to Z and Carolyn knew it. And how about the way she sits there dishing Lolly, when she stole the guy puttering about in her pool from dear ol' Lol. I guess it's all *très* sophisticated—and how I love it.

"Mr. Hayes told me Tilly was very loyal to her mistress," I said.

Carolyn laughed. "Did he now? She was very loyal to Matthew Hayes, and all that implies. Marlena detested her and the only reason she accompanied Marlena when we met was because Marlena couldn't drive."

You know the old cliché. Let a dozen people witness an event and write about it. No two will agree on what they saw. Hearing what Tilly and Carolyn Taylor had to say on the same subject was very similar. Did the truth lie somewhere between their versions, or were they both trying to lead poor Archy up the garden path?

"If Marlena didn't trust Tilly wasn't she afraid Tilly would tell Hayes about your meetings?" I asked her.

Eyes wide, she looked at me as if she didn't have a clue as to my meaning, and I believe she was being sincere. "But I'm sure Marlena told her husband about our girl coffee klatches," she said. "Why shouldn't she? He knew Marlena and I were old friends."

"Tilly got the impression that it was all very clandestine due to the rather offbeat venues you selected for your meetings."

Carolyn put her elbows on the table, clasped her hands together and rested her chin on the resulting platform. "I see," she said sagaciously, "of course, it's all as clear as mud—the kind you sling at your opponent. Tilly is being briefed by Laddy, who wants the police to believe we met in secret and exchanged recipes for foxglove cocktails. What gall.

"Listen to me, Archy. Marlena and I were roommates in Des Moines. We were both waitresses in a joint called the Cockatoo Lounge."

My face must have given me away.

"Don't look so smug, Archy. It wasn't as bad as all that. We didn't offer lap dances."

"Judge not, lest you be judged, remember?"

"Oh, shut up," she laughed. "Where was I?"

"At the Cockatoo Lounge in Des Moines."

"I left shortly after Marlena, who was then Molly, teamed up with Hayes. By the way, he didn't accidently land in her lap as his press clippings claim. He met her at the Cockatoo, started dating her, and together they conceived the plan and hired a photographer to record the phenomenon."

Clever, I mused, and typical of the man who Georgy labeled a control freak. Was he in control the night his wife was poisoned? I believe he was. Could I prove it? Not yet. Was I sanguine? No.

"I met Linton on a world cruise," Carolyn told me. "Very chic, very expensive. The ship was full of rich widows and poor Linton was practically accosted every time he stepped out of his cabin. I was one of the hostesses and we hit it off. He would hide in my cabin to get away from his ardent pursuers. This was frowned upon by the captain but who cared? He invited me to visit in Palm Beach. I did and the rest is Palm Beach history. Linton didn't know about my past in Des Moines and I didn't tell him."

She went on to say that when Marlena arrived in town she called Carolyn, who told Marlena frankly that in her new life as Mrs. Linton Taylor, she, Carolyn, didn't want it known that she once shared digs with the now rather infamous Marlena Marvel.

"Marlena, bless her, understood and we met in secret. So tell Tilly to take a long walk off a short pier," Carolyn exclaimed. "She and Laddy are pure trash, Archy. Lord knows what he promised her to get her to lie on his behalf."

But where does Hayes fit into this? I pondered. If he knew that Marlena and Carolyn were old buddies, why didn't he tell me? Or the police? Regardless of whom one believed, Tilly or Carolyn, all roads led to Matthew Hayes.

"I got more news for you, Mrs. Taylor. Tilly claims you were upstairs the night of the party. She says she saw you on the second floor just before Marlena went on as Venus."

The lady's tan glowed red and I thought she might burst something vital, like her aorta. It's a good thing I left out the water in the percolator, waiting to be tampered with.

"That is a bald-faced lie, and I can prove I never left the first floor. Billy was with me until we went out to search for the goal, and then I was joined by the reporter, Joe Gallo. They will both swear I never left the first floor of that house."

This was true, and Joe would be thought an impartial witness, but not Billy Gilbert. I didn't tell her that.

"Mrs. Taylor," I said, rather slowly, "you realize I must tell the police what Tilly told me. Playing fair, I came to you with Tilly's accusation before going to them. And I will have to tell my client, Matthew Hayes."

Her red glow turned ashen. I really felt sorry for the woman. "Do I need a lawyer, Archy?"

"You might want to talk to my father, Mrs. Taylor."

She looked pensive and then said, "Marlena called me a few days ago and said she wanted to see me because she had something amusing to report."

"Amusing?" I repeated.

"Marlena had a macabre sense of humor," Carolyn said.

"And what did she have to report, Mrs. Taylor?"

Carolyn shook her head. "I don't know, and will never know. I think she called a few days before the party and I thought I would get a chance to speak to her that night. As you know, I didn't."

But did her curiosity impel her to sneak upstairs for a quickie private chat with her ex-roomie? And what amusing news did Marlena have for Carolyn?

"Hayes never said anything to you about Marlena and me?" Carolyn wondered.

"No, ma'am. And he doesn't seem to know about Tilly's sighting—at least he never mentioned it to me."

She leaned forward as if to stress her point. "That little bastard knows everything, Archy. He's a rascal and Marlena was tired of his bossing her and his philandering. She was getting ready to dump him."

"What?" I cried. "Tilly said . . ."

She laughed, a little hysterically I thought. "Don't believe anything that bitch told you. Marlena said she was ready to leave Hayes and take most of his money with her. I will swear to that on a stack of bibles."

If true, it gave Hayes a motive for getting rid of his wife. My gut instinct told me to believe Carolyn and distrust Tilly, Laddy and Hayes. Prejudicial, the sire would accuse, and he would be right.

Before taking my leave I attempted to learn what Carolyn Taylor and Alex were up to. "Apropos of nothing, Mrs. Taylor, it's been rumored that you and the Miami newspaper columnist and political activist, Alejandro Gomez y Zapata, were seen at a marina in Miami. I ask only to ascertain if this has anything to do with my case and to warn you that people have seen you with him and are talking."

"By people do you mean that old hag, Cynthia Horowitz? She's been after Alex ever since her secretary, Connie Garcia, introduced them. She's a menace, that woman. Looks down her nose at me with five dead husbands to her credit and a past that makes the Cockatoo Lounge look like a nunnery."

Hell hath no fury like a woman looked down upon. I knew Carolyn and Lady Cynthia weren't kissin' cousins, but I never dreamed the rancor had reached the name-calling stage. Old hag? I couldn't wait to tell Connie.

"No, ma'am. Lolly told me," I confessed.

"He doesn't miss a beat, that amusing man," she said, then proceeded to tell me an outrageous lie. "I've taken an interest in sailing and Alex is something of a yachtsman. We went out in a rental a few times and we intend to go again. Would you care to join us?"

Alex a yachtsman? Since when? Carolyn Taylor was full of surprises—not to mention baloney. Who to believe in this amazin' case?

"And where did you meet Alex?" I didn't realize I had vocalized the thought until I heard myself asking.

"I introduced them."

We both turned to see Billy Gilbert in our midst. Absorbed in our fervent one-on-one, neither of us had seen him approach. Thankfully he was wearing the black shorts. His blond hair was damp, his skin a golden tan, his physique exemplary and his manner supercilious.

"I was tending bar at a club in South Beach," he went on, "and Alex was a steady customer. That's how we met and I introduced him to Carolyn."

"I wasn't being nosy . . ."

"I'm sure you weren't," he cut me off.

The guy was a punk.

"This is Mr. McNally," Carolyn said. "And this is Billy Gilbert. Mr. McNally is working for Matthew Hayes."

Billy didn't extend his hand, and neither did I.

"Are you going to question me, Mr. McNally?" Billy asked.

"I'll leave that to the police, Mr. Gilbert."

Opening his arms wide, he said, "As you can see I have nothing to hide."

Judging from the grin on Carolyn Taylor's face I had to assume that she found this amusing, but who's to account for taste in matters of the heart?

Billy was now questioning me. "Are you related to Paddy McNally?"

"Not that I know of. Is he a local?" I questioned back.

"Hardly," Billy said, as if I should know better. "He owned a ski lodge in the Swiss Alps known as the Castle. Very big with the Brits. He preceded the prince in Sarah Ferguson's affections. She played hostess at the Castle before she played Duchess in London."

The guy was a pretentious punk.

"Did you know him?" I asked.

"Of course not. I wasn't even born at the time, but I thought you might know him as you have the same name."

And are the same age, he implied.

The guy was a pugnacious, pretentious punk.

I rose to take my leave and Carolyn said, "I've asked Mr. McNally to join us on our next outing with Alex."

"Do you think that's wise?" Billy complained.

Carolyn shrugged. "Why not? Alex is bringing Connie Garcia."

Billy yielded to his benefactress, reluctantly I thought, and invited me to bring a date. "I wouldn't want you to be odd man out. We sail in two days."

"Thank you," I said, biting the proverbial bullet. "I may do just that. I'll be in touch, Mrs. Taylor."

She rose and, taking my arm, led me off the terrace and toward the front door. "You mustn't mind Billy," she pleaded. "He's insecure and responds by being pompous. I told him that bit about Paddy McNally. Linton and I met Paddy in Switzerland, and the Castle's true name was *Les Gais Lutins* but Billy can't remember that."

"Nor can he pronounce it," I ventured, not caring what she thought, "and he needs a good, swift kick in the rear of those abbreviated shorts."

What she thought must have amused her because she laughed. "Judge not, lest you be judged. Remember?"

"Oh, shut up," I scolded.

"Billy is a diamond in the rough, Archy."

"Then polish him," I advised.

"That would spoil the fun."

And we both laughed.

"I look forward to our sailing date. Call me for details," were her parting words.

I was certain Billy Gilbert did not want me aboard. Why?

15

I LEFT FLAMINGO RUN WITH MORE QUESTIONS THAN answers on my score sheet. This was not unusual after an interview, especially in a case involving opposing factions. I said I was more inclined to believe Carolyn Taylor than Tilly. This was not only because I found Carolyn more attractive and far less base, in spite of her boy toy, but because it would have been almost impossible for Carolyn to slip upstairs that evening. The operative word being *almost.*

But then it was just as impossible (that word again) for Marlena Marvel to have been poisoned and transported to the maze that night. But she was.

I am investigating the murder of Marlena Marvel, not the death of Linton Taylor, and the ensuing animosity between Linton's son and Linton's widow, but was there a correlation between the two? I mentally listed the suspects in the Marlena Marvel murder.

Matthew Hayes

Matilda Thompson

Carolyn Taylor

Laddy Taylor (and everyone else who was at the party)

Next, suspects in the death of Linton Taylor—if he was murdered, which is most doubtful.

Carolyn Taylor

Aided and abetted by Marlena Marvel

Clearly there is a correlation, and the link is Carolyn Taylor, whom I chose to believe. But then I recall several damsels I rather liked before leading them, handcuffed, to jail. It's called dancing with the devil and I so enjoy doing a two-step with an alluring succubus.

And was it just a lucky coincidence for Laddy that Marlena was poisoned with digitalis, the medication taken by Linton Taylor, giving Laddy the ammunition he needed to fire at Carolyn? Laddy was also lucky in teaming up with Tilly so soon after his arrival. Did Tilly see Carolyn on the second floor the night of the party, or did Laddy tell her she did? Birds of a feather, Carolyn had dubbed them. Was their birdseed illicit drugs? That might account for the speed with which the two connected, the drug culture being a tight-knit clan with its own buzz words, sign language and meeting places.

Enter the yachtsman, Alejandro Gomez y Zapata, who is making runs out of a marina in Miami with—guess who? Carolyn Taylor and Billy Gilbert. Rechecking my lists I find one name stands out like a neon sign in a dark alley. The lady whom I chose to believe. The lady who had come a long way from cocktail waitress to cruise hostess to Palm Beach matron. People don't change, remember, only the roles they choose to play change.

And why didn't that brat want me to join the cruise?

(Reminder: Call Georgy and see if she can get the day after tomorrow off to go yachting. Note: I must give in to the new century and get a cell phone however opposed I am to people walking about with the damn things glued to their ears and yakking like magpies.)

The only scenario Carolyn Taylor doesn't appear in is the one involving Mack Macurdy. Replacing her is the lovely Marge Macurdy. We seem to have a plethora of attractive women in this case, each with her own separate, and very distinctive, appeal. Freckles, moonlight and roses. Cockatoo Lounge, hostess and—foxglove?

Was Mack leaning on Matthew Hayes? Like the claims of Tilly and Carolyn, I have only Marge's word regarding Mack's euphoria since Marlena's murder and Mack's subsequent visits to Le Maze.

Such were my thoughts as I drove from Flamingo Run to police headquarters. I found a parking space on County Road and walked up the steps to the palace. Before you reach the information counter one passes the Crime Scene Evidence Unit. Inside the glass enclosure a group of officers were milling about, chatting and gesticulating. If there were any crime scene evidence about it escaped my notice.

The officer at the information counter, a tall blonde beauty, reminded me of my Georgy. How the physical persona of police personnel has changed in the past two decades. Will I live to see a woman president? I certainly hope so.

"May I see Lieutenant Eberhart? Archy McNally calling."

"Is he expecting you?" she asked.

"No, but if you give him my name I'm sure he'll see me."

Hesitantly, she inquired, "Are you here to report witches' covens or other strange occurrences in your neighborhood—or if you're taking digitalis, please see your doctor." It was clearly a set piece, oft repeated in the past few days.

But of course. Mack Macurdy had mentioned on several occasions that Lieutenant Oscar Eberhart was in charge of the Marlena Marvel murder. Eberhart was now a household name with a listed phone and therefore subject to calls and visits from the loony-toon fringe. The way she kept glancing at my fuchsia Lacoste and matching hat band led me to believe she thought me one of them. Impudent little thing. Give them a badge and they start taking themselves seriously.

"None of the above, ma'am. If you'll just give him my name I'm sure he'll tell you to let me in."

She picked up her phone, hit a few buttons and announced me to Oscar. She looked disappointed as she pointed to my right and said, "One flight up."

I didn't say "I told you so" nor did I stick my tongue out at the doubting Thomasina for fear that she would sound an alarm and I would end up a piece of evidence in the crime scene unit. With dignity, I tipped my boater, squared my fuchsia shoulders, and headed for the stairs.

This was not my first visit to Oscar's office so I knew my way. As I approached, a sergeant with a gray crew cut and a body that suggested he played Santa Claus at the department's annual eggnog bash was just leaving. With a nod he held the door for me.

Lieutenant Eberhart quickly closed a large notepad as I entered, but not quick enough to hide the top page which was covered with completed tic-tac-toe diagrams. Thick black lines had been drawn through the games that boasted a winner. In England they call the game Noughts and Crosses. They also call suspenders braces and pronounce clerk so that it rhymes with mark. I passed none of this on to Eberhart.

"I'm not disturbing you, I trust," I said.

Unperturbed, he shoved the notepad aside and pointed to his visitor's chair, which his opponent had so recently vacated. It was still warm. Was Eberhart the noughts or the crosses? Crosses was my guess as noughts were synonymous with nothing and Oscar Eberhart longed to be something—like the guy who solved the Marlena Marvel murder.

"I hear you're working for Hayes," he stated.

"Reluctantly, but it gives me the right to snoop. This is the first time I've been a witness to a crime and couldn't say wha'happen if I was called upon to give testimony. It irks me, Lieutenant, and I don't like being irked."

"Welcome to the club. You got anything to report?"

"I have information to pass on, strictly hearsay."

He retrieved the notepad. Was he going to challenge me? "We have nothing, McNally. Zero, zilch, nada, nothing. We've been over every blade of grass in that maze not knowing what we're looking for but it makes no difference because we didn't find anything.

"Hayes is as communicative as the Sphinx. He told us he hired you because we're incompetent. That pipsqueak's got a pair on him, let me tell you. The maid sticks to her story till I want to strangle her, and our interviews to date have done nothing for us but cost the department a wad in overtime and we haven't made a dent in the list."

"If you don't know what you're looking for, Lieutenant, how do you know you didn't find it?"

"Nobody likes a smart-ass, McNally, especially one in a purple shirt."

"It's fuchsia, Lieutenant."

"That's even worse. If I was you, buddy, I would stop having intimate dinners with Lolly Spindrift. He was on top of our interview roster and I had the pleasure of speaking to him. He knew everyone at the party by name, who they were married to, who they used to be married to, who they were sleeping with, how much money they had, and would I like to have cocktails with him in a dubious bar some evening."

Dubious bar? I suppressed a laugh which was a pity because laughs were sorely missing in this case. "You should accept, Oscar. Look at what happened to Lolly's last boyfriend. I just left him swimming in the buff in Carolyn Taylor's pool."

He flushed from neck to forehead as I knew he would. Shame on me.

"Was Mrs. Taylor watching?" When I nodded with a wink he positively glowed like a cherry ripe for the picking. "What did she say?" he growled.

"She said he was insecure and responded by being pompous."

He shook his head, the color slowly draining from his cheeks. "Everyone in this town is nuts, McNally, including you. And immoral. Spindrift said there was less to Billy Gilbert than met the eye. What do you suppose that means?"

Knowing he would drop dead if I told him, I played it safe and lied, "He means the kid is all facade and little substance. More important, what did Lolly say about Carolyn Taylor?"

"She met Linton Taylor, millionaire, on a cruise ship and he married her. She was some kind of entertainer. Strictly off the rack, Spindrift called her. Go figure. The guy even talks queer."

"Off the rack means she was not to the manor born. And she was a hostess on that liner."

"Who told you that?" he asked.

"She did. While Billy was—well, you know. And before she was a hostess she was a waitress in the Cockatoo Lounge in Des Moines. And would you like to hear who Mrs. Taylor roomed with in Des Moines?"

"Not really, but you'll tell me anyway."

"She roomed with Molly Malone, that's who she roomed with."

I got a blank stare before he almost leaped out of his chair. He reached for a manila folder, opened it and ran his eyes down the first page. "Molly Malone," he read aloud. "The deceased."

"None other, Lieutenant."

"Carolyn Taylor knew Marlena Marvel?" he questioned. "Why didn't she come forward. Why didn't you? Withholding information is . . ."

"I'm not withholding anything. I'm here to tell you what I've learned."

"Which is more than we've learned," he barked at me. "Go on, say it."

"Okay. Which is more than you've learned."

"Smart-ass," he chastened. "You said it was hearsay."

"Carolyn Taylor and Marlena Marvel were roommates in Des Moines some twenty years ago. They've stayed in touch, on and off, since then. That's a fact, the rest I have to tell you is hearsay. Meaning it's one person's word with no corroborating witnesses. Now sit back and listen."

I reported, in detail, my meeting with Tilly and my interview with Carolyn. I did not report on my meeting with Hayes as that would breach client confidentiality. Besides, Eberhart was at liberty to question Hayes. If the police didn't ask the right questions, that was their problem, not mine.

Nor did I tell him anything that was said in father's office between father and me, or the details of Laddy's last visit to McNally & Son. Laddy had blabbed to the police on that score.

When I had said my piece, Eberhart rewarded my efforts with, "You should have come here before you went to the Taylor dame. I can cite you."

"No way, Oscar. The maid's accusations are unprovable. You can't cite me for not reporting what amounts to a rumor. And isn't it obvious that she intended for me to pass it on to you? She and her boyfriend."

Reaching for his phone he mumbled, "This is the first break we're had on this lousy case." A moment later he was shouting into the mouthpiece, "I want someone to pick up Matilda Thompson. She's the maid in the Marlena Marvel case. I want her brought in ASAP. She lives in the Hayes house on Ocean Boulevard. Radio a patrol car and have them do it.

"No, she's not under arrest. I want to question her. And not a word to anyone or the press will get hold of it and headline her guilty and that nut Macurdy will have her on a broomstick." He banged the instrument in its cradle.

Well, ain't that something. One word from Archy and the entire police force is off and running—perhaps on a wild-goose chase but hey, at least I put a stop to Noughts and Crosses ennui.

"Let's take it from the top, McNally, and I want it all. You hold anything back and I'll revoke your license."

It did my heart good to see Oscar on the offensive. It made me less culpable for not coming here right after my meeting with Tilly, and I did squeeze out the info just now like a cardsharp with a poker hand.

So we went over the facts and the hearsay. I stifled a yawn.

"I don't like this Laddy Taylor tie-in. Do we have two wrongful deaths here, or one?"

"That's what I'm trying to figure out, Lieutenant."

Eberhart began scratching the back of his head. I noticed that he has been letting his hair grow a wee bit longer. Nothing dubious, mind you, but definitely more urbane. It could be the way the overhead fluorescent light illuminated his curly locks, but I could swear the lieutenant's mane had also gotten a shade or two lighter since our last encounter. Are Eberhart's pretentious longings coming out of the closet, or is a lady the impetus? I know nothing of Oscar's love life and dare not ask, but I could query Al Rogoff on the subject.

"Maybe we should have paid more attention to Linton Taylor's son. Maybe there's more to his accusations than we know," he speculated. "What do you think, Archy?"

Notice how he segued from the robust McNally to the familiar Archy without making any stops along the way. Oscar was buttering me up but I'm not easy. I had given him all I knew and he would have to make of it what he would.

He would interview Tilly, Carolyn Taylor and, given my disclosures, Laddy Taylor. They would tell him just what they told me. I didn't want to influence his conclusions with my take on these characters, nor did I believe for an instant that his judgment was subordinate to mine. On the contrary. Everything I know about this business I learned from observing the police at work—be it a case of murder, or ticketing a jaywalker.

"I have a few ideas, Oscar, but I'm not ready to go public. Can we pow-wow again after you see the leading contenders?"

"Sure," he agreed, "I'll give you a call."

"Was the digitalis in the tea water, or is that classified?"

"It was in a liquid she ingested that night. The doc can't be more specific, but we know that tea was the last thing she drank."

Standing, I considered telling Oscar what I knew about Mack Macurdy but decided to see what my client had to say on the subject before putting more fat in the fire—a decision I would soon regret. Instead, I told him, "I think Hayes is going to appear on the Macurdy show."

Oscar pulled a face. "That Macurdy is a public nuisance. I asked him to tone it down, get off all that occult nonsense, and you know what he said?"

"He told you to come on his show and have your say. What did you tell him?"

Eberhart displayed the middle finger of his right hand while asking, "Why is Hayes going on?"

"I don't know, Oscar, but I intend to ask him the next time we meet."

"And tell the horticulturist, Gallo, his nursery in Boca

is under surveillance. That's all I can say right now."

Quoting Dorothy Parker, I sallied, "You can lead a whore to culture, but you can't make her think."

"Get out of here, McNally."

16

COMING OUT OF THE PALACE I RAN INTO TILLY, ES-corted by Al Rogoff, coming in. She looked furious and Al looked determined. We passed, like ships in the night, without tooting our horns.

During my visit with Lieutenant Eberhart the bright morning sun had been obliterated by billowing gray clouds propelled by a steady breeze coming off the ocean. The weather, for better or worse, can change rapidly in the tropics. By eventide we could have a picture-perfect sunset or a torrential downpour. Not being a gambling man I raised the top on my Miata.

I made a mental to-do list as I pulled the seat belt across my lap and snapped it into its socket. Matthew Hayes was numero uno.

I had to get hold of Joe Gallo and caution him and his stringer, Binky, on the perils of wheeling and dealing in "exotic" plants. I would try to squeeze in a visit with Connie to see if she would shed some light on the yachting parties now that I was to join them, and to pump her for the latest gossip regarding our latest murder. Thanks to her boss, Lady Cynthia, Connie is a good source for upper-echelon chatter.

For belowstairs patter I turn to our Ursi, and it might not be a bad idea to swing around to the McNally manse and do just that.

I should call Lolly and tell him to stop propositioning the fuzz. Also, get the name of that dubious bar. Could be Bar Anticipation in West PB, or had Lolly discovered a more sordid sanctuary? Lolly lives by the tenet that proclaims: *There's always one step further down you can go.*

I also wanted to touch base with Marge Macurdy to learn if Mack was still riding the crest. And who was their guest on this morning's show? Count Dracula to hype the county's blood drive?

I had to check out Palm Beach Helicopters in Lantana and Ocean Helicopters in West Palm.

Last, I had to get some lunch which I decided to do first. Armies, and Archy McNally, travel on their stomachs. Thinking I could K two B's with one S, I headed for the Royal Palm Way bridge, beeping the glass and steel McNally Building as I sped past. My destination was Ocean Helicopters on Aviation Boulevard with a detour to Sandy James, the luncheonette on Southern Boulevard and S. Dixie Highway that was suddenly all the rage with Palm Beachites.

The eatery is as big as your handkerchief with a table or two for *al fresco* munching and has caught on with the people who matter for reasons best known to those who matter. At informal lunches it's become quite the thing for the hostess to announce, "The sandwiches are from Sandy James, don't-you-know." Only in Palm Beach can you get a designer sandwich.

I had the tuna melt on an English muffin with tomato, topped with cheddar and provolone and a side order of fries. I looked upon it as a last supper for the tan gabardine suit.

Nearing my destination I approached the Palm Beach Kennel Club, home to the dog races as well as the Paddock and Trophy Room restaurants, all just a stone's throw from the airport and, of all places, the Pelican Club. The young man in the small office looked like Hollywood's idea of a barnstorming stunt pilot of a bygone era. Tall, lean, skin like leather and a bomber's jacket left over from the last big war.

"You interested in hiring a chopper, sir?"

"Perhaps. I'm Archy McNally and I have some questions. Have I come to the right place?"

"That depends on the questions. Are you the police, a husband, a PI on behalf of a husband or, given the times in which we live, are you looking for the man that got away?" He raised his arms in atonement. "No offense, sir."

I laughed and so did he. He was a charmer who could charm me right out the door. I proceeded with caution. "None of the above. A friend recently employed one of our local helicopter services and I forgot which one. His name is Mack Macurdy."

"The guy with the television show," he shouted. "Sure. I flew him over that maze and would you believe what happened there? They say it was built on a Seminole burying ground and it's haunted. Mr. Macurdy had a Seminole witch doctor on the show this morning and he thinks the dead lady was the reincarnation of a warrior's squaw who rose up to claim her. The Seminoles are not happy about this."

Neither is Mrs. Macurdy, I refrained from saying. And where did Mack get the witch doctor from? Central Casting? My poor Marge. She must be ready to murder Mack.

"Yes. It's all very unnerving to say the least, Mister . . . ?"

"Martin. Like the flying dude in the comic strip, *Smilin' Jack Martin*. Only I'm Tom Martin. Are you with the network, Mr. McNally?"

"No, Tom. Like I said, I'm a friend of Mr. Macurdy and I have people coming to Palm Beach in a few weeks. Business associates. I'm in real estate, you see. I want to give them a bird's-eye view, as it were, of parcels just west of here. I'd like to take along a cameraman, as did Mr. Macurdy." I lie with great conviction, as you may have noticed, and never bother to cross my fingers. I am always believed because my face does not betray me. In the words of A.E.W. Mason's Inspector Hanaud, *It is a great advantage to be intelligent and not to look it.*

Tom nodded his head in agreement. "No problem, Mr. McNally. Would that be a video cameraman you had in mind?"

"Yes. As I said, it would be just like the run you did for Mr. Macurdy."

"I asked because Mr. Macurdy took along a telescopic camera, too," Tom informed me.

"Who was taking snaps with a telescopic camera? Mr. Macurdy?"

"That's right, sir. He said it was to show what he called tight shots on the screen but I never saw them when I watched the show the next day. Maybe they didn't come out so good."

On the contrary, Tommy boy, they came out picture perfect and I could hardly contain my excitement. I had followed my stomach and struck gold. Adding another to-do to my already busy schedule I decided there and then to fly over that maze for starters, and do it again with a telescopic camera if necessary. Where does one get a telescopic camera? From a paparazzo, who else?

"If I wanted to make a test run, Tom, would you oblige me?"

"Sure thing." He flashed me his smilin' Jack smile and promised, "I'll also charge you."

AS I MADE MY WAY BACK TO PALM BEACH I GLOATED over my discovery. Mack had taken telescopic photos of the maze, maybe even had them blown up, then pieced them together like a jigsaw puzzle and got himself a clear picture of the grid which, incidently, he did not share with his audience. He kept it all to himself and even had the audacity to brag to his wife that he would make the goal. What a devious bugger was Mack Macurdy.

He went up in that chopper days before the party, so had no way of knowing there would be a search for the goal and a prize to the winners. No. He took those photos, memorized the key, and filed away the information for whatever use he could make of it in the future, and the future had arrived sooner than even Mack himself had expected. But it seems the prize turned out to be far more than just a few gift certificates to trendy Worth Avenue boutiques.

What had Mack seen when he flew over the maze—either by the naked eye or courtesy of his high-powered equipment—to allow him to intimidate Hayes? Pay up or

I'll go public with the key to your maze? Surely not. Mack saw more than that and now Archy was going to learn what it was on Matthew Hayes's dime even if it had nothing to do with Marlena Marvel's murder.

How much did Marge know about this? Mack liked to brag. Could he have resisted telling his wife what he had done? If she knew, why was she jerking me around? Did she suspect, like me, that he had learned more than just the key to the grid which he wasn't sharing with her? Did she want Archy to learn what it was—gratis, no less?

Freckles, moonlight and—guile?

I retraced my route back across the Royal Palm Way bridge, this time pulling into the McNally Building's underground garage. I greeted Herb with a thumbs-up as I hurried to the elevator and ascended to the mail room. I purposely avoided going to my office as I was certain the monster's little red eye would be blinking furiously and should I retrieve my messages they would all be from Matthew Hayes protesting Tilly's abduction by the police.

Binky was at his desk, munching a sandwich not from Sandy James and reading a bodice ripper. Binky is addicted to the genre. His favorites seem to be sagas of virile Norsemen sailing up and down the coast of western Europe, laying waste to the land and ravishing all the farmer's daughters. He once told me there are worse things one could read and I asked him to name two. I still await an answer.

"Get your nose out of that tome and tell me how you and Joe Gallo found the exotic plant dealer in Boca."

Binky looked up at me with those brown eyes and blinked several times before saying, "Why don't you give that purple shirt a rest, Archy?"

The nerve. Since he's become a stringer for a news-hound he has lost all respect for those he used to respect—like me. "I happen to like this shirt, not that I have to answer to you for what I choose to wear. Now let's talk about that foxglove plant and the guy who sold it to you. Who told you he might have such a plant?"

"I do believe it was the lovely Fitz who knew of Romeo's nursery."

I should have guessed it was Fitz, the reigning princess of the Smart Set, who would know where to get anything exotic, be it animal, vegetable or mineral. "Romeo, is it? Well I'm here to warn you and Joe that the police are very interested in Romeo and his exotic plants. He's suspected of growing cannabis and is under surveillance by the police from Boca to Juno."

Binky shrugged his bony shoulders. "You're such a prude, Archy."

"What is that supposed to mean?"

"Everyone knows that Romeo is a dealer. But it's just grass, no hard stuff, so what's the problem?"

This was infuriating. "The problem is that it's illegal and a health hazard. Have you ever . . ."

"I refuse to answer on the grounds that it might incriminate me." With that he returned to his bacon, lettuce and tomato on toasted white with mayo. It looked scrumptious.

It was clear that his time spent in the good offices of McNally & Son were not lost upon him. I had my say and what he and Joe did with it was their affair. "A word to the wise, Binky, but I see my caution falls on deaf ears."

"Relax, Archy," he suggested. "Your generation is responsible for two world wars and that doesn't bother you as much as a little pot to dull the sharp edges."

My generation? Two world wars? "We are contemporaries, if you please." I have ten years on Binky, that's all. Well—maybe fifteen.

Binky finished his sandwich and sipped from a straw embedded in a can of Classic Coke. Such a diet helped maintain his twenty-eight-inch waist. I should have parked on the bridge and jumped off.

"Joe's no fool," Binky crowed, and I was touched with nostalgia for the days when Binky Watrous sang my praises. "Getting the plant for show and tell was a great idea so who cares where it came from? The end justifies the means, Archy."

"That, Binky, is Machiavellian."

"No it's not, Archy. It's show business."

Well, I couldn't refute that keen observation.

Not being proud I gather my rose buds regardless from whose bush they fall, so inquired, "Has Gallo come up with anything new in his investigation?"

"He has an idea but that Mack Macurdy won't cooperate," Binky complained.

Now that was most interesting. "How so, Binky my boy?"

He closed his paperback without bothering to mark his place but I surmised Binky had the page numbers of his favorite chapters etched into his memory. Binky needed a woman to dull those sharp edges and I suddenly wondered if he had tried the "personals" I understand are now so popular on the Internet. Employing code names, couples get to know each other via correspondence before actually meeting. They say many have ended in marriage, or affairs, but there are no statistics as to the duration of these liaisons.

Binky once had a gal who told me he was dynamite in the boudoir. Would she write a recommendation? What could she say? *There is more to Binky than meets the eye?*

"You heard Mack flatly refuses to have Joe back on the morning show," Binky reported.

"I have," I assured him.

"But the network is giving Joe a few minutes on the late news as a followup to the foxglove plant presentation, which was Joe's idea."

"Is Macurdy trying to get Joe canned from the evening news spot?" I asked.

Binky shook his head. "No. He doesn't have that kind of influence with the network. Joe wants to have a look at the footage Mack shot of the maze from the air and Mack is not being cooperative."

This, to be sure, was of paramount importance to me. Joe Gallo was no fool, indeed, and what did he know, or was he just whistling in the dark? I got the feeling as I sometimes do in a case that things were rapidly coming to a head, but I couldn't see the crown for the clouds.

"Why can't Joe just run the tape of the show for the morning that footage was aired? Those shots were even repeated a few times after the murder, and I bet a zillion people have it on tape, too. What's the problem?"

"You don't understand, Archy," Binky began to explain. "The cameraman took about ten minutes of film that day he went up with Mack, but it was edited down to what was seen on the show, which was exactly ninety seconds of tape. Joe wants to see the unused footage."

Now I was more than interested. I was ecstatic. "And where is it?" I asked, anticipating the answer.

"It's disappeared," Binky said. "Or the cameraman has

disappeared, according to Mack. Either way it's a dead end."

"But isn't the cameraman a network employee?"

"No," came the answer. "Like all shows, Mack's has a budget and the producer didn't want to okay the cost of the chopper and cameraman so Mack did it on his own. It's not so unusual for a star to spend his own money to boost his ratings and it sure paid off for Mack."

"Macurdy hired his own cameraman who he now says has disappeared along with the film," I finished the story. "If you believe that, Binky, you believe in Santa, the tooth fairy and the sincerity of politicians."

Macurdy had that film and he didn't want anyone to see it because it contained something amazin' about the Amazin' Maze of Matthew Hayes. "What was Joe looking for, Binky, do you know?"

"Nothing special," Binky said. "He can't get into the maze because Hayes has barred all newsmen from the place and the police aren't giving away anything they may have discovered in their search. Joe thought the unseen footage might be worth having a look at."

Or was Joe on to something he wasn't sharing with Binky, or anyone else? Everyone was playing this close to the vest. And did Macurdy just luck out when he decided to pay for the chopper and cameraman, or did he know what to look for? So many questions.

Now I pondered over what to do with Joe Gallo and his stringer who had stumbled onto something that might be injurious to their wellbeing and didn't know it. There is nothing as frightening as two amateur sleuths following a hot fuse attached to a stick of TNT. If I told Joe to forget trying to locate the unused footage, he would become more determined than ever to badger Macurdy for its whereabouts, and Macurdy might well be the TNT at the end of the fuse. If I said nothing I would be derelict of my duty. Contrary to my blabbering, I harbor a soft spot for Binky and Joe Gallo.

I compromised thusly, "I'd like to sit down with Joe and compare notes, Binky. What do you think?"

As I had hoped, he jumped at the offer. "Great, Archy. I'll tell Joe and get back to you."

17

WHEN I RETURNED TO THE GARAGE, HERB, IN HIS glass kiosk, gave me a thumbs-up. This was not sign language for "have a nice day" but to inform me that Mrs. Trelawney was hot on my trail. How did she know I was in the building? Guess.

I didn't need a clairvoyant to tell me that Hayes, tired of leaving messages with the red eyed monster, had somehow gotten through to the executive suite where he protested my truancy to our leader's girl Friday. Before getting into my Miata I answered Herb with a thumbs-down.

THE MASTER OF LE MAZE HIMSELF OPENED THE DOOR to me. This said he didn't employ any full-time help except for Tilly, who was otherwise engaged this afternoon. It also said that Matthew Hayes coveted his privacy. Those who are not fortunate enough to have a domestic staff fail to realize that their presence turns the homestead into a fish-bowl. If you doubt this, just consider the number of butlers, equerries, security guards, etc., who have penned exposés of the English royal family.

Before inviting me in, the little guy shouted, "They arrested Tilly. I need a lawyer . . ."

Father's words echoed in my head, *Don't give him my name.*

"Where have you been?" Hayes continued to rant. "I've been trying to get you all morning. What's your cell number?"

When he ran out of breath, or questions, I said, "Tilly has not been arrested. She was taken in for questioning."

"How do you know that?" he demanded.

"Because I provoked the police to do so."

He started and touched his cheek as if I had slapped him in the kisser. This, clearly, was not the answer he expected. "Whose side are you on, McNally?"

"I usually root for the Dolphins," I admitted.

"You're fired," he bellowed, loud enough for all of Ocean Boulevard to know I just got the sack.

"Good day, sir." I touched the brim of my hat and turned to go.

"Just where do you think you're going, McNally?" he cried, following me out.

"To the unemployment office. Where else?"

"Get your tail back in here, pronto, or I'll fire you."

"You just did," I reminded him.

Suddenly he was all contrite. The little boy caught in the act of something devilish and promising never to do it again if I would only spare the rod. I feared that if I applauded his performance he would actually take a bow. This was all most unseemly for the front steps of an Ocean

LAWRENCE SANDERS MCNALLY'S BLUFF 217

Boulevard villa in the broad light of day. My red Miata in the driveway was a sure giveaway as to the identity of the guy Hayes was indulging in a *pas de deux*. I thought it best to lead the little boy back into the house—by the hand if need be.

"Let's take this from the top, Mr. Hayes," I said, in the manner of a director requesting a retake. "I ring the front doorbell, you open the door and invite me in."

"No need to be surly," he had the nerve to accuse. He turned and headed back to the open door, and I followed.

No sooner were we in the entrance foyer than he attacked. "Why did you tell them to bring in Tilly? They've been questioning her for the past three days. She told them all she knows."

"Are we going to stand here, in the hall, Mr. Hayes, or can we go into the den and play this painful scene in a modicum of comfort?"

With a pout and a shrug, Hayes buried his hands deep in the pockets of his corduroy trousers and led the way. (Georgy would say he "was doing" Jackie Cooper in *The Champ*.) We passed through the great room where those gaudy, giant four-color posters still lined the walls. I took it they were part of the permanent decor and were not hung just for the party. In the words of Lolly Spindrift, "It gives new meaning to the word gauche." Forgive the cliché, but if hindsight were foresight I would have paid closer attention to those garish placards.

Once in the den Hayes hopped onto the divan as if he were mounting a horse sidesaddle. He was shod in his elevator pumps and I wondered how high he stood in his stocking feet. Knee-high to a grasshopper I imagined, perhaps unkindly.

I took the seat I had occupied on my last visit and, before he could get on Tilly's case, I got on his. "Your wife knew one of the guests at the party," was how I began the interrogation of my diffident client.

If my intention was to shock, I failed miserably. Hayes simply returned my gaze and said, "You mean Carolyn? Sure, they went back a long ways. I knew her back then, too. Marlena and Carolyn were stewardesses . . ."

"They were cocktail waitresses in the Cockatoo Lounge, Mr. Hayes. Let's cut the do-do and talk turkey. Okay? If not, I'll quit before you fire me again."

Still blasé, he uttered, "Gobble, gobble," and chuckled. "Who told you that? Carolyn, I guess. I thought she didn't want it known around this piss-elegant town where she came from. And what's this got to do with Marlena's death? That's what I'm paying you for, McNally, not to dig up gossip like that Spendthrift guy."

Was it possible that he truly didn't know the connection? To give him the benefit of the doubt, I reasoned that he was new in town and he had not been lionized by the welcome wagon ladies. In fact, he and his household had been given the PBCS (Palm Beach cold shoulder) since he had announced the construction of his maze, his profession and what he had in store for Palm Beach.

Laddy Taylor's accusations against his stepmother had never been put in print. Laddy griped to local insiders, who blabbed to each other—and outsiders, like Hayes, could very well be ignorant of the Taylor vs. Taylor scandal.

But Hayes was an actor. A superb actor, and possibly a writer and director as well. I must keep this in mind, but it wasn't easy. I was always a sucker for the underdog but, this time around, would it suck me under? So many questions.

"Did you know that Carolyn Taylor and Marlena were meeting in secret?" I asked.

"Sure," he told me. "I told you Carolyn didn't want her relationship with Marlena known now that she's a snooty Palm Beach rich widow and Marlena respected that, so they met outside the town. What's the big deal?"

"The big deal, sir, is that Tilly claims she saw Carolyn upstairs just before Marlena gave her last performance as Venus."

Finally, I got him in the solar plexus and he flinched. I followed with a jab to the jaw. "Just about the time Tilly had filled the perk for Marlena's tea and left it to attend to Marlena."

He appeared more perplexed than ever. Shaking his head, he asked, "Tilly told you this?"

"She did, sir. When I was here yesterday, Tilly passed me a note, requesting that I meet with her in our local bookstore. I did, and she told me what I've just told you."

He took this in, seemingly amazed, before posing in awe, "But why didn't she tell me? I don't get it."

"Why didn't she tell the police, sir, is more to the point. However, Tilly believes, or so she said, that your wife and Carolyn Taylor were meeting in secret. That is, without your knowledge. If Tilly told you about Carolyn Taylor's alleged trip to the second floor that night, she would be forced to tell you about those meetings and did not want to betray her mistress, or even the memory of her mistress."

Quickly sizing up the situation, Hayes immediately began defending Tilly. "She's a good kid. Always has been. Appreciates how we got her out of that diner and took her on the road with us."

He began waving that imaginary baton as he did when addressing his guests the night of the gala that ended in murder. It was a gesture more attuned to a crowd than an audience of one. There were moments when I felt the need to duck.

"Sure," he was proclaiming, "she wouldn't know that Marlena and Carolyn were old friends, and Marlena and I never discussed Carolyn in front of Tilly, and that's a fact. Poor kid. It was weighing on Tilly, so she came to you because I hired you to look into Marlena's death. She did right in my opinion."

"She would have done better telling the police what she saw."

"In our business, McNally, we don't go to the police. They come to us."

I refrained from telling him that Tilly's reason for shunning the police was fear of implicating Carolyn Taylor because I didn't believe it. Also, it would compel Hayes to again extol on the virtues of innocent Tilly.

Instead, I lectured, "I told the police because it's my duty to help, not hinder, their investigation. I work with the police, Mr. Hayes, I told you that when you hired me. But before going to the police, I went to see Carolyn Taylor and told her what Tilly was claiming she witnessed that night."

Grinning, he said, "And Carolyn denied it."

I nodded. "Who do you believe, Mr. Hayes?"

He sank back into the divan and his elevators rose from the floor. He opened his arms, looked at the ceiling, folded his arms across his chest, then opened them again. A mime depicting bewilderment. "Why would Tilly lie, but why would Carolyn want to do in poor Marlena?"

"Do you know Laddy Taylor, sir?"

He began by shaking his head before looking up and exclaiming, "Tilly's guy. Right?" Making a fist, he tapped his forehead as one would knock on wood to avert trouble. "He's Carolyn's stepson and they're at each other's throats over the old man's will. Tilly's mentioned it but I don't pay much attention to girl talk. I'm sure Marlena knew all about it from Carolyn but she never told me. So what's this got to do with anything, McNally?"

Right here, I decided that Matthew Hayes had just overplayed his hand. The competent actor had crossed the line from drama to farce, probably because farce was the mainstay of his repertoire. He didn't listen to girl talk? Sure, and Macurdy's cameraman had disappeared along with the unseen footage of the maze. Everyone is lying and no one is telling the truth now becomes, one lies and the other swears to it.

To utter yet another cliché, *What a can of worms.* But I must say I find clichés remarkably satisfying. They say it all in the fewest possible words—and everyone understands what you mean.

As they had taught me in drama class at Yale (before they asked me to leave), if you find yourself in a farce, play it for all it's worth—so going for the Tony, Obie and Oscar, I told Hayes all about Laddy and Carolyn and Marlena and digitalis, leaving out nothing including Laddy's try at exhuming his father's body.

Hayes, with eyes like saucers, shook his head in disbelief. When I had done, he pronounced it, "Manure in its purest form."

Although I wasn't sure how he would react, this denouncement of Laddy caught me off guard. I was confused, at the very least, but wasn't confusion the hallmark of farce, as well as that of a three-card monte dealer?

"Marlena wouldn't do murder," Hayes protested. "She was into the occult scam but I think she was beginning to believe she really had the gift, and she helped girls in trouble. Abortions, if you must know. It's not illegal. She used a tonic an old Waco Indian woman gave her when we camped outside of Enid one season. If it contained digitalis, I never knew it. So if Carolyn put her husband to rest, she did it without Marlena's help."

"Then Carolyn would have no reason to harm Marlena." I quickly got it.

"Of course not," Hayes responded. "But . . ."

I waited in silence and when I was sure he wasn't going to continue, I prompted, "But what, Mr. Hayes?"

"Look," he said, leaning forward, his feet touching the floor, "I taught Marlena all the tricks of our craft and she was a quick learner. Maybe too quick. She was pulling off things I would never sanction. Foolish stuff. Too risky. I've been thinking that's what got her done in. Some old score, coming home to roost. Marlena got greedy, McNally, and now I'm wondering . . ."

Another dramatic pause as I chuckled silently at the pot calling the kettle black. (For those who are keeping score, that was cliché number three.)

"How much did Carolyn Taylor come into when her husband died?" Hayes suddenly wondered.

"It's only a guess, but I heard somewhere in the neighborhood of a hundred million, give or take."

He whistled, long and loud, through his teeth. "That much?"

"Are you saying, Mr. Hayes, that Marlena might have been pressing Carolyn for a share of that money? Pay me or I go public with the life and times of Carolyn Taylor. Cocktail waitress, cruise hostess and stuff like that there?"

"Between us, McNally, the girls turned a few tricks in their time, but don't quote me on any of this. As I used to say to the sheriff when he came snooping, *I'm here to fix the copy machine, sir, and just leaving.*"

He sure did have a way with words, I'll give him that for whatever it's worth, and the more he spoke the more convoluted his reasoning. He had slowly, and cleverly, chipped away at his earlier defense of Carolyn Taylor.

"I'll keep it in mind, Mr. Hayes," I said. "And on the subject of turning tricks, as you put it, Tilly didn't waste much time getting herself a gentleman caller here in Palm Beach."

He shot me that grin which could denote amusement, innocent mischief or, like now, lechery. Remarkable. "One time, I think it was in Biloxi, Tilly went to town for aspirin and came back with the pharmacist." He laughed. I didn't.

Changing lanes without signaling, I inquired, "Are you still planning on going on the tube with Mack Macurdy?"

"You don't like Macurdy, do you?" he accused.

"I think he's using your wife's murder to advance his career and riling a lot of people who don't know any better but to believe his nonsense."

Hayes waved this off with his invisible baton. "And I told you yesterday that I liked him for just that reason. Does it sound gross because it's my wife's murder that's given Macurdy a shove up the ladder? So be it, McNally.

"I'm a grifter, second generation. Once Marlena's murder is solved, if it's ever solved, don't think I'm not going to use it to my advantage. The maze can be a bigger attraction than Disney's amusement park because there's nothing like a mystery to tickle the slobs. I'll do it not to defile Marlena, but to honor her. She would love it because she was a grifter too, by marriage. You want to see me cry, McNally, catch me on Macurdy's show."

The man was beneath contempt—a king of knaves who was proud of the title. But did that make him a murderer? No, but like his wife, he might just end up a corpse in the goal of his maze when the citizens of Palm Beach got wind of his Disneyesque caprice. The thought gives credence to the theory of justifiable homicide.

"Then I'm sure you'll enjoy hearing how Mack Macurdy made the goal that night," I announced with relish.

"How's that?" he all but sneered.

"When he went over the maze in a helicopter a few weeks ago he took along a telescopic camera. I believe he pieced together the resulting snaps and got himself a true picture of the grid. He either made a map or memorized the layout and after giving himself enough time to divert suspicion, he went straight to the mark."

For a moment Hayes's grimace seemed to express annoyance with my report but seconds later he tossed back his head and laughed with glee. "So that's how he did it," he uttered between gales of laughter. "You know what, McNally? Now I like him more than ever, but I have to reciprocate. I mean I can't let him have the last word. No, sir. I'm going on his show and when he least expects it I'm going to expose his stunt to the world and demand the return of those certificates." This brought on another fit of laughter.

"And not a word to him about this, McNally. Remember who you're working for."

While he was in this jocular mood I hit him with, "Just what else did Macurdy learn from those photographs, sir?"

He greeted this in the manner of a bartender welcoming Carrie Nation to his saloon. "What are you talking about?"

"Macurdy has been bragging about the viability of his future in show business. In short, he's got himself a backer and I was wondering if you were the guy with deep pockets."

Given Hayes's self-portrait, I was loath to use the show biz term "angel" to denote his sponsorship. The wee people with wings and harps would surely take a dim view of such a comparison and get me for it. I'm not superstitious, I'm cautious.

"How do you know all this?" he asked, not sounding very pleased with the investigative expertise of his employee. "Why are you tailing Macurdy?"

"I'm not tailing him," I protested. "I'm investigating your wife's murder at your request. The first thing one asks in a murder case is, who profits from the crime? Mack Macurdy seems to be a beneficiary, as does Carolyn Taylor if she feared Marlena knew too much about Mr. Taylor's death. Today, I am giving you the first results of my labor and you seem more perturbed than pleased."

I got the grin of atonement. "No offense," he said. "It's just that all this has taken me by surprise. Tilly seeing Carolyn that night, this Laddy guy, and now Macurdy. I don't know what to believe. But let me set you straight on Mack Macurdy. He's been here a few times, wanting to get me on his show. I never met him before and I don't know a thing about his prospects, but have you asked Carolyn if she's heard from Macurdy?"

"Carolyn?" I was nonplussed and didn't try to hide it.

"Sure. Carolyn. She's the lady with deeper pockets than mine and, from what you just told me, she's got something to hide and maybe Macurdy knows what it is."

Gadzooks! Why didn't I think of that? Carolyn Taylor. Cool, calm and collected Carolyn Taylor. She called Tilly a liar and told me Marlena was going to leave Matthew Hayes. Recalling this, I thought I should caution my client.

"You should be aware, sir, that Carolyn Taylor is claiming Marlena was getting ready to divorce you."

He leaped off the divan, raised his fists toward heaven and . . .

"I'm home, sir."

We both turned to see Tilly standing in the doorway. Forgoing what was surely to be a tirade against Carolyn Taylor, he rushed toward his maid who met him half way. They collided in a warm embrace with Hayes nestling his nose into her ample bosom. (Well, it was as high as his nose could reach.)

"Did they give you the third degree, Tilly?"

Really!

18

I STAYED LONG ENOUGH TO HEAR TILLY'S ACCOUNT OF her third degree at the hands of the Marquis de Oscar Eberhart. The story of what she had witnessed that night corresponded, word for word, with what she had told me in the bookstore. The only difference was that today her eyes were not hidden behind those dark glasses and gazed upon us as clear and unblinking as her tale.

"You should have come straight to me," Hayes said when Tilly was done. "I knew Marlena was seeing Mrs. Taylor. They were friends."

I cut in with, "You two can discuss all that when I'm gone. Right now I want to ask Tilly a few questions." When neither protested I turned to Tilly and said, "I told you yesterday I had to report your claim to the police and to Mr. Hayes. It was my duty to do so."

"I understand, Mr. McNally," she assured me.

"You told me you had confided in one other person before speaking to me. Correct?" She nodded and I continued, "Was that person Laddy Taylor?"

"It was," she said.

"And did Laddy Taylor tell you to come to me with your story?"

"Oh, no, sir. Laddy wanted me to go to the police. He kept insisting and I didn't know what to do. When Mr. Hayes told me you were coming here yesterday, and that he was going to employ you to look into Madame's death, I decided to tell you what I had seen."

"You did right, Tilly," Hayes consoled her. He was certainly solicitous to his wife's handmaiden, but that didn't mean there was anything more between them than a good working relationship. I also pondered what Tilly's position was now that Madame was out of the picture. Would she stay on as—what? Housekeeper, secretary, chauffeur, or work the box office when the maze was opened to the public? (And may the latter never happen.)

"And you still believe Mrs. Taylor went upstairs when the lights went out and the spotlight came on?"

"I only know, sir, that I saw her on the second-floor landing a moment before Madame went on," Tilly maintained, yet again.

"She saw what she saw," Hayes, at his most cantankerous, badgered me.

"My problem, Mr. Hayes," I said, turning to him, "is that Carolyn Taylor would have no way of knowing the lights would go out and a spotlight come on to illuminate your wife's tableau. Could she have come prepared with a lethal dose of digitalis just in case the opportunity presented itself? Did she know Tilly had the tea water ready to boil at that time? It all seems most unlikely, sir."

I was also sure Carolyn Taylor was not carrying a purse

that night, so she must have checked it with the attendants as did most of the women. If so, where had she hidden the vial of digitalis? Given what she was wearing, it certainly wasn't on her person. I didn't share this with Hayes and Tilly because I wasn't positive on this point and also because I wanted to keep a few cards face down for the present.

I was hardly finished when Hayes questioned Tilly. "When was the last time Marlena met with Mrs. Taylor?"

"I'm not sure, sir, but I would say it was two or three days before the party."

"In short, McNally," Hayes trumpeted with great glee, "just when we had worked out the presentation skit and began rehearsing it. Marlena told Carolyn what was going to happen that night, including the search for the goal."

"But she didn't give Carolyn the key to the grid," I pointed out.

"She didn't have it. Only I had one and now the police have it." ·

Poppycock. Hayes wouldn't have surrendered that map without a fight if he didn't have a copy someplace in the house, but this was all beside the point. Tilly's story was riddled with holes and how did Marlena end up in the maze? This last thought I uttered aloud.

"Only the murderer knows," Hayes said. "Find him, or her, and the mystery is solved."

The common denominator was always that damn maze. Was it the red herring? Like the magician's sleight of hand, were all our eyes glued to that meandering hedgerow when they should have been elsewhere? But where? That was the rub.

"Now Carolyn is saying Marlena and me were on the outs," Hayes was informing Tilly who all but gasped at the very thought.

"That's a lie, Mr. McNally," Tilly wailed. "I told you Madame and Mr. Hayes were a happy couple, and I'll swear to that in a court of law."

One lies, and the other swears to it.

I left Tilly and Matthew Hayes to talk behind my back the moment I was out of earshot. What I wouldn't give to be privy to that gabfest. I told Hayes I would be in touch.

"You think the police will arrest Carolyn?" he asked.

"The police can only make an arrest with hard, provable evidence to present to the District Attorney. Ms. Thompson's accusation is neither. Not to belabor a point, but it's her word against Carolyn Taylor's."

"I'm telling what I saw," Tilly reminded us, *yet again.*

In a manner that was more threat than question, Hayes mocked, "Who are you betting on, McNally?"

"I'm not a betting man, sir."

He let that go. "You have any leads you're not telling me?"

"I've told you everything I've learned to date, sir."

"Which isn't much," he scoffed. "I think you should question Carolyn again."

"I intend to do just that, sir."

"When?" he retorted, in that supercilious manner I so deplored.

With a smile as false as his candor, I said, "Day after tomorrow. She's taking me sailing. No, don't get up. I'll find my way out."

THE FEELING OF ELATION I HAD EXPERIENCED AT OCEAN Helicopters was fast ebbing. Hayes had that effect on my psyche. I was spinning my wheels on this lousy case.

Slip-sliding away from a solution with every step I took toward it.

Who profits from Marlena Marvel's death? I had given Hayes two prospects: Macurdy and Carolyn Taylor. I had purposely omitted two others. The lady's husband—if she was going to leave him and take the better part of his fortune with her. And, indirectly, Laddy Taylor, if Carolyn was found guilty of Marlena's murder.

As I pulled out of Hayes's driveway I returned to pondering over the uncanny luck Laddy Taylor had in Marlena Marvel's death by digitalis poisoning, and teaming up with Tilly who saw Carolyn Taylor on the second floor landing that night. Was it luck, or happenstance—or clever plotting?

Macurdy seemed to have fallen into a pot of jam, too, and I couldn't ignore Hayes's suggestion that Carolyn Taylor could be Macurdy's angel.

But all of them—Matthew Hayes, Carolyn Taylor, Laddy Taylor, Mack Macurdy—were with me, in a crowded room, when Marlena was poisoned. This left Tilly to administer the fatal dose of digitalis and Tilly was the only person who didn't appear to profit from the crime. I could hypothesize that Laddy promised Tilly a generous reward if she lied, saying she saw Carolyn Taylor upstairs, because it was after the fact. I simply refused to consider that Laddy hired Tilly to poison her lady boss.

And then we had that maze. Always the maze, looming in the background like a grinning hyena. For the first time in my chosen profession I feared I had tackled a case that would never be solved.

*   *   *

I WAS NEAR ENOUGH TO LADY CYNTHIA HOROWITZ'S
ten-acre oceanfront spread to pay my respects to Connie
and erase another to-do from my list. I drove round to the
service entrance of the mansion because I didn't want to
chance running into Lady C and being coerced into listening to her plans for the Halloween ball. Lady C, whom
Lolly has dubbed the Hostess with the Leastest on the Ball,
puts slightly more effort into prepping a party than the
Windsors put into preparing for a royal wedding.

But Lolly and Lady C are the best of friends, in spite of
Lol's wicked tongue. The two share gossip, men and cos-
metic surgeons. Lolly has had a nip and a tuck (but who
hasn't?) and Lady C, according to Lol, has cornered the
market on Botox.

The housekeeper, Mrs. Marsden, let me in. "Long time
no see," she said as she welcomed me into her spotless
kitchen.

"I'm a working man, Mrs. Marsden."

"I hear you're now living in Juno with the policewoman," she asserted as if speaking of the weather. There
is nothing reticent about our Mrs. Marsden and there is
nothing sacred in Palm Beach, except one's bank balance.

I confirmed her pronouncement with the sardonic
comment, "I see you and Ursi are still in daily communication."

"What makes you think that?" she asked, and I believe
she meant it. Subtlety was lost on Mrs. Marsden or so she
pretended. "How come you're using the back door? Has
Lady Cynthia banished you from the kingdom?"

"I'm here to see Connie, and no one else, Mrs. Marsden," I said hopefully, forgetting that he who only hopes is
hopeless. "Is she in her office?"

"Where else would she be? In the pool?"

I believe Mrs. Marsden gets her repartee from lines Hollywood writers foisted off on poor Marjorie Maine such as the memorable "Cabbage has a cabbage smell."

Connie looked harassed as she usually did when in the throes of one of Lady C's extravaganzas. Her telephone console, which is the envy of the White House, thc Pentagon and NASA, blinked red, green and blue lights. She deftly put callers on hold, removed others from call waiting and deported several unfortunates to call forwarding limbo.

"I told you," she barked into the microphone she wore around her head like a telephone operator of yore, "the dancing pumpkins are to be in tights and tutus and tell the boys if they must pad themselves to do so modestly; the skeletons who auditioned are too fat, put out a call for anorexics; don't try to substitute children for genuine munchkins; the mummy must wear briefs under his wrappings, last year two drunks pulled off the bandages and it was most embarrassing; make sure the cages holding the bats are securely bolted; the blood samples you sent are too watery and the vampire wants more air holes in his coffin if he's to stay in it until midnight.

"Thanks, Max. No, Max, the heads are to roll in to the tune of 'I Ain't Got Nobody,' not the headless horseman."

She disconnected Max with a touch of a finger displaying a perfectly manicured purple-passion-painted nail. Seeing me she threw open her arms and cried, "Archy, have you come to take me away from all this?"

Bending, I planted a brotherly kiss on Connie's cheek, taking in the sweetly erotic aroma of roses which always left me feeling anything but brotherly. Georgy is lavender and jasmine, Connie is roses and *caliente* spices. Georgy is fair. Connie is exotic. Georgy is the girl next door. Connie is the girl father warned you about. Combined, they represented the greatest threat to monogamy since the pill.

Today she wore white jeans that showed not a wrinkle, and a black blouse that I believe is called "off-the-shoulder." Hardly a working girl's ensemble, but then Connie Garcia is not Mrs. Trelawney and Lady Cynthia is not Prescott McNally—praise be to Zeus.

"I came, my dear, to gaze upon your lovely person and to learn what the upper echelons are saying about the murder of Marlena Marvel."

"In other words you're here to use me. You always used me, Archy. Alex worships me."

I tilted my boater back on my head like Dana Andrews in any Dana Andrews picture. "We used each other, Connie."

"I didn't need cooking lessons and boring old movies."

"I didn't need padding."

With that she burst into peals of laughter which was the unkindest cut of all. "If we're going to be shipmates, Connie, I think we should call a truce. It's very easy to lose someone at sea and, as I recall, you don't swim. Carolyn Taylor has invited me to join the cast and crew of the next voyage into the wild blue yonder."

"So Alex told me. By the way, Archy, we whisper the name Carolyn Taylor in this house unless we precede it with a fitting expletive."

"What's with her and Madame?"

"I think it has something to do with both of them coming from the wrong side of the tracks and giving a goose to their social status by marrying well. It took Madame five husbands, four with ready cash and one with a title. It took Carolyn only one to achieve the same position and Carolyn might be even richer, but she sure is younger."

"And which does Madame envy most, the money or the youth?"

"I hope you're kidding." She reached for a box of Godiva chocolates and tempted me with, "Have a truffle."

"Nix. I'm on a diet."

Biting into the delicious morsel she said, "Don't tell me Georgy's learned how to cook."

Defending my turf, I crowed, "She made a delicious roast chicken the other night, with a salad of fresh greens. And don't you dare have another truffle."

With a malicious laugh she picked another Godiva nugget out of the box. "Even I could make a roasted chicken."

"Then why didn't you, dearheart?"

"Because you always cooked, dearheart."

"Truce," I said.

"Truce, it is." She closed the box of Godiva as the first step toward détente in the McNally/Garcia wars.

"Now tell me about the sailing parties with Carolyn Taylor of all people and that foolish boy."

"Billy? Isn't he a doll?"

"No, he is not a doll. He's a pompous brat. And since when did Alex become a yachtsman?"

"He's not a true yachtsman but he can pilot a boat. His uncle is an officer on a cruise line."

"Really? My uncle is a veterinarian but I can't bark. So what's the story? Should I bring my rod and reel?"

"Honestly, Archy, I can't tell you. It's up to Alex—if he wants to bring you in on it. I've been sworn to secrecy."

I didn't press the issue because Connie would not break her word if her life depended on it. However, this only piqued my curiosity. How many mysteries could a guy ponder before his brain exploded? "Can you tell me what you hear about the Marlena Marvel homicide or did you take an oath on that, too?"

"It would be easier to tell you what I didn't hear, Archy," she said. "The husband, the maid, the lover . . ."

"Lover? Did she have a lover?"

"This is Palm Beach, Archy. It's assumed she had a lover. Have you heard about the alien from the UFO, the Seminole warrior, the voodoo zombie, the . . ."

"Spare me, Connie. I came for erudition and I get malarkey. You know Mack Macurdy?"

"Of Mack and Marge? Sure. Not in the flesh, but I've seen the show. He's responsible for most of the rumors, as I'm sure you know."

"Have you ever heard any rumors about him and Carolyn Taylor?"

"Macurdy and Carolyn Taylor? Now that is hot news. What do you know?"

"That woman would bed a wooden Indian if she thought she could squeeze a nickel out of it," came the sage words of Lady Cynthia Horowitz who stood in the doorway looking like a pillar of salt in a silver lamé jumpsuit, gold sandals and much glitter in her red (the color of the week) hair. "Why are you and Connie discussing that tart?"

"We weren't," I said. "I stopped by to ask Connie . . ." Here Connie, very casually, put a finger to her lips which signaled that I was not to say why I had stopped by. Lady C did not know about the sailing trips with Carolyn, I guessed, and it was worth Connie's job if she found out. "I came by to see how you were getting on with your party and I was just leaving."

"Tarry a while, lad. I hear you're working for Matthew Hayes." Before I could confirm or deny this, she moaned, "I've been trying to get him on the phone and all I get is that maid or the answering machine. She swears he's always out and he doesn't return my calls. I want him as my guest of honor."

The nerve of the old biddy. "He's prostrate with grief," I challenged, hoping to embarrass her. (Ha!)

"Nonsense. I buried five husbands and never missed a party. My last, Sir Nigel, fell out of a tree where he was watching beetles fornicate and broke his neck on the very day I was having twelve to dinner, including royalty. Simms, he was the butler, and I put Nigel in the deep freeze and I told my guests Sir Nigel was indisposed, which wasn't exactly a lie. It was a most successful dinner party."

The woman has ice water flowing in her veins. "You were very brave, Lady Cynthia," I complimented with great solemnity.

"Moxie, lad. It's called moxie. Now what's this rumor about Mack Macurdy and Carolyn Taylor?"

"Archy heard Carolyn Taylor is going to be a guest on Mr. Macurdy's show," Connie said, saving the moment, and her job. "Just a rumor, of course."

"And not true," Lady C declared with an assurance particular to the very rich. "Mack is going to bring a camera crew to the party and treat his audience to a look at the lifestyle of the Palm Beach elite." To Connie, she announced, "I've decided to come as Helen of Troy. Get the Gallo boy on the phone and tell him to come as Paris. I believe Paris wore a pleated skirt and little else." She hummed a few bars of Porter's "I Love Paris."

Deciding to rain on her parade, I asked, "But what about Fitz, Joe's significant other? Who will she come as?"

"Yes, the charming Fitzwilliams gal," Lady C sighed. "She's not coming."

"You mean you're not inviting her?" I cried.

"Oh, I'm inviting her," Lady C declared, "but she can't make it."

"Why?" I asked.

"Because her father's bank handles my estate and if they wish to continue to do so, she can't make it. Now Connie, you must call the undertakers and have them arrange the flowers . . ."

WHEN I GOT TO THE JUNO COTTAGE I LAMENTED TO Georgy, "I just remembered that I forgot to call you."

"Well, you can give me the message now or forever hold your peace. What's up?"

"Can you get the day after tomorrow off?"

"Archy," she chastened, "the day after tomorrow is my day off. We're going to Riviera Beach and taking the *Palm Beach Princess* casino cruise. The boys tell me the one-dollar slots have a twenty-five-thousand-dollar pay-off."

"Well, we're going sailing, but not on the *Princess*. Connie and Alex are taking a yacht out of Miami and they've invited us. So hoist the mizzenmast, or the spinnaker, and anchors aweigh, mate."

"Where is Alex getting the money to rent a yacht?" Georgy always asks the right questions.

"Actually, Carolyn Taylor is the hostess."

"Carolyn Taylor? The woman in the Marlena Marvel case? What's going on, mate?"

"I'll tell you all about it over dinner, including my day in the salt mine." I looked around our rather empty kitchen. "What have you done about dinner?"

"I made a reservation at Capri."

"We can't afford Capri," I reprimanded my blonde goddess.

"I assumed we were going on the *Princess,* and if we hit the jackpot we could buy the Capri."

"Oh, Georgy girl!"

19

I'M STANDING IN LAKE WORTH'S BRYANT PARK, JUST
at the foot of the bridge that connects Lake Worth to
Palm Beach island. This tranquil oasis with acres of lawn,
inviting benches and piers that extend into the intracoastal
waterway, is a favorite site for joggers, mothers with babes
in strollers and senior citizens taking the sun and a snooze.

It is also the site favored for the town's municipal and
social events, such as the annual Finnish Day festival cele-
brating Lake Worth's Finnish population which some say is
the largest outside of Finland, and more recently, the annual gay day's colorful parade down Lake Avenue that ter-
minates in Bryant Park.

This morning, as you can see, the area just behind me
has been cordoned off with the police department's familiar yellow tape. The joggers, mothers and seniors are
milling about in awe and wonder, for their haven has been

rudely violated by the discovery of a body lying, almost hidden, under the sloping structure of the bridge.

A jogger, Ms. Marilyn Anderson of Lake Worth, passing a few yards from the spot, saw what she thought was a homeless vagrant—most unusual for this community. Cutting short her run she left the park and hailed a passing patrol car. Office Kert Johanson immediately entered the park and, following Ms. Anderson's directions, approached the man, tried to rouse him, and ascertained the man, who was well-dressed and clean-shaven, was in fact dead.

Officer Johanson returned to his car and radioed for help. In ten minutes an ambulance, paramedics and three patrol cars arrived on the scene. It is believed that one of the paramedics recognized the corpse as Mack Macurdy, co-host of the popular morning show aired on this network, Breakfast with Mack and Marge. This was confirmed by the driver's license retrieved from Mr. Macurdy's wallet.

For those of you who have just joined us expecting to see Breakfast with Mack and Marge, this is Joe Gallo for WPBQ reporting live from Bryant Park in Lake Worth where the shocking discovery of Mack Macurdy's body was found by an early morning jogger. These are the facts to date: I received a call from Mrs. Macurdy an hour before show time asking if I could come to the studio and go on with her in place of Mr. Macurdy who had been missing since last night.

Mr. Macurdy left his apartment in Palm Beach last night, directly after dinner, telling his wife he was meeting with a prospective guest for their show. According to Mrs. Macurdy, it was not unusual for him, or her, to interview people before inviting them on the show and due to conflicting schedules, these interviews were often held in the evening. When Mr. Macurdy did not return home by three *this morning, Mrs. Macurdy notified the Palm Beach police who ran a check of car accidents in the vicinity and queried local hospitals—all to no avail.*

This morning, the police advised Mrs. Macurdy to go on the air and report his disappearance as the most likely way of locating him, or persons who may have seen him. Mrs. Macurdy called me to assist. Minutes before the show was to air, we received the call from the Lake Worth police telling us of Officer Johanson's startling find.

Viewers may recall that Mr. and Mrs. Macurdy and I were present at the home of Matthew Hayes when his wife, the theatrical artiste Marlena Marvel, was felled by a fatal dose of digitalis poisoning. Since, both Mr. Macurdy and I have been reporting on that incident, now officially declared a wrongful death.

I want to make it perfectly clear, as do the police, that at this time there is no link between Mr. Macurdy's death and that of Marlena Marvel. I spoke to Lieutenant Oscar Eberhart of the Palm Beach police who is here because Mr. Macurdy was a resident of Palm Beach and because it was to the Palm Beach police that he was reported missing.

The cause of Mr. Macurdy's death is not yet known. Lieutenant Eberhart disclosed that there are no marks on the body to suggest he was brutally attacked and nothing missing from his person to suggest a mugging or robbery.

If Mr. Macurdy died of natural causes, such as a fatal heart attack, one must ask what he was doing in such a remote and almost inaccessible place.

For those of you who have just joined us . . .

20

WE STOOD TRANSFIXED, STARING IN DISBELIEF AT the small screen, no doubt as stunned as a host of viewers in the area who had tuned into *Breakfast with Mack and Marge* this morning. In our terry robes and holding mugs of Georgy's dreadful instant coffee, we listened to Joe Gallo repeat his spiel for a second time, perhaps to verify what we thought we had heard.

It began as another overcast day with a slight chill in the air, both typical for late autumn in southern Florida. Waiting for Georgy to come out of the shower, I turned on the TV to see what terrors Mack Macurdy was perpetrating on his eager fans this morning and got Joe Gallo telling me Mack Macurdy had met his maker.

"Do I hear Joe's voice?" Georgy called as she exited the bathroom.

"Come here, quick," I shouted.

And here we are.

Last night, over the pasta *aglio e olio,* piccolo portions if you please; followed by *pollo alla cacciatora*—chicken fricassee with peppers and tomatoes, for the unilingual; followed by espresso ice cream with hot chocolate sauce with one spoon as we shared; followed by a tab that Mrs. Trelawney will swoon over, I brought Georgy up to snuff on my investigation into Marlena Marvel's murder.

Nonplussed, we continued to stare at the spectacle in Bryant Park that resembled a scene-of-the-crime sequence in a police procedural film—yellow tape proclaiming in black letters, POLICE LINE DO NOT CROSS—POLICE LINE DO NOT CROSS, TV newsman with mike in hand, a dozen cops in uniform scurrying aimlessly, patrol cars and, finally, the gawking masses.

"What in God's name is going on in your playground, Archy?" Georgy broke the spell.

"My guess is that Macurdy's angel turned out to be an avenging angel," I said, sipping the cold brew in my mug and wincing.

"I'll lay you seven to five that he died of digitalis poisoning," Georgy speculated. "And I'll go twelve to seven that Matthew Hayes was home all last night with his maid to vouch for him."

"He's smarter than that, Georgy girl. I'll bet Hayes was home last night with several guests to prove it. And one, a lady no doubt, even spent the night to give him wall-to-wall alibis."

"I thought he was prostrate with grief," Georgy said.

"I'll buy the prostrate part, but no more."

"Beware the guy with the airtight alibi," my police person warned me. "And don't forget, Hayes had a house full of people the night his wife bought the farm. Maybe it's his modus operandi."

"We don't know that Mack was blackmailing Hayes. Maybe he just got lucky and his luck ran out last night."

"Under the bridge in Bryant Park? He was dumped there, Archy, with a belly full of digitalis, and you heard it here first. You might also want to find out where the widow Taylor was last night."

I started to laugh. "Maybe she spent the night with Hayes and Bob's your uncle."

"And Laddy Taylor?"

"He was in bed with Tilly," I teased. "A *ménage à quatre* at Le Maze."

"What about Billy?"

"Okay, a *ménage à cinq*, if you will."

"That's gross," Georgy reproached me.

How strange women are. There was nothing gross about the *quatre*, but the *cinq* got her. Maybe it was the odd number that repelled.

"Joe didn't tell us who Mack went to see last night, or maybe his wife never asked him," Georgy noted.

"They know more than they're saying," I called, heading for the shower. "You know as well as I do, maybe better, that Joe is reporting only what the police are willing to give out at this point."

"Joe is really good, isn't he, Archy?" she said, looking at Gallo's handsome face. I must say the TV camera is very kind to Joe Gallo. He's one of those rare people who photographs even better than he looks. And talking about people who profited from Marlena's Marvel death, Joe Gallo takes the blue ribbon. From stringer to anchorman over two dead bodies. Hummmm? I wonder. No, Georgy would kill me.

Suddenly in a rush, I was out of my robe before I reached the bathroom but had no idea where I was rushing off to. Marge was my first choice, if I could see her. I didn't have a chance of getting near Eberhart this morning, but maybe I could meet up with Al Rogoff. I should check in with my father and could I see Joe and . . . ?

"Look, there's Binky," Georgy screamed.

I ran back into the parlor, my robe shielding me fore, but not aft, and sure enough, there was Binky Watrous not five feet from where Joe was reporting. It was now after nine and our mail person should be in the McNally Building, sorting the morning delivery, this very moment. I'll have him fired, I will.

"And there's Al Rogoff," I pointed, losing the robe.

Georgy grabbed it from the floor and refused to give it back. "Finders keepers, losers weepers," she recited, running off to the bedroom to dress. Life with Georgy has its ups and downs.

Did I hear her humming "I Love Paris" just before closing the bathroom door?

GEORGY WAS OUT OF THE COTTAGE BEFORE I FINISHED dressing. Given my mission this mournful day, I pulled on a pair of black jeans and a black tee. I reached for a black shirt, thought better of it, and settled for a white-on-white number, topping it with a zippered black windbreaker. Stepping into a pair of white Jack Purcells, I appraised myself in Georgy's full-length mirror which hangs behind the bedroom closet door, and declared myself perfection. The outfit made a statement without dwelling on the morbid.

I called Marge before leaving and got a busy signal. Driving south, I stopped at a pancake palace for breakfast. Florida abounds in pancake palaces which differ only in name. Making up for last night's feast, I went easy with a scrambled egg sandwich, one egg, on rye toast, and a glass of grapefruit juice. I had a cuppa and took a container to go.

Back in the Miata I opened the glove compartment and extracted a pack of English Ovals. I actually had one between my lips before returning it to the pack and replacing the pack in the glove compartment, which I locked. Victory? I do think so. Did it make me feel happy and healthy? Hell, no. I felt depressed, jittery and in need of a cigarette. I put the container in a holder I had attached to the dashboard and drove unhappily off.

At the office I listened to my messages. Three from Hayes, yesterday; two from Mrs. Trelawney, yesterday; one from Hayes, this morning, and ditto from Mrs. Trelawney. In a burst of creativity I got a roll of masking tape from my desk, cut out a one-inch square and pasted it over the red light. Depression and the jitters disappeared.

I called Marge and got a busy signal.

I called Hayes and got him. "Macurdy croaked," he bellowed, piously. "What do you make of it?"

"I've no idea, Mr. Hayes. I doubt if I can talk to my police connections this early and I can't get his wife on the phone. What do you make of it?"

"You thought he was leaning on someone. Well, could be they leaned back, real hard. Where was Carolyn last night?"

"I'll ask when I see her. Where were you last night, sir?"

"You're working for me, McNally."

"You keep reminding me of that fact, sir. I ask only because Mrs. Macurdy has stated that Mack went to interview a potential guest for their show. Was it you?"

"Me? I had company last night. The carnies who worked my party. They're folding their tent in Miami and moving on. A few stayed the night."

Just as I thought. I wished Georgy were here so I could

gloat. "What do they think of your wife's death? Do they have any idea how she got from the house to the goal?"

"They offered their condolences, nothing more. In our trade you don't pry, McNally, and you expect others to reciprocate."

The carny version of judge not, lest you be judged. "Do you think Macurdy's death has anything do with Marlena's?" I pried.

"Not directly," he said, "if you rule out Carolyn. But those telecasts of his attracted a lot of kooks—you know what I mean?"

I knew, and I had had similar thoughts. So, I'm sure, had the police. "When was the last time you saw Macurdy?" I pried once more.

He hesitated as if trying to recall. "I think it was day before yesterday. Yeah, it was. He was here just before you came that day. Why?"

"Just curious." Hayes gave no indication—nary a hint—that Macurdy was in any way troublesome to the residents of Le Maze or that Macurdy was in any way connected with Marlena Marvel. And, beware the guy with the airtight alibi.

"Let me know what you find out, McNally. I'm curious, too."

"Of course I will, Mr. Hayes. I work for you, remember?"

I got a cynical "Ha-ha," before he cut me off.

I called Marge and got a busy signal. How many busy signals must one get before conceding that the lady's phone is off its cradle?

I called Oscar Eberhart and was told he was not available. "No, sir. I have no idea when he will be available."

"Is Sergeant Rogoff in the station house?"

"No, sir, he is not."

I called Al's home and got no response and, being a very wise man, Al does not subscribe to voice mail. "If I ain't at home, they'll call again if it's important. If it ain't important, screw it. That's how I see it, buddy."

Al, like clichés, says it all in twenty-five words or less that leave no doubt as to where he stands on the subject.

Enter Binky Watrous. Enter a very excited Binky Watrous. "What do you think, Archy?"

"I think you should get to work on time, young man, that's what I think."

"They closed the bridge until they removed poor Mack. I was stuck in Lake Worth," he lied. Binky lies almost as well as yrs. truly because of those liquid brown eyes. Now, he appeared to be crying over the bridge's interference with his work ethic.

"Since when do you take the Lake Worth bridge to work?"

"Since they found Mack Macurdy's body practically under it."

Such insolence. I imagine this comes with being on television at nine o'clock in the morning. But I rather liked this new Binky and perhaps women younger than Mrs. Trelawney would now find him more attractive. Had I lost a son and gained a competitor? I have heard of worse things, but I couldn't think of two.

Taking my cue from Georgy, I said, "I think Macurdy was murdered and his body dumped in the park. What does Joe think?"

"The police are not telling all they know," Binky confided.

"They never do. Was Joe able to learn anything?"

"There's something fishy about Mack's body, Archy."

"Other than its odor? He was a few feet from the lake."

Corny, I know, and perhaps a bit irreverent, but I can't help myself. Is there a twelve-step program for punsters? If not, there should be.

Binky, so enraptured by his news he kept bouncing up and down on the soles of his Wal-Mart sneakers, gushed, "The body was covered, Archy. Joe said when he got there he asked if he could see the body since he was Macurdy's colleague. Just him. No video cameramen. They refused.

"Then one of the people in the park told Joe that he was there when the police arrived and they immediately formed a blue wall, actually arm in arm, to keep the body hidden. When the ambulance arrived the paramedics put a blanket over Mack and the police broke ranks."

"But the police told Joe there were no marks or bruises on the body," I said.

"I know, Archy, but why wouldn't they let Joe see it? When Joe got hold of the woman who first saw Mack lying there, he asked her if she had got a close look at the body and she said she was told by the police not to answer any questions. Remember, it was all confusion at this point, but when the chief saw her talking to Joe, he came over, took her by the arm, and led her out of the park and into his car."

Now that was news. Very strange news. I had to see Marge. She would have viewed the body to make the formal ID. "Was Marge in the park, Binky?"

"No. She stayed in the studio until Eberhart came for her. He must have taken her to the morgue for ID."

"Just what I thought," I said. "Has Joe been in touch with her?"

"Sure. They spoke several times after Joe got off camera. He has her cell number."

Which is just what I wanted. I would have kissed Binky, but with his newly found confidence I wasn't sure how he would take it. "Can you get Joe on his cell? I need Marge's cell number."

No sooner said than done. Binky pulled his cell out of his jacket pocket and punched out Joe's number. "By now he must be at the studio, getting into makeup for the noon newsbreak."

Makeup! So that's how he does it.

"I'm with Archy, Joe. He needs Marge's cell number. He doesn't know anything. I told him about the body." To me, he said, "When can you meet with Joe?"

"Today is out. I've got to see Marge and my father, and try to get Eberhart or Al to sit down with me." I didn't mention that I also wanted to see Carolyn Taylor because I didn't want to give Joe any more fodder for the noon newsbreak. "What about tonight?"

"Tonight, Joe?" Binky said into the new millennium marvel. Pause. "No can do. He's been invited to dine with the Fitzwilliams's."

Well, well, well. Joe was certainly rubbing shoulders on Ocean Boulevard. I never remember Fitz asking a boy to dine with the family. Lolly would report this with great relish, and envy, as I'm sure he had given Lady C the Helen of Troy/Paris suggestion just to get Joe in that pleated skirt—and nothing more. As Billy S so aptly put it, "Oh, what fools these mortals be."

Tomorrow, Saturday, was out as I had that boat ride. "Tell him Monday is the best I can do. And get Marge's cell number."

Binky took a pad and pencil from my desk and jotted it down for me. "I'll catch you on the noon newsbreak," he said to his new idol. Well, at least he wasn't humming "I Love Paris."

When I got Marge on the phone my heart went out to

her. "Archy," she sobbed, "it's so horrible. I'm home. Can you come right over?"

"I'm on my way," I promised.

"Do you know where I live?"

"As a matter of fact, I don't."

"My dear Archy, you can always make me smile. Bless you."

She gave me the name of her condo complex which I knew very well. The Macurdys were not poor.

21

A S I PULLED INTO THE VISITOR'S PARKING SPACE, I
noticed a clique of men, about a half dozen, chatting
and smoking just across the street, all but blocking the entrance to the Everglades Club. Reporters—distinguished
by their inability to stand still, the pencils tucked behind
their ears, and the slouch hats perched in a variety of an-
gles on their heads.

Mack Macurdy had happily attained national attention
with his unorthodox coverage of the Marlena Marvel murder and now his new widow was going to reap the dubious
rewards. The Everglades regulars, who like to keep a low
profile, would frown upon this conclave of fourth-estaters
on the steps of their temple.

The doorman asked my business and I told him I was
there to see Mrs. Macurdy.

"Your name, sir?"

"McNally."

Looking a bit apologetic he asked, "May I see your ID, sir?"

"Are things that bad?" I griped, pulling my wallet out of my back pocket.

With a nod toward the front door, he answered, "That crowd out there storms the gate every half hour. In case you don't know, several are her brothers, two are her uncles and one is an insurance claims adjuster." He looked at my driver's license photo, glanced at me, and handed it back.

"She's expecting you, Mr. McNally. Four A. Fourth floor."

Marge checked me out through the peep hole before unbolting the door. I walked into a spacious entrance foyer carpeted in a plush, teal blue, wall-to-wall. Beyond was an immense living room with a row of unadorned windows facing the Atlantic. It was all light, bright and airy, but the now solitary resident was anything but.

She fell into my open arms and sobbed hysterically. I patted her back, stroked her hair and said not a word. What could I say?

"I was mad at him," she got out between sobs. "I hated what he was doing on the show—the way he was bossing everyone at the studio, including me—I wished him dead and now he is dead."

More tears have been shed over answered prayers than those that go unfulfilled.

"We all have such thoughts," I whispered into her hair. "Don't dwell on it. You're not responsible for what happened to Mack."

She had been with the police all morning and I suspected this was the first time she was out of the public eye and able to vent her emotions. She felt soft and warm and vulnerable in my arms and I had to keep reminding myself the reason I was here. "Let's go inside and sit, Marge."

Standing back I was shocked to see her red, swollen eyes and pitiful face. She must have been made up for the show this morning and never removed it. Her tears and a succession of tissues had streaked the mascara and grease paint, leaving her looking like a little girl who had gotten into Mommy's vanity case.

The large room was furnished in white leather couches and easy chairs. The tables were glass and chrome. The wall art displayed postmodernism at its nadir, and a bar at one end of the room (more glass and chrome) was backed by a mirrored wall.

Seeing my rather startled gaze, Marge said, "It came furnished. Mack loved it." This caused her to giggle nervously, and I joined in.

I declared the decor "As warm and cozy as an igloo."

"The network rented it and they pay the monthly tab. It's one of the perks of our contract."

I wanted to ask her if I could see the bedroom, but didn't dare. We sat on the slippery leather couch, Marge's hand in mine. "I heard Joe's coverage this morning so we can skip all that. Did you ID the body?"

She nodded and shuddered. "It's horrible, Archy." I feared she was going to resume the crying jag but, thankfully, she didn't.

"You mean Mack's death?"

"No," she cried. "I mean, yes . . ."

"Would you like a drink?" I offered.

"No. I don't want to start that. Not now. It's too early."

"Can I brew a pot of coffee?"

"No, Archy, thank you. If I have another cup of coffee

today I'll be awake for the rest of my life. Have you ever tasted the coffee at the county morgue?"

I thought of Georgy's instant blend as I shook my head. Horrible was a strange way of expressing grief, so I asked again, "What was horrible, Marge?"

"What they did to him," she said, her eyes glassing over.

"I thought he wasn't abused physically. That's what Joe reported."

She was crying again. "He wasn't." She touched her forehead. "Here. It was painted here."

"A message?" I was stunned.

"A sign," she said. "An occult sign. A five-pointed star within a circle."

A pentagram within a circle—where had I seen that before?

"It was painted on his forehead," she sobbed. "It was grotesque."

"Painted with what, Marge? Lipstick, crayon, ink?"

She buried her face in her hands. "Blood—it was painted in blood—the medical examiner confirmed it was blood. And there was something in his mouth."

"Easy, easy," I pleaded. "You don't have to tell me now. Take a deep breath and look up at me."

Raising her head she turned to me and recounted, "There was a leaf stuffed into his mouth. Do I have to tell you what it was?"

Foxglove. It couldn't be clearer if the murderer had left a calling card. Or had he left a calling card? The pentagram and circle. I could see it in my mind's eye. Could see it branded into human flesh. Whose? When? Where?

Had some crazy satanic cult taken revenge on Mack for blaspheming their beliefs? Or had some clever assassin planted the red herrings to make the police think just that? Any more red herrings and we could open a fish store.

It was now perfectly clear why the police were keeping this under wraps. After the way Macurdy had incited the public with his dark forces routine they would have a riot on their hands if this went public.

First the maze, now an occult sign and leaf, to keep our eyes on the hole instead of the donut.

"The police are putting out a call for that silly witch and Zemo the nut, as well as the poor old Seminole Mack dug up and a few others he had on the show," Marge was saying with disgust. "They're all phonies and the police know it."

"But they must do it," I told her. "They can leave no stone unturned because under the one ignored could lie the answer."

"You don't believe this was the work of some demonic cult or coven, do you, Archy?"

"No, my dear, I don't. I think there's a connection between Mack and Marlena Marvel."

"I told you Mack's euphoria began the day after Marlena's death and you said it began when Mack found the goal." She was more composed now, her interest in the mystery usurping for the moment her anguish over this morning's cataclysm. "You wanted to know the name of the helicopter service Mack employed for his ride over the goal. You think he discovered the key to the grid from that ride, don't you?"

"I think, Marge, he discovered more than that. Remember I said Mack knew something, but he didn't know what he knew until after Marlena's murder. I'll qualify that and now say he didn't know the *value* of his discovery until after her death."

"He knew who killed Marlena," she concluded.

"No," I said, "but I think he knew how it was done, which might, or might not, be the same thing. I've learned that Mack took a telescopic camera with him on that helicopter trek and from those photos got a clear picture of the grid. Hence, he found the goal." Not wishing to speak ill of the dead, I didn't tell her that her husband took those photos for no other reason than to snoop and obtain a key to the grid.

"He hired the copter and the cameraman at his own expense, but he never told me about the still photos," she assured me. "I should have known he was up to something when he kept insisting that he would make the goal."

"I think he also found something else," I repeated.

"If he was killed because of what he knew about the maze, isn't it obvious who his killer is?" she cried.

"You mean Matthew Hayes, and I'm afraid it's anything but obvious, Marge. All I'm doing is guessing that Mack found more than the key to the grid on that romp. A wild guess at that. I talked to Hayes this morning and he seems as shocked by Mack's murder as the rest of us."

I purposely downplayed my distrust of Hayes and his maid because I wanted to broach another candidate for Mack's elusive angel. Given the time and place, it was a most delicate undertaking. Carefully choosing my words, I asked, "Can you think of anyone who might have wanted to help Mack financially? I mean put up money for his TV pilot?"

"You mean a woman?" she shot back, a teasing smile on her lips. I must have forgotten I was talking to a very perceptive lady. "Don't be embarrassed, Archy. Mack had a lot of female fans and given our venue many of them were rich and unscrupulous—and Mack wasn't faithful."

"I didn't ask you that," I cut in.

"But I'm telling you anyway. Mack and I have not been getting along since we came down here to do the show. In fact I would have left him in New York if the deal with the network hadn't included the two of us, as a team."

Was she telling me this as a way of saying that if I wanted to make a pitch, the road was clear? To say that I wasn't interested would be a lie. But again, this was neither the time nor the place to test her motive, tempted though I was. Am I a cad, or only human, or is there no difference?

"This doesn't mean his death is any less traumatic for me. Especially the way he died. We had many good years . . ." and she again broke down.

I waited for the moment to pass before asking, "Was Carolyn Taylor one of those women?"

"You mean the woman who was left a fortune when her husband died? She was at the party, wasn't she? Mack never mentioned her to me—but then he never discussed any of his liaisons. Mack was crude, not sadistic. Why do you think he knew her?"

"Just another wild guess and too complicated to explain at the moment, so forget I asked. Do you know who Mack went to see last night?"

Marge shook her curly head. "I don't know. The police have asked me that again and again, and I don't know. I was furious with the guests he was booking so when he said he was off to interview a prospect I pretended disinterest and never asked who it was. I'm sorry."

"Don't be," I assuaged her. "What will happen with the show?"

She shrugged uncaringly. "Tomorrow is Saturday, and

we're dark on Saturday. After that, who knows? Reruns until something is worked out."

"Will you continue alone?"

She shook her head. "I don't know what I'll do, or even if they'll want me without Mack. Would you like to be his replacement?"

Was the double entendre intended or accidental? She looked at her hands and I at the ceiling. It was time to leave, or perhaps past the time to leave. "Have you thought about the arrangements? For Mack, that is."

"Private. I don't want a circus. Does that sound selfish?"

"Not at all. You're been through hell today, and it's just beginning. More of the same you don't need." I began getting up. "Now I think you should get some rest, but first take a long hot soak and scrub your face. Your freckles are beginning to show."

"Sally, the makeup person at the studio, tells me it takes more grease paint to hide my freckles than they had to use on Katharine Hepburn. I was flattered."

"You should be," I said.

"Are you going to ride over the maze in a helicopter?" she suddenly blurted.

"I intend to do just that, Marge."

"Please be careful," she implored. "If that secret got Mack killed . . ."

"We don't know what got Mack killed," I said. "It could very well be just what it appears to be—the work of a madman."

"You don't believe that," she challenged.

"Go wash your face."

* * *

"IT'S AN OUTRAGE," MRS. TRELAWNEY CHARGED THE moment I stepped off the elevator. "That nice man. What is happening to our town, Archy? Are there demons among us?"

How many of Mack Macurdy's loyal fans were in a state of shock and fear this day? Now I could clearly understand why Marge wanted a private interment. Ancient photos of the weeping women queuing up to view the remains of Valentino were here evoked.

"We don't need demons, Mrs. Trelawney. We have just plain folks to do their work."

"Who would do such a thing?" she persisted.

"Someone who didn't like your matinee idol. Is the boss in?"

"Yes, and he's asking for you. Oh, yesterday that awful Mr. Hayes called several times and was most rude."

"It's his nature," I said, "and I got back to him. I'll register your complaint when next we meet."

"Please do," Mrs. Trelawney ordered.

Father looked up from his work as I opened the door and lectured, "The first thing I want you to do is go see your mother. She's frantic over this new atrocity and worried about you. They say this Macurdy was defaced with a witch's mark. Is it true?"

So it was already public knowledge and you didn't have to be a whiz kid to figure out how that came to be. One of the policemen whispered it to his wife, or girlfriend, or boyfriend, and he or she whispered it to their—etc. etc. etc. And let us not forget the jogger who was probably on the horn with everyone she knew as soon as the police released her from custody. By now the rumor had reached Miami and was on its way to Key West.

I sat, wearily. "It's true, sir." Then I unburdened my mind as well as my feet.

"This is a bad business, Archy."

"You're not telling me anything I don't know. I'm not sure if Macurdy's death has anything to do with my case, or if the altercation between Laddy Taylor and his step-mother has anything to do with either murder. I've ex-hausted all the few leads I had and now my only hope is learning something from up there," I said, jerking a thumb to heaven.

"Don't tell your mother you're going up in that infernal machine," he warned.

"I won't, sir."

"And, Archy . . ."

"Yes, sir."

"Do be careful."

I STOPPED IN MY OFFICE AND CALLED SMILIN' TOM Martin.

"Have you heard about Mr. Macurdy?" Tom gushed with macabre relish when I identified myself. "They say he was scalped and his private parts taken for a souvenir. Don't mess with them Seminoles, Mr. McNally."

Was I to be spared nothing this dastardly day?

I made an appointment to fly with Tom on Sunday at ten in the morning.

"Where are we heading, Mr. McNally?"

"To the Seminole reservation for lunch."

"You got some sense of humor, Mr. McNally."

"My grandfather was a comic with the Minsky circuit."

"You're kidding," Tom laughed.

"My father wishes I were, Smilin' Tom."

* * *

MOTHER WAS IN HER GREENHOUSE, TENDING HER BE-
loved begonias, and, as always, I paused to look in on the
tranquil scene before entering. She wore her garden bonnet, apron and gloves as she snipped and fed and talked to
her charges. How they flourished under her care. One almost hated to intrude upon the rhapsodic setting I have
long thought should be captured on canvas.

She saw me and waved. I entered the sanctuary and
kissed her florid cheek. "I'm so glad you're here, Archy,"
she said.

"Not as happy as I am to be here, Mother."

"Another murder," she sighed, "and such a cruel one. I
hope you're not looking into it."

I avoided answering and cautioned, "Don't concern
yourself with such things, Mother, and keep away from the
television and Ursi's news flashes. It's all more hearsay
than fact, anyway."

"If it were up to you and your father I would shut myself
off from the world and take up residence here in the greenhouse. Well, I'll do no such thing, Archy. I may be a little
forgetful and my blood pressure may be higher than I'd
like it, but I'm perfectly capable of looking, listening and
interpreting for myself what I see and hear."

I laughed and kissed her again. It did me good to hear
her putting me in my place while proclaiming her independence. I must warn father to be less solicitous with his
bride as it only encouraged her to rebel. "I'll get you a
soapbox," I teased.

"A new pair of garden shears would be more appreci-
ated. These have seen better days—as have their present
owner," she added with a wily smile.

"Your wish is my command, Mrs. McNally."

"Are you staying for dinner, Archy? It's rack of lamb, your favorite."

"I'd love to, Mother, but I promised Georgia I'd dine with her. However, I will take a rain check."

"How is Georgia? It's been so long since I've seen her."

"She's well. I've invited her to New York for that long weekend I told you about and she's very excited about going."

"That is splendid. It's been so long since father and I have been to New York and I miss it," she said.

"Why don't you come with us and made it a foursome? Georgia would love it, I'm sure."

She brushed this aside with a wave of her hand. "Two's company and four is a crowd. Isn't that what they say?"

"It's close enough." I glanced at Mickey's hands and announced, "Now I really have to go."

When I bent to kiss her, she whispered, "Was there really a hex sign branded on that poor man?"

After her declaration of independence speech I saw no reason not to speak frankly. "Not exactly a hex sign, Mother, and it was painted, not branded." I was grateful that she didn't ask in what medium the artist worked. "And don't tell father I told you. He'll take a strap to me."

"Do be careful, Archy."

I PRACTICALLY CRAWLED INTO THE JUNO COTTAGE ON my hands and knees. "I'm home, dear."

Georgy, standing at the dining table, returned my greeting with, "You look like the wrath of the Medusa."

"I've had one hell of a day and I need a drink, not your lip."

"Martini?" she suggested.

"No, woman. A real drink. Four fingers of bourbon over rocks." I had set up a small bar on a converted tea trolley in our small breakfast nook/dining area, which was just off our small galley kitchen in our small cottage. "Do you want a martini?"

"No. I'll have a white wine. It's in the fridge."

There were two Cornish hens sitting in a baking dish on the table. "Aren't they cute?" Georgy cooed.

"Charming," I said. "Are they for show or eating?"

"I was just about to put them in the oven. I'm waiting for it to reach the correct temperature. It's very important to preheat, Archy."

I guessed she had a cookbook hidden someplace in the cottage. I also guessed that fowl, in many sizes and guises, would be her specialty. I got a tray of cubes out of the fridge along with a bottle of white wine. As I poured the wine and my bourbon I envisioned Ursi's rack of lamb.

"Cheers, my love." I drank the amber liquor and immediately felt almost human. "So how was your day?"

Putting the cute hens in the oven, she said, "Connie called. We're to pick her up at nine tomorrow morning. We'll be meeting the others at the marina. The dress code is informal. Now sit down before you keel over and tell me all about it."

"You got a full report, I trust."

"We did," she said. "And so did every police precinct in the area. It's gruesome. A pentagram within a circle. Where have I seen that before?"

"Funny, I had the same thought," I told her.

"Do you want to talk about it? I have some ideas."

"Not right now, Georgy. I've been thinking about it all

day. I want to wash, change and eat the hens. Then we'll talk."

"I bought a new brand of bath salts. Lilac. Why don't you give them a try."

I finished my bourbon and indulged in a refill. "That sounds like just what the doctor ordered, Georgy girl. Join me?"

"No, Archy. That's the last thing you need right now."

I agreed.

"ARCHY!"

I jumped up out of a sound sleep. "Georgy? What's wrong?"

"I just remembered."

"It's the middle of the night. What did you remember?"

"The pentagram and circle."

"You did? Where does it come from?"

"Lawrence Talbert."

I was now fully awake and sitting up. "Who in the name of all that is sacred is Lawrence Talbert?"

"Lawrence Talbert as portrayed by Lon Chaney in *The Wolf Man*. The wolf bites Talbert and the next day, on the back of his hand, we see the brand. A pentagram inside a circle."

"Swell," I grumbled. "All we have to do is look for a werewolf."

"Or a theatrical enthusiast—goodnight, love."

22

Is THERE ANYTHING MORE REPRESENTATIVE OF OPU-lence than a marina in full swing? What could be more unnecessary to the sustenance of life on this planet than a pleasure craft? From the zippy speed boats, called cigarettes, to the modest Grady Whites, to our forty-foot Hatteras, the marina is a celebration of the winners in the *laissez-faire* sweepstakes. They who come out with less don't think it's fair, but a pox on the spoilsports.

And what could be more picturesque, exciting and exulting, than a marina at high noon under a cloudless Miami sky and radiant sun? As they say in these parts, *nada, chico, nada.*

Walking along the narrow boardwalks to our floating alcazar, I noted the proud owners scraping, painting and hosing their man-o'-(corporate)-wars. It's said the happiest two days in a boat owner's life are the day he buys his first boat and the day he sells it. I saw no for-sale signs but perhaps, like previously owned diamonds, discretion is the better part of value [*sic*].

Surveying the bobbing sloops, skiffs, dories and dinghies, I am pleased to say we made a handsome sextet. The ladies in shorts which showed their gams to advantage, the gentlemen in white ducks which showed we were more swells than salts. Billy boy's had the traditional thirteen buttons and flared bottoms which caused my Georgy to nudge me in the ribs and gush, "He's darling."

"You can't afford him," I snapped.

"I can window shop," she snapped right back. This shameless brazenness I attribute to women's lib, a movement that heralded the decline of Western civilization. Its fall is imminent.

Carolyn wore a white blouse that resembled a middy and her sailor's cap restyled into a cloche. Georgy had commandeered my navy Polo and my authentic New York Yankees baseball cap. Connie was in a black halter and an outrageous sombrero; however, one's eyes never ventured above the halter.

Billy boy had gotten into a tank top (really!), Alex in a silk dress shirt with sleeves rolled to the elbows and opened to the waist (really!), and Archy in a sea-island lime shirt with a heliotrope ascot at the throat (splendid!).

As stated, we were a handsome sextet.

A dingy took us to our Hatteras (called the *Bonnie Belle*) as Alex explained that it takes great skill to maneuver a forty-foot luxury vessel from its berth to the open sea. For this reason it's done for the less experienced renter who is shuttled to and fro, compliments of a marina pilot.

"When did you learn to navigate a big ship?" I asked Alex.

"All the men in my family have taken instructions in navigating boats of all sizes, and we're licensed," he said, proudly reiterating the achievements of the Gomez y Zapata clan as the dinghy plowed through the blue water. "I encourage all the boys and men of Cuban extraction here in Miami to do the same. We must be prepared for the invasion."

Connie and Carolyn looked at Alex, who stood tall in the dinghy like Washington crossing the Delaware, with great admiration. He did resemble a swashbuckler of vintage Hollywood fare as the sea breeze blew his dark mane roguishly across his forehead while his eyes looked hopefully into the wild blue yonder.

We boarded on a lift that rose at the press of a button, depositing us at the ship's rear (forecastle?) that was furnished with all the comforts of an upscale cocktail lounge. Blue-and-white pin-striped sofas, teak captains' chairs, bar, television, stereo equipment and a telescope, slightly smaller than the Hubble, that did not contain a coin slot.

"Tally-ho," Georgy exclaimed as she stepped onto the well-appointed deck.

"You've got the wrong sport," I upbraided my fair lady. Turning to the others I apologized, "You can't take a policewoman *no* place."

They all laughed, none more heartily than Carolyn. It was remarkable how quickly she had established a rapport with Georgy, as I'm sure she had done when first meeting Alex and Connie. Carolyn Taylor, *nouveau* millionaire, had not forgotten her roots and reminded us of the fact, saying, "When I was a hostess on a luxury liner catering to the rich and infamous, I would order the *grenouille* every time it appeared on the menu. One evening the waiter asked me if I was going to have the frog legs as usual and I told him I never ate the awful things."

More laughter, except for poor Billy who didn't get it.

Alex and Billy had toted hampers they now stored in a refrigerator behind the bar. "Sandwiches and salads for lunch," Carolyn announced, "from Sandy James, don't-you-know. The bar is fully stocked with beer and booze and even champagne if you can take the bubbly before sunset. It also comes with a real live captain and a wine steward, whom I imagine is also alive, but for our purposes they're not necessary."

And just what were our purposes? I thought, fearing we might be the forerunners of Alex's Spanish Armada. We all went to the bridge and gathered around Alex who, with an assist from Billy, turned on the engines and we were off—where? Why?

A huge compass under glass told me we were headed south which, I believe, would put us on a collision course with Cuba. "How far are we from Havana?" I asked our captain in the silk shirt.

"Two hundred miles as the crow flies," he answered.

"How close can we get before they start shooting?"

"Relax," Billy advised. "We go about five miles and turn off the engines."

"Then what do we do?"

"Fish," Billy said, winking at Alex before they burst into laughter. I did not like this.

Carolyn hustled the girls back to the lounge to start lunch and as soon as they were gone Alex, his eyes on the endless expanse of sea and his hands on the huge wheel, said, "When we reach our mark I can let it drift while we have a drink and lunch. Then I'll tell you our mission."

"Fair enough," I acquiesced, but what else could I do? Swim to shore?

Leaving Billy and Alex to count miles, I joined the

ladies, taking a comfy chair and ordering a Campari and soda. Connie played bartender, Carolyn fussed with plates and silverware, Georgy, sitting beside me, took a deep breath and exhaled, "It's so beautiful I want to cry."

"Go right ahead," Carolyn called, "I did my first night on that liner. There was a full moon as I recall."

"It makes me think of the night we fled Cuba, not knowing if we would make it to Miami," Connie reminisced.

It made me think of werewolves.

Connie served my Campari in a tall tumbler, its rim decorated with a slice of lime. "To go with your shirt," she remarked maliciously, and began singing, in Spanish, "The day that I left my home for the rolling sea, I said, Mother, dear, O pray to thy God for me . . ."

"Can you get us some proper music on that stereo?" I requested of our hostess.

Carolyn, emerging from behind the bar with a tray holding three drinks, said with a wry smile, "Alex told me you two were old friends."

"They go back ages," Georgy chimed in, getting a scowl from our homegrown Carmen Miranda.

Carolyn cheerfully served the drinks, "Bloody Marys, ladies, with a spicy blend of tomato and celery sticks for swizzle sticks. Original, no?"

"No," we replied in unison.

Settling down with our drinks we silently took in our briny, and very privileged, milieu. The Miami skyline was slowing sinking into the ocean as seaworthy crafts of all genres drifted in our wake. The sparkling water accommodated water-skiers, scuba divers and fishermen. Sailboats, leaning precariously into the wind, performed their aquatic ballet with a chorus line of catamarans, to the annoyance of the scullers. Saturday traffic, I was amazed to learn, is not confined to the highways and byways of this great nation.

The sea was exceedingly calm, the swells hardly more than ripples, which may have accounted for the fact that none of us had come down with *mal de mer*—so far, that is. Georgy looked a little pale around the gills but it could be the sun block she lavished so generously on her fair skin. As our captain pushed southward our fellow seafarers, as well as the comforting Miami skyline, began to diminish. I could hear Coleridge's ancient mariner wailing, "Alone, alone, all, all alone, Alone on a wide, wide sea!" and searched the sky for an albatross.

"Mack Macurdy," Carolyn said, giving me a start. "What a loathsome business. Is it true, Archy? I mean the witch's mark and all that rot?"

"I'm afraid it is," I said. "Did you know him?"

"Not personally. Only from his show. Didn't he make the goal the night of the party? He and Penny."

"Lady C is furious," Connie gossiped. "Mr. Macurdy was supposed to bring a camera crew to the Halloween extravaganza and air it on his show."

"Just like that dreadful woman," Carolyn accused. "Me, me, me. Did she express one word of sympathy for the poor man and his wife? I don't know how you put up with her, Connie."

"It's a living," Connie answered, "but I'm looking to retire in the near future." To make her meaning clear she began to stroke the ring Alex had given her as if it were a household pet. Far be it from me to be catty, but you needed a jeweler's loupe to see the stone, and I've extracted more precious gems from a box of Cracker Jacks.

The girls ooohed and aaahed as women do in the presence of incipient brides.

"Have you set a date?" Carolyn questioned.

"Not exactly," Connie confided, "but Alex's mother told me she favors spring weddings."

I will fly to the nuptials of Alex and Connie on the back of a pig, but I kept my mouth shut on that score. Carolyn just repudiated any association with Macurdy and I believed her, which left Hayes as the prime suspect of Macurdy's blackmail—*if* he was blackmailing anyone, and *if* he wasn't killed by a lunatic, acting on his own.

I also think it was evident that Carolyn saw no link between Macurdy and Marlena Marvel and as much as I'd like to, I didn't dare press the issue. Carolyn's association with Marlena was known to me and the police, and she might suspect I had told Georgy, but that's as far as it went.

Georgy knew better than to raise the point and Connie, engrossed in wedding bells, couldn't care less.

Shortly thereafter we were joined by Captain Courageous and Billy Budd. I guess we had gone the required five miles. Looking around I could make out some craft on the horizon, but the shoreline was gone. In fact I would be hard-pressed to say where the shoreline had been. It was disorienting and scary.

The boys drank beer, the girls brought out the sandwiches, salads, pickles and slaw, and our floating picnic was underway. The conversation ran the gamut from the sublime to the ridiculous, avoiding politics, religion and the reason we were lunching on a luxury yacht rental, five miles from our home base. When we were down to the brownies and almond cookies, I spoke my mind. "Now will you tell us what this is all about?"

Alex looked at Carolyn who looked at Billy. who volunteered, "I'll tell them, but first they must swear they'll never repeat this to anyone."

"Not in blood, I hope," I protested, and got a laugh. "But I give my word as a gentleman."

"Can't you do better than that?" Connie heckled, and got a laugh.

"My word as an officer of the law," Georgy joined in.

It all seemed rather silly and sophomoric until Billy enlightened us.

In his days as a bartender in South Beach, Billy Gilbert had befriended many Cubans who, like Alex, still had family and friends in Cuba. Most were political activists. One of them told Billy he had a contact in Cuba (in effect, a spy) who had been outed and had gone into hiding. He now had to defect to Miami and planned to do so in a small speed boat, leaving Cuba in the dead of night and arriving off the coast of Florida the next day. He would travel as far as the fuel he could carry would take him.

This man, himself a covert operator between Cuba and Miami, asked Billy if he would rent a boat on the appropriate day, rendezvous with the man at sea and smuggle him into the country.

"He asked me," Billy explained, "because I'm an American with no connections to Cuba or the movement in Miami to oust the Cuban regime."

"We are under constant scrutiny by the CIA and the Coast Guard," Alex said, not sounding too thrilled with either branch of our government. "It is most important that the man be brought in without fanfare. He is to go underground on his arrival and those in charge will see that he is at some point assimilated into the Miami Cuban community."

Billy said, "I went to Alex because of his column in the Miami paper, and his outspoken opposition to the present Cuban regime."

"Why didn't the man who came to you go to Alex?" I asked Billy.

It was Alex who replied, "Because he's an operative and must never reveal himself, even to those who are active in the cause. If any of us are questioned by the authorities, as we sometimes are, we can swear on the holy book that we don't know any names. He took a chance on confiding in Billy because he had no choice. His counterpart in Cuba must get out or he will be killed."

Like the tale of the ancient mariner, they had us all enthralled.

It was Alex's idea to rent a pleasure boat for their purpose, for what is more common out of a Miami marina than a pleasure boat, preferably carrying some rich man or woman out for a lark on the high seas. Alex's first thought, because of his association with Connie, was enlisting the help of Lady Cynthia Horowitz.

"I nipped it in the bud," Connie got in, "because Lady C can't keep a secret if her life depended on it. With someone else's life, it would be twice as risky."

"So I turned to Carolyn," Billy said with a grateful look at his live-in patroness.

"Isn't it thrilling?" Carolyn maintained ecstatically, taking Billy's hand in hers.

Thrilling? Perhaps. But even more satisfying to have usurped her competition from the running and emerge in the history books as the Mrs. Miniver of the Cuban counterrevolution.

Thus began the weekly rentals of the *Bonnie Belle* to establish themselves as regulars at the marina so that on the day of the rendezvous it would appear to be business as usual.

"I told Carolyn to invite others before the crucial run to

establish our aim as revelers and so that it would not always be just we four the pilot ferried," Alex told us. "When the four of us go out that day and return with an extra passenger the pilot will be less likely to take notice."

"In fact," Carolyn said, "I spoke to Alex the morning you came to see me, Archy, so it was you who got the invitation. Aren't you pleased?"

I wasn't sure if I was pleased, but as I recall Billy was not pleased to have me along. Was it because he knew I was in some way connected with the law? And now here was Georgy, who was the law. Billy didn't seem upset by our intrusion into his mission of mercy, but then what could he do about it?

It was all most edifying—but did I believe it? "Shouldn't you have gone to the proper authorities?" I questioned.

"Never," Alex raged, "they have their spies here as well as we have in Cuba. Another Bay of Pigs we don't need, Archy."

"When is D-day?" Georgy asked.

"That we will not tell you," Alex said, standing. "The man we pick up will be a stranger to us and we will not ask his name or recall what he looks like. We will deliver him to a safe house and *adios,* the job is done." With that, our captain rose and commanded, "And now it's time to return."

"It's been such fun," Connie piped up with the zeal of a cheerleader at a pep rally. "Alex is coming north, so why don't we all go to the Pelican for dinner?"

I could have fed her to the fishes.

CONNIE AND ALEX GOT INTO CAROLYN'S BENZ, LEAVING Georgy and me alone in my Miata. As we started north I asked, "Well, what do you think?"

"About what?" Georgy said. "Connie's chapeau, Carolyn Taylor or mission improbable?"

"The only thing bigger than Connie's hat is her mouth. You know who's going to pay for this dinner? Connie and I are the only chartered members of the Pelican and I can't ask her to split the tab. That would be gross."

Georgy laughed. "You can write it off, sport."

After our dinner at Capri the other night and now this, Mrs. Trelawney would go into cardiac arrest at the sight of my expense report. "Mission improbable," I mused aloud. "You think Billy's story is malarkey? Alex doesn't think so."

"Alex is such a zealot for his cause he would believe anything," Georgy stated, and rightly so. Billy's story was tailor-made for Alex's bombastic ego. "But spy stories, the real ones, are the fodder of novels and films—hard to believe, but true. Then I think of that little boy, remember?, the only survivor of a Cuban exodus, clinging to a piece of wood for days before he was rescued. It gives me the chills. Those people are desperate and men here, like Alex, are their only hope."

That gave us both pause to reconsider Billy's tale, and count our blessings. "What about Carolyn?" I finally ventured.

Georgy dubbed Carolyn Taylor "A nice lady. Certainly not a killer, Archy, and if she knows anything about Mack Macurdy's murder, I'll eat Connie's hat."

PRISCILLA, THE PELICAN'S MAÎTRE D'/WAITRESS, WELcomed us to the club with "The wrecks of the Hesperus. Do come in. Mr. Longfellow will be so pleased that not all of you went down with the ship."

"Do we look that bad?" Georgy cried.

With a provocative glance at Billy, Priscilla said, "Not him."

"You can't afford him," Georgy quickly remonstrated.

From the look on Carolyn Taylor's face, I would say she thought it was all very funny. This was born out when Connie asked her, "What do you think of the Pelican?"

"It's not the Everglades, but it's most amusing," Carolyn offered.

And it's a tad classier than the Cockatoo Lounge, I was tempted to rebut, but instead turned on Priscilla who had wrapped her perfect form into a flowered sarong, stuck a gardenia in her hair and looked breathtakingly lovely—as always. One thought of a South Seas princess. What Billy and Alex were thinking I'd rather not say.

Taking charge of a fast-deteriorating situation, I ordered, "We would like a table for six, young lady, and no lip, if you please."

"Yes, sir, Master Legree. Right this way."

The Pelican, which is a converted clapboard house of generous proportions, was surprisingly quiet this evening. Despite the fact that it was Saturday, we were late diners. The early evening rush had most likely been and gone.

By the time we were seated, everyone was in a jovial mood. "I want to join the Pelican," Carolyn announced as Priscilla passed out the menus.

"Good idea," Billy encouraged, eyeing Priscilla. Seeing his gaze, Carolyn did not pursue the subject of membership.

"I think we should have champagne," Alex suggested. "Yes?"

Before I could shout NO!, everyone applauded the idea, including Georgy. I would put lye in her bath salts. My wallet was hemorrhaging and no one seemed to care.

"Tonight's dinner is the traditional ribs of beef," Priscilla recited, "*avec* mashed potatoes, French style beans and Leroy's famous brown gravy."

"And the appetizer?" I asked the princess.

"The appetizer is red herring."

23

"HAVE YOU EVER FLOWN IN A CHOPPER?" SMILIN' TOM shouted.

"No," I shouted back.

"It can be scary," Tom shouted.

"It can also be noisy," I shouted back.

"Oh, that. You get used to it. Check your belt and don't look down. Here we go."

Naturally I looked down as we went up and the *mal de mer* I had been spared on the *Bonnie Belle* threatened to make up for lost time. Unlike a conventional plane, we didn't appear to be rising as much as the earth seemed to be pulling away from us. It was more than scary, it was nauseating.

This, I had told my pilot, was my test run before taking aboard my imaginary clients. "Let's fly over the A1A and that maze," I had instructed, "just for the hell of it."

"Could be bad luck," he warned me. "Look what happened to Mr. Macurdy."

"I'll chance it, Tom."

He took a sting of beads from his jacket pocket and hung them around his neck. "Seminole worry beads," he said. "They ward off evil spirits."

Is that so? I thought they made you worry.

"I keep a four-leaf clover in my wallet," I told him, "and so far I've never had a mishap in a chopper."

"I thought you've never been up in a chopper."

"I haven't."

He looked a bit perplexed but, as intended, it ended the conversation. Tom was in his jeans, bomber jacket and necklace. I was going to wear jodhpurs, riding boots and accessorize with one of Georgy's white silk scarfs. Modeling the finished product I asked, "Cary Grant?"

Georgy gave me the once over and said, "Tom Mix."

So I got into army fatigues, white turtleneck pullover, I-Like-Ike battle jacket and boots that were made for walking. "John Wayne?" I asked.

"Marlene Dietrich in drag?" she guessed.

I replaced the fatigues with a pair of chinos but kept the rest of my outfit intact and made a mental note to pick up a can of lye on my way home this evening.

Once we were up, up and away, it was rather thrilling to see so may familiar sights from a bird's point of view. Lake Worth—one of the bridges was up but that didn't stop us—the roof of the McNally Building, Palm Beach's myriad golf courses, private and otherwise, and Ocean Boulevard skirting the coastline like a meandering serpent with bugs on wheels agitating its spine. And, finally, the Amazin' Maze of Matthew Hayes.

We couldn't put the flying machine in park, so I told

Tom to circle the maze a few times. Touching his worry beads and his private parts he began to circle the maze. As I recalled from Mack's film, one could see it was a maze but we moved too quickly to get a comprehensive picture of the grid. I saw the goal thanks to the sundial at its center and . . .

"Go back," I ordered, Tom.

"Again?"

"Yes, again."

There was something lying next to the sundial. It was long and narrow and . . .

"Can you go lower?" I shouted.

"No, sir."

"Why the hell not?"

"There are laws, sir. We're over a residential area and this is as low as I'm allowed to take it. There are a lot of influential homeowners down there and I know I'll get complaints flying over them even at the legal altitude. We always do in this air lane. If we dropped a foot they would have my license."

"Then take me back to the heliport as fast as this crate can go."

"You okay, Mr. McNally? You look like you're going to be sick. I showed you where we keep the sick bags."

I didn't need a sick bag. I needed the police. If that long, narrow thing wasn't a dead body *I'd* eat Connie Garcia's hat.

THE CRIME SCENE EVIDENCE BOYS AND GIRLS WERE still sauntering about behind their glass wall. Was the foxglove leaf found in Mack Macurdy's mouth now in their dominion? I had no time to cogitate on this depressing thought as I raced across the lobby of police headquarters. There was now a young man behind the information counter who proved no more helpful than his female colleague.

Approaching him I demanded, "I must see Lieutenant Eberhart at once."

"Your name, sir?"

"Archy McNally. Look, officer, just get him on the phone and tell him this is an emergency."

"And what is the nature of the emergency, sir?" he asked as if I were selling subscriptions to the *Police Gazette*. This was maddening. The kid was a minute past puberty and still battling zits. I also didn't like the way he kept staring at my Ike jacket.

"The emergency will be history if you don't get Eberhart on the line and tell him I have to see him now. Right now, Officer."

"I must know the nature of your business, sir."

This guy was a real Johnny-one-note. "Murder, officer. I'm here about a murder."

"Whose murder, sir?"

"Yours, if you don't get Eberhart on that phone in the next ten seconds."

"What are you ranting about, pal?" I swung around to find Al Rogoff directly behind me. I almost threw my arms around the big lug.

"Al," I cried, taking him by the arm. "I've got to see Eberhart, quick. Come on, I'll explain on the way up." With that I pulled him toward the staircase.

"I ain't seen one of them jackets in a month of Sundays, pal. Where you been? To a V.F.W. rally?"

"I've been flying all over Palm Beach, Al. Really flying."

"You want help, Sergeant?" the kid behind the counter called after us.

"It's okay, Bruce. I'll take responsibility. He ain't no nut."

Bruce?

Thanks to Bruce, Eberhart was expecting us. Once inside his office he questioned, "Flying, McNally? The kid thinks you're high as a kite."

"I was up in a helicopter . . ."

"Helicopter," he exploded. "Was that you in the helicopter? What are you up to, McNally?"

"How do you know about the helicopter?" I asked, now somewhat baffled.

"How do I know? We got a dozen complaint calls, that's how I know. You were snooping on private citizens."

"I was snooping on the maze, Oscar, and I saw a body. A dead body in the goal of the maze."

"Whose body?" This came from both the lieutenant and the sergeant.

"How should I know?" I cried. "I was too far up to see a face. Now let's get moving. If people noticed the helicopter this morning so did Hayes and he's had enough time to remove whatever he's hiding in that damn maze. Is your patrol car outside, Al?"

"Hey, mister, I'm in charge here," Eberhart protested, then paused, as if making a momentous decision, before asking, "Is your car free, Al?"

"Free and clear, sir. You want we should go to that maze?"

"I want," Eberhart said to Al, "and on the way there, McNally, I also want to know what possessed you to go over the maze in a helicopter."

Bruce looked startled as the three of us sped past his counter and made for the exit. When we got to Al's patrol car Eberhart got in the front passenger seat, which placed me in the rear, behind the metal grate that separates the good guys from the bad guys in a squad car.

"Give," Eberhart ordered before we had pulled away from the curb.

I gave him everything I knew and got accused of holding out on the police.

"Not true, Lieutenant. If Macurdy learned anything from his helicopter tour of the maze I didn't know what it was, and I still don't. I was just playing a hunch."

"And stumbled over a dead body. Nice." Eberhart wasn't pleased. "So if Macurdy was leaning on Hayes, you think Hayes done him in, and maybe there's a link between Macurdy's murder and the Marlena Marvel murder."

"If and maybe sums it up," I carped. "And *if* we don't hurry, *maybe* Hayes will have removed whatever I saw in the maze."

"If he did," Eberhart concluded, "all we're doing is spinning our wheels—or Al's wheels."

"Not really," Al said. "Hayes will know we saw something and are on to him, and we can gauge his reaction. We can also search the maze and the house."

"Been there and done that," Eberhart grunted. Turning to me, he said, "You think Hayes is the heavy, but I don't see how he can be. In fact he was with you at the time of the murder."

"I know a werewolf isn't the culprit, Lieutenant."

"You heard about the mark on Macurdy's forehead, eh?"

"Lieutenant," I sighed, "everyone in Palm Beach has heard about it."

We didn't have to ring the doorbell. Hayes, in his elevator oxfords, met us at the door. "What the hell is a police car doing in my driveway?" he ranted. "And was that a police chopper disturbing the peace this morning?"

"No, sir, it was me," I confessed.

"You, McNally? That does it. You're fired."

Eberhart took charge. "I want to inspect the maze."

"You got a warrant?" Hayes retaliated.

"It's a crime scene under investigation. I have an ongoing warrant to search it and your house, sir."

"What are you looking for?" Hayes looked anything but distressed over our surprise visit.

Without answering, Eberhart fired instructions at his subordinate. "Check out the house. We'll walk around to the maze." A meaningful nod passed between the two officers.

I followed Eberhart up the driveway, past the delivery entrance where Tilly was peeking, eyes wide, from behind the door she had opened a crack. Hayes followed Al into the house. The lieutenant took the map of the grid out of his jacket pocket and we went, in fits and starts, directly to the goal. Except for the sundial in the center of the opening, it was empty. We walked about, examined the ground and shook the hedges. Nothing.

Eberhart gave me a disdainful glare and said, "Let's walk around the passages we missed on our way to the goal."

We walked, and found nothing. "He hid it," I said in defense of my allegation. "He had plenty of time to get rid of it."

"It's not so easy to hide a body, McNally, and why did he put it in the maze in the first place? To air it?"

"I saw something next to that sundial," I insisted, feeling not a little foolish. The maze was constructed purposely to confuse and confound and was succeeding on both counts. The guy who built it was, by his own admission, a grifter, a con man, a swindler and a conjuring artist *par excellence*. He was making fools of me, the police and the town of Palm Beach. For the first time in my career I despaired of bringing a case to a satisfactory finale.

"I still think the answer is here in the maze," I said to Eberhart, making the most of a lost cause.

"If it is, McNally, it's invisible."

When we got back to the patrol car we waited, in silence, for Al. When he emerged from the house I could just see Tilly closing the door behind him.

"You guys look like doom and gloom," Al criticized his boss and his friend with good reason.

"We got zilch," Eberhart reported. "What about you?"

"I looked around, lower level to attic, and didn't see no body," Al said.

I wanted to scream, *a double negative makes a positive.* If you didn't see no body, you saw a body. But the boys were not feeling too kindly to me this day and more of my helpful tips might push them over the brink.

"I questioned them," Al told us, "and got nothing. But the peanut and the broad ain't the kind to cave in at the sight of a uniform. Personally, I think they're both lying, but they do it so well you want to applaud." Al saved the punch line for his swan song. "And he's going to report this illegal raid to the commissioner."

Eberhart opened the patrol car's back door and motioned for me to get into the cage. "You know what, McNally?"

"What, Oscar?"

"I wish I could fire you."

JOE GALLO PLACED A HUGE BOWL OF STEAMING BEEF stew in the center of the table. We guests inhaled the aroma, made the appropriate sounds and complimented our host.

"The stew is my specialty," he stated with pride. "The

trick is not to serve it before its time which is three days. I made it Friday, when Binky told me we would get together on Sunday. It's been hibernating in the refrig since then, assimilating the juices of the meat and vegetables."

"It looks good enough to eat," Al Rogoff commented, which is about the zenith of Al's wit in social situations. He reached for the ladle and got his hand slapped by the cook.

"Not yet, Sergeant," Joe scolded his neighbor as if Al were a child being taught table manners. "First the noodles."

Joe went to the kitchen which, in a trailer, is about ten feet from the dining area. Come to think of it, it's about the same distance from table to sink in our Juno cottage. Using pot holders, Joe took the boiling cauldron off the stove and poured the water into a sieve, retaining the noodles. These he placed in a bowl which already contained a generous amount of melted butter, tossing the noodles in the butter before presenting them to Al, Binky and Archy.

"A dollop of noodles," Joe instructed, "then a dollop of stew over them. There's a baguette, sliced and warm, and a salad which we'll have after the meal because I'm Italian, and also because the table isn't big enough to hold four salad and dinner plates at the same time.

"Binky brought the salad, Al brought the beer and Archy brought his august presence. *Bon appétit,* gentlemen."

We dug in and it was excellent. Beef stew is a man's meal, and for our beverage we drank ale (Bass, in fact) which is a man's drink. Wine at a stag dinner in the U.S. of A. would be frowned upon. The background music, *sotto voce,* was classical and included a variety of arias, some familiar (the suite from *Carmen*) and some only a buff like Al Rogoff could name.

His musical choices, and the beef stew, had assured Joe Gallo lifelong tenure in the heart of his crusty neighbor. As the trumpets blared the Triumphal March from *Aida,* Al declared, "You can't beat them Eyetalians when it comes to music."

Joe Gallo knew how to charm the rattle off the snake.

"Georgy never told me you were a cook," I said between piquant bites of the three-day-old ragout.

"Georgy has spared you many of my talents," Joe replied, "cooking being the least of them."

Al Rogoff let out a ribald laugh. Binky Watrous blushed. I helped myself to bread. "I hear you're going to Lady Cynthia's ball as Paris. True?"

Joe treated us to a lackadaisical shrug. "She's having my skirt tailor-made. What do you wear under a skirt?"

"Ask a Scotsman," Al told him.

Not letting Joe get away with such indifference to his entry into Palm Beach society, I blasted, "And what of Fitz? I hear she's not going."

I got a smug look and a boyish grin. Joe Gallo has become famous for his boyish grin. I find it boring. "Paris will arrive with a wooden horse on wheels. A big wooden horse. Once inside the gates, the stallion's belly will open and out will pop Fitz, as Cleopatra."

Binky looked at Joe with great admiration. "What does Cleopatra wear?" he wanted to know.

"Very little, Binky. Very little," his idol assured him.

"When they do *Les Troyens* at the Met they bring out the wooden horse. It's incredible." Al hummed a few bars from *Les Troyens,* or *The Trojans* to the common folk.

"What does Paris wear at the Met, Al?" Joe asked.

"A skirt, pal. What else?"

"Watch your step, Joey," I warned. "Hell hath no fury like Lady Cynthia Horowitz deprived of Paris in a skirt. She'll get Lolly Spindrift to trash you in print."

"I can handle Lolly," Joe boasted with a ribald snicker. Ribald laughs, snickers and hoots, as you now know, are what stag dinners are all about. I find it boring.

"On the subject of romance, if that's what we're talking about," Joe began, "Binky has something to report."

"I do not," Binky denied, his face pink.

"Binky has a girl, Binky has a girl." Joe teased. "Her name is Marilyn Anderson."

"Anderson?" Al questioned. "You mean the dame that found Macurdy's body?"

"None other, Sergeant," Joe said. "I sent Binky to talk to her about doing an interview with me and they hit it off, right Binky? She and Binky went to the flicks last night."

Resigned to his fate, and rather pleased with the attention, Binky told us, "We have a lot in common, Marilyn and me."

"Give me a for instance," I said.

"Jogging," Binky announced.

"Since when do you jog?" I badgered.

"Since I met Marilyn Anderson."

And we all gave this more laughter than it deserved. As you must have noticed by now, the four of us were in a playful mood that bordered on the giddy, thanks to having just spent the better part of two hours discussing the murders of Marlena Marvel and Mack Macurdy—all to no avail. We rehashed, again and again, what we knew as fact, only in this case the facts came to a preposterous conclusion.

Al Rogoff made the definitive statement. "The body in the maze was that of Marlena Marvel. That is a provable fact. The person you saw posing as Venus was not Marlena Marvel because she could not have gotten from the house to the maze, dead or alive, without being seen. Period, finished, over, done, the end."

Fine. Who was posing as Venus and where did she, or he, go after the show?

Fact. Marlena's body was not in the maze when we all ran through it in search of the goal. When and how did it get there?

We learned from Al that Macurdy was not poisoned. He was smothered to death, probably with a pillow. Hence no marks on the body. Who done him in? A nut or a cunning murderer?

We learned from Joe, via his astute research, that it takes an excess of ten milligrams of digitalis to cause cardiac arrest in a healthy adult.

Ultimately, we learned that we were stumped. One hundred percent stumped. Joe's dinner rescued us from mental languor—and shame.

OVER THE SALAD, AL ROGOFF BROKE INTO THE BANAL conversation and muttered aloud, "It wasn't empty." Gaining our attention, he repeated, "It wasn't empty."

I've known and worked with Al Rogoff a long time and am keenly attuned to his sudden bouts of inspiration. The hairs on the nape of my neck began to tingle. "What wasn't empty, Al?"

"The goal. It wasn't empty this afternoon. It's never been empty. The sundial is in the goal."

Maybe Al was losing it or the Bass had gone to his head. "The sundial? You think it's a Trojan horse, Al?"

"No. Ain't I taught you nothing, pal? That monument has a base about two feet square. What does it cover? Maybe a trap door like they use on stages in magic acts to make people pop up or disappear.

"A trap door over a hole you could hide a body in and make it disappear—or pop up."

Al's idea was like a call to arms. We stopped licking our wounds and began arming for a counterattack which took the form of hopping about like bunny rabbits and all talking at once. When the elation evaporated into reality one thing became clear. We had to go back to the goal and move the sundial.

"How can we do it?" Joe questioned. "Hayes won't let us near his place."

Looking at Al I mouthed the name, "Eberhart?"

"After today? You gotta be kidding. He'd have me pounding a beat just for asking."

"We're out," Joe reasoned, "because Hayes knows all of us."

Still munching on his salad, Binky said, "He doesn't know me."

We all stared at Binky and as we did a plan began to form in my devious mind. "We need a key to the grid, Al."

"Not from me," Al blared in a tone that said he meant it. "It's now police property and classified."

"I know where there's a key to the grid," Joe divulged. "Mack had one and now we know how he got it, thanks to Archy. He showed it to me and told me where he kept it in his office at the studio. I can get it tomorrow. You have a plan, Archy?"

Did I have a plan? "Put down that salad fork, Binky my boy, and let me tell you how you're going to play *Les Troyens*."

24

I AM FREE TO TAKE ADVANTAGE OF THE STATE-OF-THE-art resources of McNally & Son, human and otherwise, as long as I don't toss a monkey wrench into the works and send Mrs. Trelawney into a tizzy. Therefore, the day after Joe's dinner party and Al's epiphany, Binky sorted the first-class mail and delivered it, as usual, shortly after ten.

He then met me in the garage, got into the trunk of my Miata, and we were off and running. Herb, observing this from his glass tower, immediately picked up the phone and dialed Mrs. Trelawney. As I drove out I imagined I could hear him reporting, "Archy's abducted Binky. What should I do?"

The plan, well thought out and timed to the minute, was simple. However, as the poet said, the best laid plans of mice and men—etc. etc. etc.

I would drive to Le Maze, parking as far up the drive-way as possible, which would be past the delivery door, and go round to the front door. Binky, armed with the key to the grid, would give me time to ring the bell, get in the house, and distract Hayes and Tilly with foolish banter. Then Binky would get out of the trunk and hurry to the goal. Once there, he would tilt the sundial and inspect beneath it.

I gave Binky five minutes to find the goal—even with the key it's tricky—five minutes to inspect the sundial, and five minutes to get back into the trunk. "Don't dally," I directed. "Hayes is a wily rascal and I doubt if I can hold him and the maid still for more than fifteen minutes."

"I hope that monument doesn't weigh a ton," Binky grumbled.

"All you have to do is tilt it, not carry it on your back like Atlas."

Tilly answered the door. "I thought Mr. Hayes fired you," was her welcoming salvo.

"I would like to speak to Mr. Hayes and you. I've been with the police, as you know, and have something to report that is of paramount importance to both of you."

Unimpressed, she said, "Mr. Hayes is meditating. I can't disturb him."

If he meditated with his eyes closed I was batting a thousand. "I'll wait," I said to Tilly and practically pushed my way in.

"He might be hours," she warned.

These people are extraordinary in every way. I thought my ploy about the police would have them at least curious. Obviously, it didn't.

"Wait," Tilly said, and politely turned her back on me.

I looked at my watch. Five minutes. I strolled into the great room and began to examine the posters as if I were in a museum. There was Marlena as Venus, just as we'd seen her the night she died. I glanced out the French windows and observed the maze. Binky, at this very moment, must have made the goal. I continued to inspect the artwork. There was the fairway with its Ferris wheel, strollers and the guy hawking a girly show. I walked past, stopped, returned, got on tiptoe to take a closer look and gasped.

Was I seeing things? No, I was not—and I had to get Binky and me out of here like right now. I checked my watch. Twelve minutes. I prayed Binky was ahead of schedule.

"What do you want, McNally?" Hayes had surfaced.

"I was just leaving, sir."

"You some kind of nut, McNally?"

"You could say that, sir."

I raced to the door, got out and went to the Miata. I could see that the trunk was a tad open. It was now more than fifteen minutes since our arrival. Confident, I got into the car and backed out of the driveway.

I headed for the parking lot of the Publix supermarket where I had arranged to meet Al after my stint at Le Maze. I spotted the patrol car and parked next to it. Getting out I ran to my trunk and opened it. It was empty. No Binky. Oh, my God!

Al sauntered over and saw what had happened. "Where's Binky?"

"He must still be in the maze. We have to get back there, Al. No time to explain—in your car—put on the siren . . ."

"You sound hysterical, Archy. Calm down."

"I am hysterical. Take me back to that damn maze."

"After yesterday . . ."

"This is today, Al. If you don't want to see Binky dead with a pentagram etched into his forehead in blood, get in your car and go like a bat out of hell to that diabolical labyrinth."

The sign of a good general is his ability make a quick decision, for better or for worse, in the line of fire. Without blinking, Al started for his car. I followed. We were out of the parking lot and tearing up the A1A, siren blasting, in minutes. We arrived at Le Maze making enough noise to draw Hayes, and a few of his neighbors, outdoors.

Hayes was squawking, but we weren't listening. "Take us to the goal," Al ordered.

Hayes responded with, "Screw you."

Al touched the hilt of his weapon. "Now, mister."

With a sneer and a shrug Hayes headed for the backyard. "The police have my key to the grid." The guy had nerves of steel—or else he knew he had us beat, yet again.

"Move," Al answered.

After a few false leads, unnecessary I'm sure, Hayes led us to the goal. Except for the sundial, it was empty. "Where's Binky?" I shouted.

"Who the hell is Binky?"

"He's here someplace, you bastard. Now where is he?"

"You men are nuts and I'll have your job for this, Officer . . ."

"Archy?" It was Binky's voice coming from no place. "Archy? Is that you?"

"Binky? Where are you?"

"I'm here but they tied me up."

Hayes began to run. Al grabbed him by the collar, almost lifting him off the ground. "Where is he?" Al demanded.

Hayes was squirming like a monkey on a leash. "You're choking me."

Al took out his gun and put it against the back of Hayes's head. "Where is he?"

"Okay. Okay. Let me loose." Al let go and Hayes went

out of the goal and into the passageway. We followed with Al's gun still pointed at the shrimp's head.

Hayes reached into the hedge and pulled a lever, and before our eyes the hedge began to slide, closing off the goal we had been in and creating an opening to a twin goal next door.

Binky was on the dirt floor of the second goal, his hands and feet bound. Miraculously, he had managed to bite through the tape over his mouth. Next to him was an alabaster statue of Venus de Milo with glass eyes and a red wig.

"Archy," Binky cried, "there's no trap door under the sundial."

"WHEN I SAW LADDY TAYLOR'S FACE IN THAT POSTER I knew we were in trouble—or Binky was in trouble. Laddy was part of Hayes's carnival and probably in the house, or even worse, in the maze, which proved to be true. Carolyn Taylor told me Marlena had a bit of gossip to report but died before she saw Carolyn again. I believe Marlena wanted to tell Carolyn that her, Carolyn's, stepson, newly arrived in town, was a working member of Hayes's traveling carnival."

Al Rogoff, Joe Gallo and I were in Oscar Eberhart's office congratulating each other on the arrest of Matthew Hayes, Laddy Taylor and Matilda Thompson for the murders of Marlena Marvel and Mack Macurdy.

"Laddy didn't come to Palm Beach with Hayes because he didn't want people here to know he was a working member of Hayes's troupe. Old man Taylor was still alive and Laddy was still hoping to get his share of Daddy's estate. When the old man died and Laddy got skunked in the will, Laddy came here to harass his stepmother.

"At the same time, Marlena told Hayes she was leaving him and taking half his fortune with her. This, I'm sure, is when Hayes and Laddy put their depraved heads together and hatched the plot to get rid of Marlena and frame Carolyn Taylor for the murder. Hayes had the two goals and sliding wall constructed to fool the public when the maze opened because conning the public is his métier. Now he would use it to con the world."

Joe, who had been taking copious notes, picked up the story. "They poisoned Marlena with digitalis, the medicine Linton Taylor was taking, the afternoon of the party and put her body in the concealed goal. The statue, which they had used before instead of Marlena, appeared on the balcony. The red wig and those staring glass eyes had us all fooled."

Eberhart interrupted with, "But where did the statue disappear to?"

"The maid, Tilly, put it in the magician's box in the attic," Al Rogoff told him. "And I saw it. But all that was visible was the head and feet sticking out of each end so I had no way of knowing it was an armless statue of Venus. The wig they shoved in a drawer and we didn't search no drawers looking for a body."

"After our search for the goal that night," I said, "I noticed Laddy was missing for some time when we all returned to the house. Now we know that he was transporting Marlena's body from the hidden goal to the goal containing the sundial, or he could have moved the sundial to the goal where Marlena was hidden. You see, the sundial was the prop that had us so sure we were always in the same goal. By the way, it's a stage prop and weighs about fifty pounds."

"You saw the statue from the helicopter," Joe said, "but why did they put it in the goal?"

"To get it, and the red wig, out of the house before the police, or maybe me, got wise," I explained. "Al kept telling us that we didn't see Marlena posing as Venus. Given time we would have figured it was a statue and maybe connect it with the statue in the magician's box. They were too clever to take such a chance. The goal was the best place for it before chopping it up or smuggling it out of town. Their one mistake was to put it in the goal with the sundial which I spotted from the air.

"Laddy Taylor was in the house when I was talking to Tilly and he saw Binky go into the maze. He went out the French doors, caught up with Binky, knocked him out and put him in the goal with the statue, moving the sundial to the other goal and closing the sliding panel. They would have taken Binky to some desolate place and done him in, like they did Macurdy, when the coast was clear, never figuring Al and I would return in ten minutes. All three were in the house when we got there and Hayes came out to greet us, confident that we would find nothing."

Eberhart was shaking his head. "They thought of everything. And Macurdy saw the two goals with his telescopic pics and said nothing because he figured it was some carny trick and liked the idea of having something on Hayes. The night of the murder Macurdy knew exactly how Marlena Marvel's body popped up in the goal and couldn't wait to use it to his advantage. Hayes was a rich man and Macurdy needed an angel. It was a marriage made in hell.

"It was also Macurdy, with his reporting, that gave Hayes and Laddy the idea of putting the bloody pentagram on Macurdy's forehead and have us believe it was the work of some cult group or a kook."

We basked silently in our glory for a few minutes before Joe wondered, "And where's our hero, Binky?"

I looked at my watch. Mickey's small hand was on three and his big hand was on twelve. "Binky is making his three o'clock rounds at the McNally Building, where he should be," I stated.

"You ain't got no heart, pal," Al Rogoff rebuked me.

A double negative makes a positive.

25

GEORGY LOOKED LIKE A SUPERMODEL IN HER NEW suit, purchased especially for our junket to New York. Navy blue, skirt just knee length, tailored jacket, with princess seaming accentuating a nipped waist. And with it she wore a striped silk blouse in jewel tone and pumps with a modest heel. Navy blue was made for blondes.

As we were stopping at the Yale Club (yes, the seigneur booked us into a suite for three nights), I got myself into chinos, blazer, oxford button-down with a narrow knit tie (maroon) and wing-tip brogues. Boola-boola for us.

I engaged a limo to take us to the airport and after checking our luggage we indulged in a bon voyage drink in the lounge to steady our nerves. When our flight was called we queued up to be searched for bombs, box cutters and weapons of mass destruction, went through the metal detector and finally got to board.

Traveling business class, we had comfortable seats side

by side with Georgy taking the window seat. The steward instructed us on emergency protocol as his stewardess teammate showed us how to use a life jacket once called a Mae West. (I longed for Smilin' Tom's Seminole worry beads.)

We fastened our safety belts and held our breath as we taxied down the runway and gradually left terra firma. When we were airborne the stewardess passed out newspapers and magazines for those who wished them and asked if we wanted coffee before lunch. We did.

I got a *Post* and Georgy got a *Herald*. Waiting for the coffee we scanned our dailies.

Moments later I heard Georgy exclaim, "Oh, no!"

"What's wrong? Are we crashing?"

"Worse," she said, handing me her *Herald* and pointing. "There, right on the front page. I can't believe it."

Following the perfectly manicured moving finger, I read:

SOCIALITE AND POLITICAL ACTIVIST DETAINED IN MIAMI

Palm Beach socialite Carolyn Taylor and Miami columnist and political activist Alejandro Gomez y Zapata were arrested by the Coast Guard yesterday, along with Consuela Garcia and Billy Gilbert. All four are being detained by the Miami police.

Yesterday afternoon, the party boat, rented by Mrs. Taylor, while out on a run with her guests, picked up a lone passenger piloting a speedboat. Spotted by the Coast Guard, they boarded Mrs. Taylor's yacht and were told the man had escaped from Cuba. The man, who has not been identified,

*carried only a leather satchel. Upon examining it,
the officer discovered two dozen bags of uncut
heroin, worth millions on the illegal drug market.*

*Mrs. Taylor insisted that she believed the man
was a Cuban refugee they had been alerted was
coming. Mr. Gomez y Zapata and Ms. Garcia confirmed Mrs. Taylor's allegation.*

*Billy Gilbert stated that he was a guest of Mrs.
Taylor's and was totally ignorant of any planned
rendezvous at sea.*

*The spokesperson for the Coast Guard de-
scribed the ensuing scene as "a three-ring circus."*

Oy vey.

The *New York Times* bestselling
Archy McNally Series by

LAWRENCE SANDERS

**Available wherever books are sold or at
penguin.com**